COLLAPSING THE DIVIDE

Kirasu Rising
Book Two

KRISTEN ILLARMO

Le Bovier Publishing

DEDICATION

For Judi, Meighan, and Jen. Thanks for spurring me on.

For Eric. Thanks for asking, "What's next?" Just enough to keep me going, but not enough to make me scared.

CONTENTS

CHAPTER 1

PRAYERS FOR BEDA ESS

Sweat rolled down Miranda's back as the gyrating mass pressed closer. Too many. Too close. Sweet and spicy aromas clashed in the sticky air. Her knees buckled. She stumbled.

Samsara had been partying for days since the funeral, as if honoring the woman who'd saved Nibiru from a black hole was a contest they didn't plan to lose.

So carefree, so sure there would be no repercussions.

"Come out and see the city," Monrovia had said. "You can't spend the rest of your life hiding in bed."

But ten minutes outside the house, she'd lost Monrovia in the crowd. Now Miranda regretted few things more than leaving the safety of her covers.

Three boys hammered out a driving beat on drums strapped to their chests, so close she could touch them. Her cells vibrated with each strike. The mass swayed and stomped in time, moving with practiced rhythms, jostling her like a ball in a pinball machine. With shallow breaths, she stumbled, searching for a way out of the hot bodies.

If they knew the black hole had never been headed to Nibiru, they wouldn't be dancing. They'd be furious.

Breathe.

Miranda moved to squeeze past a tall woman blocking her escape from the crush, but Miranda misjudged her next dance move and she rocked back, crunching Miranda's foot. Searing pain shot up her leg while the woman swooped down to help, her eyes wide with unsaid apology. Miranda brushed aside the sympathy and tried to limp through the gap.

"Wait! You're—" She seized Miranda's hand, trapping her in the thick and hoisted her arm into the air. She shook Miranda's fist above both their heads. "Toast to Beda Ess!" she shouted.

Nearby horns ripped out a tinny retort, and half the woman's drink spilled on Miranda's shoe as she fought the tight grip on her wrist. *No attention.*

She wanted to shrink, not be fawned over for her mother's sacrifice.

The pack swung, and a new hole opened. Miranda pried her wrist from the woman's grip and lurched out of the scrum. Lumbering to the sidewalk, she leaned against a wall and pressed her cheek to the rough brick, thanking whatever gods of chaos and revelry deposited her in this empty spot.

Miranda dug her fingers into the grooves of the bricks while she watched the mob. Since she'd stood next to Carl for his impromptu interview on the day of the Gathering, people had occasionally recognized her. For these revelers, the Gathering had been the day they had used their ancient strength to help Beda stop the black hole from ending their world. For Miranda, it had been the day Beda died.

The scent of buttery bread wafted toward her, and she squinted against the sun to read the sign. Two Buns, Monrovia's favorite bakery. Miranda hadn't done a lot in these past few weeks on Nibiru, but she'd sampled their treats more than once with her sister. Maybe she'd show up here.

A woman in the bakery kneaded dough on a long wooden table, so much like the one Nathan had used. Miranda's heart tightened. He'd punch and flip the dough, flour up to his elbows, and he'd always make sure a few rolls came out too small for selling. The rejects. And what else could they do with the rejects but eat them? She touched the glass with the tips of her fingers and bit back tears. Is he really gone? Are they all gone?

How could she live like these people? Like everything was ok? The banner 'Prayers for Beda Ess' rippled over the crowd.

"I thought I'd never find you." Monrovia's voice startled Miranda, but she grabbed her sister in a tight hug. Monrovia awkwardly patted her back. "You okay?"

Miranda dropped her arms, stepping back, trying to act casual. *Too much.* She pointed at the throng of dancers. "I can't handle that."

Monrovia nodded. "There won't be as many people where we're going. I hope you're hungry."

As she hustled to keep up with Monrovia's long strides, Miranda's stomach answered with a loud growl. She'd been eating small portions at Carl's house just in case he might rethink bringing on another child. But he'd been nothing but loving, accepting, since she'd first shown up on his balcony. And she knew he had all the money they needed to live comfortably, even though he'd left his job at the Interstellar Research Group.

No, it wasn't the fear of Carl's rejection stopping her from getting out of bed to eat. Her stomach twisted as the realization crystallized. Lying in bed pretending to sleep was easier than meeting their concerned faces. The unsaid: are you ok?

Everything would have been different if she hadn't followed Beda to Earth that night so many years ago—but she couldn't take that back.

Monrovia stopped to let Miranda catch up. "After the noodles, I have a surprise for you." Monrovia's eyes sparkled with a flare Miranda had not seen before, but the word 'surprise' sent a hot shot of panic racing through her. After destroying Earth, losing her mother, and trying to settle into a new planet, surprises were not on the top of her list. Instead of running screaming, she took a breath. "What kind of surprise?"

"Let's just say I'm sure you've never done it before."

Miranda's mind raced with things she'd never done, eaten in a fancy restaurant, swam in the ocean, tied her shoes underwater. "Can you give me a hint?"

Monrovia ignored the entreaty. "Just try to keep up." She weaved through a group of people clustered around a man holding a pink-and-green bird.

Miranda couldn't look away from its bright feathers and sharp, black beak. A child reached out nervously with pudgy fingers to touch its feathers. The bird held its head high, enduring the encounter until the trainer produced a wriggling worm. Pointed teeth flashed as it scarfed the treat. Miranda shivered, and the child jerked his hand back. She broke her gaze and caught the edge of Monrovia's flowing skirt turning down a side street.

"Hey, slow down!" Miranda jogged to catch up.

The crowds had thinned to only a few passersby. Monrovia waited by a cottage marked with a short fence and a small yard. The quiet hopefulness of this street made Miranda wish she could remember life here before she left at only three years old. They all lived together then, perhaps in a house like one of these. If Monrovia remembered the day her sister and mother disappeared, she'd never mentioned it. Miranda watched her, staring into the garden. They had both been so young.

A creeping plant with delicate white flowers grew along the fences, filling the air with a complex aroma unmatched by any chemical concoction. Miranda drew in its sweet smell as she strolled beside Monrovia.

A woman appeared in her doorway, sweeping the threshold. As Miranda blinked, the woman became Beda, with her long, white hair catching the ash rain as she swept the soot out of their cinder-block shack in the Trash Lands.

A sharp pang stabbed Miranda's chest. She gripped the fence tight. Beda gave this up to go to Earth to save people she didn't know or even understand. But the black hole had taken Earth, anyway. *Earth gone. Beda gone.*

Could they have stopped Alois another way? Was he really gone?

Still gripping the wood, Miranda focused on a beam of sunlight playing on a patch of flowers near her. She felt the woman watching her and leaned down to a blossom, lingering in the smell, feeling the warm sun on her face. Her chest released, and she straightened up, giving the woman a wan smile.

Monrovia moved closer, whispering, "You okay?"

Miranda loosened her grasp, nodded, and followed Monrovia through the winding streets, wandering to tangy smells.

They came to a wide street with back-to-back huts filling its middle. Monrovia barreled through the maze of scents with unmatched focus. Miranda ambled behind, her mouth watering as she imagined what delicious treats might be in those boiling pots and searing woks. Monrovia stopped at the counter of a sagging hut, its dingy bamboo walls struggling under the weight of expectations.

"This one is the best." Monrovia held up two fingers to the stooped woman, who nodded and filled two nubby-looking bowls from a blackened pot. A board painted red hung over the pots on the back wall, and in yellow letters it declared: Be Here Now.

The words stung. *There's nowhere else I can be.*

Monrovia placed some large coins on the counter as the woman set down the steaming bowls. Miranda scooped one up and sniffed hard. Pepper seared her nose. She sneezed into her soup, sending hot droplets sailing into the air. The old woman chuckled.

Monrovia handed her two sticks. "Can you eat and walk?"

Miranda took them, bewildered by the mechanics required. "I can try." She trailed Monrovia, shoveling hot noodles while trying not to look like a person who grew up in the Trash Lands—but the slippery food was too delicious for decorum.

Monrovia paused at a set of bamboo poles that each held a red lantern painted with black symbols. Miranda slurped down her last noodles as she gazed at the sharp strokes. Were they words? She'd seen nothing like them. The lanterns marked the entrance to a staircase that descended into a dark jungle. She shivered.

"Your surprise is down there," Monrovia said, then took a confident bite out of her bowl.

Miranda didn't know which was stranger, walking into thick, dark foliage or eating one's dinnerware. "You want us to go down there?"

"Of course," Monrovia said, taking another bite.

"Why are you eating that?" Miranda asked, distracted now by the spectacle.

Monrovia cocked her head, looking at Miranda like she was the strange one. "It's made of rice. Eat it, and you have less waste."

Miranda studied the nubby bowl, red from the juices and spices that had soaked in, then looked back up at her sister as she finished her own with a last bite. Miranda cautiously nibbled and found it had a nice crunch, but the concentration of the chili oil scorched her mouth as if she'd eaten a burning match.

"See, it's fine." Monrovia started down the darkened stairs.

Miranda waited at the top while she gobbled her bowl. Her eyes watered from the heat, but she would not be outdone. She swallowed down the last of it and gestured at the stairs. "Is it safe?"

Monrovia did not turn around but tilted her head like it might help her understand the question.

"There could be spiders, I guess. You should watch out for those."

"Why would they recreate spiders?"

Monrovia moved further into darkness. "We remade Earth's ecosystem. Spiders are an important part of that."

Miranda stepped into the gloom, watching for trouble on eight legs, but as the sun broke through the leaves, it lit up Monrovia's long, white hair, making it a beacon in darkness. Miranda watched it shimmer, so much like Beda's. She touched her own mass of black curls.

What if Monrovia had followed Beda that night instead of me? Would they have been able to save Earth together?

Monrovia paused on a landing, looking out over a clearing in the jungle. As Miranda caught up, she saw a massive wooden structure rising from the clearing like three giant hats woven together and wet from the rain, suspended in gentle sweeping curves and peaks. It seemed impossible that anything so fluid could be a solid structure, the opposite of the harshly lined buildings she'd left behind in Bubble City.

Miranda's skin tingled and, for the first time in a long time, everything felt right. Shadows from lanterns and burning torches played among the trees as a song floated on the breeze. "It's beautiful," she said, wishing she could better describe the completeness that filled her. She wanted to hold on to this moment, to put it in a box to save for when she might need it later.

People glided under the curved structure, not walking or running, but moving in smooth motions. Miranda couldn't pull her eyes away. "How are they moving like that?"

"They are skating. That's what we came to do."

Miranda watched the people effortlessly gliding. Was there some magic trick to it, like the way Beda and Monrovia had taught her to transport to Nibiru? Jitters danced in her stomach.

As they descended, the hairs on Miranda's arm stood up. The faces of the people were familiar. She only had to imagine them in a shiny silver suit or dusty rags. She rubbed her eyes and blinked hard. It must be her mind making sense of the new place. Clearly, these people were not from Bubble City or the Trash Lands.

Monrovia searched the crowd, much more subdued than the revelers celebrating Beda. "I know he's here somewhere."

Stalls with grass roofs dotted the clearing around the giant curved wooden structure. A band played a lively tune, and it surprised Miranda to find her foot tapping out the rhythm.

"I found you." A boy about Miranda's height gave her a quick wink as he tapped Monrovia's shoulder.

"Tan!" She pulled him into a hug, and he fit neatly under her chin.

Monrovia seemed so open to that hug. Miranda couldn't help but think how differently her own attempt had been received earlier.

He broke away and turned to Miranda. "I'm Tan, and you must be the famous lost twin?"

He had an open, easy smile. Miranda reached to shake his hand, and he shoved a pair of worn, wheeled boots at her. She took them with both hands, surprised at their weight. "What are these?"

"Skates!"

Miranda looked back at the skaters. "Those people are rolling around on these?"

Tan grinned, which was surely meant to be reassuring, but Miranda had deep doubts. "It's easy! I'll teach you."

"Oh no." She tried to pass the skates back. "You guys go ahead. I'll just watch."

"Nope, doctor's orders. You need to move around and do something different."

He had a bubbly energy Miranda would have normally hated, but rather than being annoying, it had an endearing quality.

"What doctor?" She looked to Monrovia for help, but she just shrugged and smiled.

Miranda followed him to a bench near a small rink. The soft grass sprang back under her toes, making each step satisfying.

Tan tightened his skates in one practiced motion and Miranda did her best to copy. She got a firm hold on the back of the bench and stood. Her legs wobbled like they would fly out from under her at any second. "But really, why are we doing this?"

"Because it's fun." Tan's face glowed as he said the word and motioned for her to let go and take his hand.

For half an hour, Miranda clung to Tan's arm, falling on her butt between brief bouts of unconfident rolling while Monrovia watched from the sidelines like a proud parent. Safe on the bench now, Miranda breathed in the evening air. The light scent of flowers mingled with the peppery smells from more bubbling pots, forming a fragrance that wrapped around her like a blanket. Miranda touched a few coins in her pocket. She could have anything she wanted. It was all right here at her fingertips.

She whipped her head, sure she'd heard Nathan's easy laugh. Only leaves danced on the breeze. She whispered to the darkness between the trunks, "You'd do so much better here than me. You'd make friends and appreciate the food, and I bet you'd be running your own bakery in a few weeks." A cool breeze brushed a tear on her cheek.

I'll try. For you.

CHAPTER 2

FAMILIAR FACES

The streets were quiet as Miranda and Monrovia made their way home. The syncopated rhythms of the band still reverberating in Miranda's brain, the taste of the sweet, thick mango drink still coating her tongue.

Her butt ached from the effort of learning to skate, but her skin buzzed. She was living like the rich in Bubble City on Earth, before—

She swallowed hard but tried to hold on to the lightness.

No one skated there, but they did things just because they wanted to, and now here she was, not on the long commute to work or home from it, not scrounging for water so they would make it through the night. She had done something frivolous, something just for fun.

Monrovia punched in the door code to Carl's apartment. As it swung open, Miranda heard voices. One was a woman's—familiar, though she couldn't place it—and another, deeper voice.

"Hey girls," Carl said, his voice lighter than usual. "Sophia and her family stopped by to check on us. Miranda, come meet Brian and Oren."

Miranda left her shoes beside Monrovia's and steeled her nerves. It had been good to think about other things for a few hours, but these people were here to whisper and cry over Beda. She would do that again, but not now, and not with strangers.

"You remember Dr. Roma." Carl motioned to the woman standing beside him.

"Oh, please, call me Sophia." She smiled warmly.

Miranda hadn't seen her since the day Carl had convinced the people of Nibiru to come together and use their energy, the same energy their ancestors had wielded to create their world, to collapse the black hole, sealing Earth to its fate. They called it the Gathering.

When Nibiru shifted to take Earth's coordinates after the black hole collapsed, Sophia had called several other labs to confirm her instrument readouts. They all verified the unbelievable—Nibiru had moved.

She looked more relaxed out of her lab coat with her hair down. Maybe she was coming to terms with the improbable.

Miranda gave a little wave. "Hi."

"And this is Brian and her son, Oren."

Miranda looked past the husband and thought she might melt through the floor.

Her whole body shook.

Nathan stared back at her; his hand outstretched to shake hers like it was the most normal thing in the world.

***

Miranda stepped onto a square pane of pink glass, which lit up under her boot. *On the bridge in Bubble City. On my way to work.* Time flashed on the building front: 8:10 am.

11

"I'm late!" Miranda moved to run, but her boots were stuck tight to the pink square. A woman materialized next to her, as if from mist. *Familiar.*

The woman reached toward Miranda. "Help me!" Her eyes filled with desperation.

A sound like a gurgle rising from deep water circled them and the woman's feet left the bridge. She clawed the air for anything to anchor her as she floated up. She called again, but quieter this time, as if she knew it was wasted breath. "Help me."

Miranda dove for her, but her hand went right through the woman's arm, like she was a ghost. She floated like a loose balloon to the top of the dome.

While Miranda watched her outline fade, the blocks that made up the bridge fell away under her feet. Bubble City receded in shadow, and she hovered in darkness.

Alois was before her, holding Beda in his hands, stretching her limbs like taffy.

"You do not know what you are doing!" His words echoed through the darkness as he cracked Beda's body.

***

Miranda tore at something wrapped tightly around her arm and leg. She fought with it, kicking and flailing. Where was she?

A bright light filled her vision, but her eyes were closed. An acute sharpness stabbed her head. Her heart raced. A moan broke through her panic. Miranda tensed, ready to strike with her one free hand, but the throbbing made it hard to focus. Something shifted in the darkness.

Concentrate.

She willed her vision to focus on her surroundings, starting with what she was tied to. It was soft under her. She tugged at the thing squeezing her wrist and it fell away. A sheet?

A dresser, a closet, another bed. Monrovia's room.

She took a shaky breath and kicked off the sheet curled around her leg. A dream. She'd been under the dome—and then Alois. Why did she have to see that again?

And why did her head hurt so badly? She gently touched the tenderest spot and felt a knot. The last thing she remembered before the dream was seeing Nathan. Did she hallucinate? Her throat was dry; there was no going back to sleep tonight.

She tiptoed down the hall, trying not to wake Harold. She wanted to get her own glass of water. The machine stayed dormant in the corner while she rustled in the kitchen, completing her task as quietly as possible. A bright moon hung over the balcony, drawing her past the tin assistant, out into the night air. Luna slipped out behind her, swishing her tail, making clear it was the night she came for, not affection.

The woman's face from her dream hung in her mind, pained, scared. Miranda had tried to keep her on the ground. She sipped the cold, sweet water. It was the same as last time, before Earth was destroyed, when Kirasu took her there. Miranda had grabbed for the woman then too and had to watch as she floated helplessly up, only to come crashing down when gravity shifted. Miranda shuddered. So many of them had come crashing down, scattered among the debris.

On the balcony, she trained her eyes on the tops of the trees in the park below, honing in on the details in the dark, pretending to count the leaves. Anything not to see her mother's body in Alois' hands again. Anything not to see her snapped in half, to hear the sound. Luna jumped in her lap, and she petted her sparingly, hoping she would stay while she waited for the edges of night to fold into dawn.

***

Carl told her she'd fainted and fallen backward onto the wooden coffee table.

How ridiculously embarrassing.

Sophia had collected her family and left in a hurry, as if what Miranda had might be catching. Carl had taken her to bed and sat with her until Harold had finished whatever version of medical checks a robot more accustomed to making lunch could manage. It was enough to satisfy Carl that she'd probably wake up just fine.

The sun was all the way up and she'd traded her water for tea. Harold had brought it to her with a bag of ice for her head. She begrudgingly accepted both.

She blew on the steaming cup and her headache eased. But a nagging thought filled the gap left by the pain.

Did Sophia's son really look like Nathan? How was that possible?

Monrovia had spent time with Nathan on Earth. She would be able to tell Miranda whether Nathan's double had been sitting in Carl's living room—or whether she was cracking up. The possibility gave her goosebumps, and she rubbed her arm against the chill.

Wake up already, Monrovia.

Miranda cradled her tea and watched the faithful gather for their morning meditation, forming a semicircle of brown tunics and linen pants. She had seen them do this before, sit for hours—not moving—like Beda used to, tapping into something beyond themselves. Something still beyond her.

She watched their still bodies. They'd come to this spot every morning since the Gathering, forming their circle in front of a giant tree whose roots dangled from the top, as if it searched for sustenance from the air instead of soil.

Do they come to atone?

"Do you want to go down?" Monrovia's voice broke her concentration.

Miranda jolted, spilling some tea on her lap. She jumped up at the searing pain.

"I didn't mean to scare you. Are you okay?" Monrovia asked.

"I'll be fine."

"Do you want to go with them?"

Miranda squinted, hoping it might help her make sense of these words. She'd been waiting for hours for Monrovia to wake up to ask her about the boy, and here she finally was, but what was she talking about? Miranda gave up trying to understand and grunted, "What?"

"We have a custom to thank the universe after a successful Gathering," Carl said.

Miranda whipped around to see her father filling out the frame of the sliding door. How long had he been there?

"We could join them," he said.

The image of Beda sitting on the dusty floor of their shack, unmoving, back straight, utterly silent, filled Miranda's mind. Beda seemed untouchable, unknowable in that state.

"I'll pass."

Miranda searched Monrovia's face for a sign. Was she holding something back? Did she not want to talk about the Nathan lookalike around Carl? But Monrovia's face gave nothing away. She blithely sipped her tea and pet the cat as if everything was normal.

That means I must be losing it.

"Okay then, go pack. I'd like to leave soon," Carl said.

The announcement startled Miranda. She clutched her cup, stifling the immediate urge to scream, *I'm not leaving!* Instead, she offered a measured, "Where are we going?"

"Beda's favorite waterfall, remember?" Carl said. "If you're well enough for the journey."

The journey. The final funeral.

His plan came back to her. Since the Gathering, he'd been wanting to hike to her special place, where they would see her off in their own way, with no crowds.

He'd wanted to leave immediately, but Miranda had told him she needed time for her side to heal, which was true, but she was also terrified to say a real goodbye to Beda. It would be closing the door to any chance of her coming back.

She's not coming back.

Miranda touched the tender bruise on her head, then pulled up her T-shirt to look at the wound on her side.

Carl screwed up his face in a pained expression. "How's it looking?"

She gently patted the tender skin peeking around the edges of the thick scab where the banshee had sunk its stark, white finger-bone into her side to keep her from going after Beda. And if she had been able to break that skeleton's grip, she would have dropped into the black hole to face Alois by Beda's side.

And then I'd be dead too.

She glanced up at Carl and dropped her shirt. His eyes were wide. "It's getting better."

Miranda searched for another excuse not to go there yet, but she'd already delayed him almost three weeks.

"I'm so ready for the woods," Monrovia said, and ran inside.

It's done then.

Carl held out a bag to her. "I have a present for you." His cheerful voice sounded forced.

"A present?" Miranda ran a quick inventory of every time she'd ever heard those words directed at her. As expected, the results came back as zero. She took the bag with an excitement she found irritating and pulled out a brown boot with a green sweater trim around the top. It was clean and soft—and brand new. "This is for…me?"

"Of course, and there should be another one in there." Carl winked.

Miranda took both boots out and let the bag fall. They were even nicer than the plastic boots the rich wore in Bubble City, and far nicer than anything a girl from the

Trash Lands could ever dream of having. But she had never been a girl from the Trash Lands, not truly. She had to keep reminding herself of that.

"They're too nice to wear outside. They'll get dirty."

"Their job is to protect your feet. They don't need to stay clean. Try them on," Carl said.

She dropped into the chair and slid one on, then the other. They were a warm hug for her feet.

"Walk around. We need to make sure they fit because we'll be walking a lot."

Miranda stepped around the balcony, bouncing as if she was walking on a cloud.

"They're perfect." She stared at the crisp boots on her feet. Surely these feet were not hers. "I've never had new shoes."

Tears welled up in Carl's eyes as he tucked a mass of dark, unruly curls behind her ear; curls so much like his own, before his had gone gray. "You have, you just don't remember."

In that moment, Miranda wished she knew this man as her father, wished she could recall a time when she wasn't learning his reactions and habits; a time when he was familiar. "Thank you."

He recovered and straightened up. "It's my pleasure. Now, go pack. And bring extra socks. You should always keep your feet dry."

Miranda joined her sister in the room they had shared for the last three weeks. If Monrovia regretted letting her move in, she was good at hiding it. A new green canvas pack lay on Miranda's bed.

"Dad and I picked this out for you a few days ago," Monrovia said. "We got you some new clothes, too. I hope they're okay." She tapped a short stack of gray T-shirts and black cargo pants. "I didn't want to break you out of your comfort zone, so we stuck to dark colors."

A wave of relief hit Miranda. "Thanks."

She tried on the empty pack. The thickly padded straps sat comfortably on her frame. A tingle washed over her and she grinned. *New boots, new pack.* Life in the Trash Lands would have been a lot different if she'd had these supplies.

"Fill it up." Monrovia threw several rolls of socks on the bed. "And here is your bed roll. You tie it to the bottom." She unfurled her own sleeping bag and rolled it tightly again, sliding it under the two straps at the bottom of the pack, then cinched it tight.

Miranda wrestled with whether to ask her about last night. Surely, she would have said something by now if he really had looked like Nathan. She rolled a pair of pants and shoved them down into the pack. Better to leave it.

Monrovia packed some socks for herself. "Sophia's son's name is Oren."

Miranda's heart beat faster. Why would she say that? She focused on breathing evenly, trying to keep her cool, and smoothed out her bedroll, tightening the straps around it as Monrovia had. "Oh, yeah?"

"I hadn't seen him in years before last night. It's so strange that he looks so much like..." Her voice dropped.

Miranda's legs weakened, and she sat.

"You okay?" Monrovia asked.

No.

Her tongue lay dry and useless in her mouth. Why had she taken so long to say something? Monrovia had casually confirmed that a mirror image of the boy she loved, the boy she'd lost forever, had appeared and she'd fainted onto a coffee table.

No. I'm not okay.

Monrovia put her hand lightly on her shoulder. "Miranda?"

"Why does he look like Nathan?"

Monrovia shook her head. "I wish I knew. You need some water. I'll be right back."

She hurried out of the room and Miranda stared at the clothes, waiting to be packed. She touched a soft shirt and buried it in the bag. *What does it mean?* Did he act like Nathan, too? When would she see him again? A shiver ran down her arms. It would be so hard to wait until they got back.

But she had crashed onto a table. He must think she was demented.

She slid in the rest of the clothes—shirts, pants, socks and rolled the top down. A sense of control bubbled up as she laced the straps through the fasteners. She breathed a little easier as she tightened them. She would carry her own bed and wear clean clothes that fit and walk in new boots. Whatever this Nathan lookalike meant, she would face it.

She took a step to feel the weight and accidentally kicked some socks under the bed. She dropped the pack and fell to her knees, fumbling under the bed to get them. But instead of soft cotton, her fingers brushed the surface of a hard-backed book. Her heart quickened. She knew what it was before she saw it. The cover would be worn brown linen and most of the pages would be blank, waiting for a warm touch. She wanted to pull her hand away—to leave it there forgotten—but she couldn't.

She trembled as she pulled out the book and ran her fingers lightly over the pages, careful not to press her palm to the surface. The pages were cold, no trace of energy. Her conversations with Alois were wiped clean.

When she had first found this book buried in Monrovia's backpack, he had seemed a friend. He'd helped her save Monrovia and Beda through these pages. Her chest tightened. Why had he done that only to destroy Beda later?

"Alois died when we collapsed the black hole. Beda killed him." She whispered the words to convince herself. *He's gone. She's gone.* It had to be true.

"What are you doing with that?" Monrovia's words came out clipped and fast.

Miranda shut the book on her thumb. "I just found it under your bed."

Monrovia motioned and Miranda handed it over, watching her closely. She flipped through, scanning the pages.

"I guess the conversations are gone because he's dead," Monrovia said.

Miranda didn't want to give voice to the persistent thought burrowing a hole in her brain, but it burst out. "What if it's a trick? Getting rid of him was too easy."

Monrovia snapped her head up and slammed the book closed. "Beda died to stop Alois from continuing his cycle of torture. What was easy about that?"

Miranda bit her lip and nodded.

"You girls almost ready?" Carl sang out from the kitchen.

Miranda snatched her boots and pack from the bed, eager to put some distance between herself and Monrovia's certainty. Maybe Miranda accepted the possibility that not everything had gone as planned in that black hole, fighting a near-god, because she knew the real woman—the flawed woman.

She joined Carl and Harold to help wrangle the last of the supplies. Ten minutes later, they waited for the rover on the balcony, Miranda in her new clothes, new boots, carrying everything she owned on her back. *You don't deserve this.* The thought crept up, loud, but not unexpected. Why should she have so much when Earth was gone?

She looked over at Monrovia, who was watching the sky for a glimpse of the rover. She seemed anxious to leave.

Harold waited behind the balcony doors. Was it watching them? *Did it do that?*

Earlier, Carl had proclaimed with glee they were going to rough it. No robots, no food generators. Harold couldn't roll on uneven ground, anyway. *Roughing it.* Sounded familiar.

The sleek silver pod arrived to take them to the edge of the woods. Its door opened and a ribbon unfurled, hardening into stairs.

"That's hard to get used to," Miranda said, trying to shake a hollowness taking hold in her gut.

"Electrocrystallization," Carl said. "I love it. It would have been nice to share some of our advances with Earth, but they weren't ready for our ideas."

Miranda stepped in behind Monrovia and Carl came in last. She noticed a lemon scent as she settled into her seat. She'd been in several of these pods by now, and they had all been small, but this was the first one with a scent. Was that a special touch by the company for Carl? His old job had made him a kind of celebrity. *Strange.* She fought to cram her pack under the seat.

The door sealed shut with a satisfying whoosh, and Miranda's stomach fluttered as the rover rose into the air. Flying would never be her favorite. The machine powered in a straight line, following the street below, and she peered out of the window as the city raced by.

Orderly apartment buildings like Carl's gave way to small houses, then the space between the houses widened, becoming fields separated by clusters of trees.

The flutter in Miranda's stomach grew, and she had to admit it was more than flying in the rover. Since the Gathering, she had no connection to Beda, not even a whisper. She had tried, in the silence of night, in the business of day—in many ways—to catch hold of the feeling, the memory of her mother. But each time only the realities of her new world came back to her. Maybe this life of plenty had dulled her senses. She chewed at the skin by her thumb nail as the fields gave way to trees.

What if Beda's special place wasn't special at all for her? What if there was no magic, only rocks and trees, with no unexpected shiver she could tell herself was a hug from beyond? No buzz past her ear she could pretend was a whisper?

The rover slowed and descended.

"We could fly closer, but we'd miss the full experience if we did," Carl said. "It will mean more because we've earned it."

That sounded like the sentiment of someone who has never had to do without, but Miranda did not protest.

The door opened slowly, and Carl hopped out first, followed by Monrovia, each of them carrying their backpacks. Miranda tugged at her own, ripping it out from the hold. She perched on the edge, holding it tight to her chest.

If I can't feel her here, then she's really gone.

A heaviness settled on her shoulders as she stepped down into the bright day.

CHAPTER 3

PINK ROCKS

They piled out of the rover and onto a patch of gravel that extended to a small wooden fence. A gentle breeze rustled the tall grass in the field beyond. The air was cooler here than in Samsara; the sun warm but not yet hot.

"The trailhead is about a mile that way." Carl pointed at a line of dense trees. Gravel gave way to wet grass. Miranda's boots sank in the soft, rich mud. Her head spun, and the ground seemed to roll under her feet. She'd been here before—but that was impossible. Still, she couldn't deny the familiarity slapping her in the face. Darkness clouded her vision, closing in until only a pinprick of light broke through. She threw out her hand to keep from falling and connected with Monrovia's arm. Miranda clung tight, words stuck in her throat. She fought for her bearings, but the field spun.

A memory came into focus in her mind. She'd been here, but when she was on Earth, with Nathan. She'd sat on the milk crate in the cafe's kitchen and been transported in a vision to a field so much like this one. Mud had covered her boots and water had seeped into the holes, soaking her feet.

"What's wrong?" Carl's voice floated. "Are you okay?"

Miranda shut her eyes tight and focused on his voice, willing herself to open them to a sunny day. Monrovia was talking, too, but her words sounded garbled, like she was underwater.

Carl leaned closer. "If you can't do this yet, it's okay, Miranda," he said.

She breathed deep, and the spinning slowed, then stopped. Both their faces, framed by bright-blue sky, stared at her, their heads bobbing like balloons with painted eyes, silently staring. She blinked hard and they returned to normal. Her legs were sturdy on the ground. Wildflowers bent in the breeze. She let go of Monrovia's arm. Her grip had left red marks.

"I'm okay, I… explaining what she just experienced wouldn't convince either of them she was ready for this journey. She decided to go with, "I'm fine."

Carl brushed a curl out of her face, his mouth set in a firm frown. "I think being in Beda's place will help you, but we can wait if you need more time."

Miranda wanted to believe him, and not to disappoint. She quickly wiped away the unexpected tears. "I can do it."

He gave her hand a tight squeeze then faced the tree line, reporting in his Carl-the-man-in-charge voice, "We'll camp at the Green River tonight. It's five miles away, so we better get a move on."

Miranda fell in line behind Monrovia as they carved a path through the high grass. She thought of Nathan with each step. Was any piece of him left? A soul? She cleared away the tears sneaking down her cheeks.

Carl stopped at the edge of the forest.

"If we keep a good pace, we'll have no problem making Green River before dark. We'll set up camp and have a good dinner. It's another half-day's hike to the waterfall from there." He gave Miranda's shoulder a playful squeeze. "How ya feeling, Randa?"

She'd never seen him so relaxed. She wished she could soak up his energy. Maybe pretending was enough.

She tried a convincing smile. "Fine," she said.

He nodded. "Let me know if you need to slow down or rest." He turned heel and sprinted into the dark woods.

The temperature dropped under the thick canopy, and a blanket of wet leaves muffled the soft thud of their steps. Miranda tried to feel something different in the air here, something different from the detached confusion of Samsara. She peered between the trees, examined the carpet of leaves and needles under her feet. No tingle, no magic. Her mouth went dry.

I don't feel her.

She caught a glimpse of something large moving quickly. She whipped her head in that direction, searching the shadows between the trunks, but there were only tall, skinny pines. Carl yelled something, but his words were lost in the rustling leaves.

She tripped and flailed for a hold but landed face first in the dirt.

Carl doubled back. "I said watch out for that root." He helped her back to her feet.

"Pthh." She spat out wet leaves.

Her shin throbbed, and she looked back where he pointed. A mid-shin height, gnarled root. *How could I miss that?* "Sure, next time." She carefully dragged her pant leg up over the tender spot. "It'll just bruise."

Carl gave her a look like he was worried she might break. "You have to step carefully out here."

"I've never been in the woods, you know."

"Of course." His face settled, as if he was reminding himself that she was not like Monrovia. She was different, strange.

"Well, pay attention to where you step out here."

"Noted," Miranda said.

"Wait there. I'll go find something to help that bruise." Monrovia darted off the trail and came back a few minutes later with a handful of pulpy leaves. She gingerly rubbed the juice of one onto the bruise. The pulp was ice cold, and Miranda wanted to pull her leg away, but she bit her lip instead.

"Your bruise will heal much faster now," Monrovia said.

The pulp quickly dried on her leg. Monrovia offered her hand and Miranda took it, standing cautiously, testing her weight on her leg. Carl had his arms folded tightly across his chest, his eyebrows knitted, gauging her progress.

Miranda dropped her sister's hand, suddenly aware that she was delaying the mission. She took a step on her own. Hot pain shot up her leg, and she winced, but quickly covered her grimace and gave a thumbs up. She waited for them to turn away before hobbling a few more steps, trying not to put her full weight on that leg. She trained her focus on the trail.

Forest sounds came alive around her—the beat of a bird's wings, the rustle of leaves on the trees, and the patter of their soft steps on wet ground. She settled into the repetition of walking and the throbbing became part of the scenery. They hiked in silence for a long time before she spoke. "How much farther?"

"We're getting close to the campsite now. Can you hear the river?" Carl asked.

Miranda listened but could not pick out the rush of water from the muted forest sounds.

"When was the last time we camped, Dad?" Monrovia asked. *Was she tired of walking in silence?*

"When you were about twelve or thirteen, I think. It's been too long. Workaholic Carl is a thing of the past, girls."

Miranda remembered her first night in Samsara. Carl had been called to the lab almost immediately. His long-lost child showing up after years wasn't enough to give him the night off. But he had been trying to save Earth from the black hole. Miranda shrugged. *Priorities.*

"We'll see about that. I have my doubts," Monrovia said.

"Me too," Carl mumbled.

Another twenty minutes of trudging brought them out of the trees to a riverbank.

"We made it." Carl flung his arms wide as if introducing them to a thing he had built himself. "Green River gets its name from the moss that grows on the rocks." He pointed to a spring-green mound under the fast-moving water. "But be careful because the moss makes the rocks slippery, and the top of the waterfall is just down there." He pointed downriver. "You wouldn't want to be dragged." He dropped his pack and began unloading poles and canvas.

Giant rocks dotted the riverbed, their green strands flowing like an off-kilter princess's mane. "We'd have to stand on the rocks to slip off them, right?" Miranda asked.

"That's right!" Monrovia stripped off her shoes, laughing as she bounded into the rushing water and hopped on top of a rock, then slid into knee deep water, squealing with delight.

Miranda had never seen her be so free.

Carl laughed. "There will be time for that later, but first we have to make camp. Come on, Rona, you've got to show Randa the ropes."

He'd only used that nickname with her a few times, but always when he was in a good mood. It still sounded strange to her ear, but she hoped for a chance to get used to it.

"Okay," Monrovia came back to the rough sand, her pants soaked.

Miranda stepped aside as Monrovia and Carl worked through a series of practiced moves, handing off poles and setting up the canvas until Carl tossed Miranda a small roll of twine. "Tie the rivets to the poles."

She caught the roll and rubbed her sweating palms along her legs. A mess of fabric stared up at her, daring her to make it something useful. A circle of metal outlining a hole in the corner of the canvas caught her eye. "Is this a rivet?"

Carl glanced up. "Yep!"

She breathed a sigh of relief and fed the piece of twine through, wrapping it around the pole, then fought with it to tie a knot. Carl leaned over her shoulder.

"Tie it so it's tight, but can be loosened easily later, like this." He held both ends together and looped them around two fingers, then yanked down. "Now you try."

Miranda looped the twine the same way. It held.

"Nice job."

"It took me years to master that knot," Monrovia said.

"You were also much younger," Carl said.

He patted Miranda's back and warmth enveloped her. She sat back, tired from the day, but without the hollowed-out exhaustion she'd gotten used to. A fully constructed tent stood in front of her, and she'd helped.

"Now, everyone claim your spot in the tent."

"I'll take the middle," Monrovia said as she disappeared into the tent with her bedroll.

Miranda dragged her pallet in behind her and threw it against the side. The tent seemed smaller inside than she expected. "This is going to be weird."

"Sleeping all together, you mean?"

"Yeah."

"It's just different. I'm going back in." Monrovia ran out of the tent, toward the glistening, green water.

Miranda followed her out but paused by Carl as he fussed with starting a fire.

"Go ahead." He nodded at Miranda. "I'll get dinner together."

She left her boots and socks in the damp sand at the river's edge and rolled up her pant legs, sticking one foot in. Icy water bit her skin, and she jumped back. "It's freezing, Rona!" She liked using Carl's pet names. It seemed right here.

"Comes down from the mountain. What do you expect? You can handle it, come on." Monrovia balanced on two bright-green rocks, grinning.

Miranda took a cautious step onto a bed of pebbles. Her toes rippled under the clear water. She climbed onto a soft, furry rock, its green hair brushing against her toes. Monrovia hopped from rock to rock. She tried to imagine Beda doing the same. Her stomach tightened. She couldn't remember ever seeing her mother do something for fun.

Miranda stepped from her rock to the next large one, closer to Monrovia. Her foot slipped, and she landed knee deep and gasped as her chest tightened from the cold. Monrovia hopped as if each rock had a Velcro top. *How is she doing that?*

Small silver fish darted in and out of Miranda's legs. She snatched at one, but it swam away. She took a step closer to Monrovia and a perfect square of pink lit up under her foot. Instinctively, she jerked her foot back, but the pink square glowed up at her defiant, demanding to be seen. A perfect pink square just like on the pedestrian bridge in Bubble City.

She looked up, horrified that she might see the woman being lifted. Leaves rustled in the wind, the smell of dinner cooking on the campfire filled the air. Everything was in its place.

She rubbed her eyes, begging to see anything else when she opened them, but the square glowed unflinching. Her heart pounded in her ears louder than the racing current. She tried to shut out the image of bodies crashing onto shattered bricks in the dome.

Not here. It can't be here.

Monrovia splashed too far upstream for Miranda to call her back. *And what if it isn't really here?* Miranda fought the current to the riverbank, refusing to look down.

***

"You're shaking! Is it that cold?" Carl asked when she fell by the fire. He hummed while he stirred the contents of the pot.

The words fell out of her mouth before she could stop them. "I saw something under the water."

Carl put the spoon down, his forehead creased with worry lines. "What do you mean? You seem scared."

She'd ruined his relaxed night. Her stomach knotted in a tight ball. She could say she was kidding. *It was nothing.* But she couldn't hold it in. "There's a piece of glass from a bridge in Bubble City over there." She pointed, shaking. "It lit up pink when I stood on it. It's at the bottom of the river." She searched his face for understanding.

"Pink?"

Miranda nodded. He relaxed, stirred the contents of the pot again.

"That's just flat quartz. When the sun hits them, it makes them light up. Some can be as pink as a rose. Pretty, right?"

He wrapped a towel around her, and the tension of the last few days melted out of her muscles. *Pink quartz.* She'd never been so happy to learn about a rock in her life. She didn't want him to let go.

He held the ends of the towel and looked into her eyes. "You're safe here. Do you believe that?"

Miranda knew there was a right answer, but she also knew there was no point in lying. "I hope you're right."

Carl sighed and went back to stirring the bubbling pot of bean chili he seemed to have conjured.

"When did you first come here?" Miranda asked.

He looked around the beach and out to the river, an almost shy smile curling on his lips. "Your mother brought me out here not long after we met."

He pointed to a rock just breaking the surface of the rushing water. "On a night with a full moon, she stood on

30

that rock. The moonlight made her hair glow silver. She balanced perfectly, like she was standing on the water." His eyes misted. "That's when I fell in love with her." He sniffled and added, "I should have known she'd be trouble."

Miranda watched the reflection of the crescent moon dance on the river and pictured the scene. Beda in her glory, at one with the river, pulling power from the moon. She had never thought of her mother as trouble. Crazy, yes—but never trouble.

But of course, she was. She left her husband and daughter and raised their other daughter in a dying foreign world just for the off chance they could save it. It's a brand of trouble.

Miranda hesitated, but she needed to know. She let the words tumble out. "Would you have stayed with her if you knew she was going to leave and separate us?"

Carl sucked in air and didn't answer right away. Miranda tucked her legs under her and leaned in just a little closer. He watched the river. The water gently lapped at the rocks and silence hung for several minutes.

Miranda decided he would not answer—almost an answer of its own, but then he said, "I think it's better not to know how things will work out."

His answer stung. He would not have chosen Beda if he had known. He would change it all if he could. Why should that surprise her? It was the logical decision. Or maybe he was glad he didn't know. Glad he was free to make the choice he did.

"She was fearless," he said, still looking out over the water.

Monrovia sniffled. "I'll get the bowls. It's time we ate." Miranda hadn't realized she was even there.

As Monrovia scooped chili into bowls Carl said, "She cried for weeks after you both left. She kept asking where Mommy and Randa went and when you'd come back. I didn't know what to tell her. Eventually, she stopped asking.

That almost made it worse, like one day she woke up and forgot you both, so I didn't talk about you in case that would start her pain again." He wiped his face and suddenly looked older. "I didn't know what to do."

Miranda stared out over the rushing water, feeling empty. "I don't remember Nibiru at all. I wish I did."

***

Silence. Darkness. Teeth-rattling cold seeped under Miranda's skin. Drifting. Helpless. She shouted until her throat was raw, but the sound came out as a whimper.

Then, no more drifting. Now tearing through space at blinding speed, stars streams of light. Tears slashed her cheeks, ripped from her eyes by the force of the wind.

Earth hovered, expectant, watery and blue. She smashed into the ruins of Bubble City. Heaps of gnarled metal and broken cinder block. She'd come down past the bridge where the woman would float up.

Nathan, inside the cafe, clawing at the countertop, fighting being Lifted. As his feet rose higher than his shoulders, he lost his grip. Miranda reached out for him, but, like every time they had to replay this, he was just beyond her reach.

His face twisted with pain as his body contorted at an impossible angle. Light streamed around him, and he screamed her name as he reached for her, until his body crumpled as if crushed in the palm of an unseen hand.

She shook with rage. "*Nathan!*"

Her scream would not leave her.

Bubble City melted into darkness, and now it was Beda in battle. Her body thrashed as an unseen enemy ripped her limbs from her torso. Tissue and bone floated aimless in the air.

Miranda lunged at the faint outline, determined to rip apart the assailant she could not see, but instead of grabbing hold, her feet went tumbling over her head. She hurtled through darkness, head over heels, faster and faster until she slammed into a cold stone floor. Or was it rock?

***

A slippery wet rock. She fought for breath. It hadn't happened that way.

But—what is that?

Cold water rushed over her feet. Mountain, night, river. She balanced perfectly on the green rock in the middle of the rushing river.

How did I get here?

The poise that held her paralyzed in her nightmare fell away. Every muscle in her body slackened. She slid off the rock and her head slipped under the bracing water. Black. Cold.

A blind panic gripped her.

I can't swim.

She thrashed for the surface. The current that had been lazy and slow earlier in the day now raged. She found the surface and the thundering boom of falling water was all around her. So close.

The top of the waterfall.

Carl's warning banged in her head as tons of rushing water pushed her closer to the precipice, as if the river had claimed her. One quick breath of air and then under again. She flailed for a handhold under the water, grasping for anything to stop her from going over the edge.

Her lungs burned. She needed another breath.

Is this the end?

Her fingers touched something sturdy, like a metal rope running under the surface. Sharp spikes sliced into her hand as she gripped it. She yelled, taking in water, but held on, using it to pull her head above the surface. She sputtered, coughing up the river while stealing gulps of air.

33

Barbed wire.

Her hand burned, but she squeezed tighter as the river pulled at her. White-hot pain shot up her arm. She fought the water to grip her other hand on the twisted metal. It landed between the spikes.

Mercy.

She clamped down on the rope, hauling herself a few inches further from the falls, battling to breathe air, not gulp water.

If I slip, it's over.

She could barely feel her legs. The freezing water pounded her face, and the thundering falls battered her ears. It was so hard to hold on. Her grip slackened.

I'm sorry, Carl. I didn't mean to.

Would he think this was somehow his fault?

No, not like this. A surge of adrenaline kicked in, and she let go of the blade, reaching blindly under the black water for a spot higher up the rope. Her cut hand landed on the braided metal, and she heaved herself forward. Letting the other hand go, groping for a safe place to brace, she dragged herself farther upriver. Her muscles quivered against the strain.

"Miranda!" Carl's voice cut through the darkness.

"Miranda! Where are you?" Monrovia called out.

Miranda's heart leaped. *They're looking for me.*

She clutched the barbed wire with her good hand and splashed with the other. Shouting over the rushing water, she yelled, "I'm here!"

"She's in the river!" Carl sounded panicked. "Where are you?"

She wildly chopped at the surface with her free hand, hoping one of them would find her before the river tore her loose. "Over here!"

He's coming to save me. Miranda's senses sharpened. *I will make it out of this.* She pulled higher out of the water and, by the light of the moon, saw Carl sink under the surface. Her mind froze, unable to process why he'd disappeared. Her heart thudded against her rib cage until he crested the water close to her. He wedged himself against a rock.

"Give me your hands," he said, reaching out to her.

She released one hand and locked into his outstretched grasp. He motioned for her to release the other. She hesitated. *Will we both go over?*

"Come on."

She released the thick wire, and he tugged her close.

"Climb on my back."

Miranda clung desperately to his shoulders as he took two powerful strokes. Monrovia watched from the shore. Her scream split the night as the current pushed them farther downstream, closer to the roaring drop off.

She cannot watch us die.

Miranda clasped his shoulders and stretched her numb legs out behind them, kicking furiously to act as a motor.

Carl pushed through several stronger strokes, and they made it to shallow water, where they collapsed onto the pebble shore.

Miranda heaved up river water onto the rough sand until only a sticky yellow fluid was left. It burned her throat. She sat back on her heels, shaking. Monrovia wrapped a towel around her shoulders. Miranda met her gaze. Monrovia searched for understanding but must not have found what she expected. She slowly shook her head.

Carl took a deep breath, then voiced the question she knew was coming. "What were you doing out there?"

Miranda stared at the river like it was an unsecured weapon. "I woke up, and I was standing on a rock in the river. Then I fell."

"I put you on the inside so I would know if you left the tent," Monrovia said. "How did you get out without waking me up?"

"I don't know what happened." Miranda blinked a few times as if it might help her better understand her sister's casual confession. *I think you're crazy and need to be watched.*

Carl squinted, forming new wrinkles on his forehead. "Sleepwalking."

Depressed planet killer. So many labels.

"You two need dry clothes. It's cold tonight." Miranda let Monrovia help her up.

They hobbled back to the tent by moonlight. Miranda changed into the warm clothes Monrovia had found for her and crumbled onto her sleeping bag. Monrovia slathered slime on her wound and wrapped it in shreds of a shirt. Miranda closed her eyes, but the second she did, the weight of the dream slammed into her like a punch.

She snapped her eyes open. "Nathan was being crushed and Mom was torn apart. They were in agony, screaming in pain, and I... I couldn't do anything. I just watched them be obliterated." The words, the memory, weighed her down. She wondered if she'd ever have the strength to get up.

Monrovia squeezed Miranda's shoulder. "It wasn't real. It didn't happen that way."

"It seemed real." Miranda let the tears flow until her lids were too heavy to keep open.

CHAPTER 4

THE FINAL FUNERAL

Spoons clanked against tin as Miranda climbed out of the tent. The recognizable whiff of coffee hit her nose—Bubble City, working alongside Nathan, luxuries she couldn't have. Like so many things on Earth, coffee was for others. "Good morning," Carl said.

She squinted into the early morning sun to see his face. Monrovia stood behind him, cautious, like she was afraid Miranda might break if she approached too quickly.

He put an arm around her and squeezed her shoulder. "How are you feeling?"

Miranda buried her toes in the sandy soil. "Hungry."

Carl's face broke into a grin. "I can work with hungry."

Monrovia popped out from behind him, still watching Miranda warily, and handed her a bowl of brownish mush. "Would you like some coffee?"

Miranda took the mush and shivered with a rush from the question. In this life, she was allowed simple pleasures. In this life, she didn't steal food or water, both were plentiful. She ate a spoonful of the hot, bland food, and nodded to Monrovia. "Sure." She was on the other side now.

Last night's dream and fighting for her life in the river still clung to her like a shadow, but the bright morning sun faded the memory. Monrovia passed her a cup with steam swirling to the sky. She leaned in for a sip. The bitterness curled her tongue, and she crinkled her nose, searching for water.

Carl laughed. "You can try it with milk at home."

"No wonder people put sugar in this stuff." She slurped another cautious sip. The pungent flavor spread over her tongue, but it was growing on her.

"Finish up. We need to get a move on. I want to make it to Beda's waterfall by midmorning."

She shoveled down the bland food, appreciating that it lacked the fire of last night's dish. Monrovia and Carl worked with precision to break down the tent, rehearsing practiced steps.

Miranda repacked quickly with her good hand, careful not to be a burden—*more* of a burden. She took in the river view as she secured her pack. The water was calm. Enough to make her doubt everything that had happened—and she would have doubted it if Carl and Monrovia weren't witnesses. The deep cuts on her hand also stood as proof.

Miranda fell last in line as Carl led the way into the forest. After only a few steps, the dark patches hiding behind trees hooked into the shadow of her dream, stretching the landscape until only Beda's contorted body ripped apart in front of her and the echo of Nathan's scream drowned out any other sound. She squeezed the sides of her head to make it stop. *It didn't happen that way.*

"What's wrong?"

Monrovia's voice jolted her. Her sister cocked her head with a worried look, but also one that demanded, pull it together.

Miranda tried to shake off the icy chill of torture.

"Come on, girls!" Carl waved for them to catch up.

"Coming," Monrovia yelled back. "You okay?" *Was it a question or an accusation?*

Miranda took a careful step. *Focus on the patches of light, not shadow.* Maybe Beda's special place would help wipe away these images. "He likes a goal, doesn't he?" Miranda asked.

"In everything," Monrovia said.

The woods were quieter and cooler than the river. They walked in the shadow of the mountain. Miranda scanned the trail, but she also peered through the trees, wanting to glimpse whatever might be there.

Pockets of sunlight played on the forest floor, golden brown with pine needles and fallen leaves and—

Miranda slammed into Monrovia's back, startled. She peered around her sister to find Carl kneeling with his finger to his lips. He pointed to the path ahead with a silly grin.

Miranda's gaze followed where he pointed and she caught her breath. A gray bunny sat on the path, rapidly twitching its nose. His silky ears stood at attention as he watched them warily.

She'd seen jackrabbits with long skinny legs, matted fur, and red eyes in the Trash Lands. Their tall ears stood up, too, but that was the only similarity with this gray ball of what seemed to be the softest possible thing in the universe.

Miranda's fingers itched to touch his fur. The wind shifted, rustling the trees, and his ears tilted.

"He's like the drawings. I thought they were a lie because the desert rabbits never looked like that. I can't… Why is he so cute?" Miranda whispered.

He hopped off the path, disappearing into the undergrowth.

"I like that line of thinking," Carl said. "But being cute doesn't stop the hungry fox."

Miranda winced at the idea of the plump, furry rabbit being someone's dinner, but peeked under the branches, wanting another glimpse. "Where did he go?"

Carl patted her back. "He's long gone."

The sun climbed higher as they walked, and dank air settled deeper into the trees. Dry leaves gave way to spongy moss as the path curved up, gradually at first, then became a steep climb. A slate wall stretched along one side of the trail in this section. Ferns jutted from cracks, and small rivers of water washed down its face, spilling into a pool lined with rounded, flat stones.

She ran her fingers under the drips, stroking the slick moss. *Like the moss from the river.* Her cuts stung under the bandages, as if the memory made the wound deeper. She pulled her fingers away and looked around for Monrovia and Carl. *No sign.* They must have rounded a turn. She jogged up the trail. *Hiding?* She listened for their footsteps and the rustling of fabric.

Silence.

Miranda's heart beat harder.

They are here. Somewhere.

Monrovia stuck her head out of a thick patch of trees. "Through here."

Miranda stumbled back and uttered a soft curse but followed Monrovia into the chill. The dank air seeped through Miranda's thin jacket. "It's here?" She shivered but stayed close behind Monrovia as she hurried over the moss-covered boulders and knotted roots.

Perched, cross-legged, on the edge of a flat rock, Carl faced a rushing waterfall that ended in white caps of bubbles in a pool below. The musty dankness evaporated in the warm sunlight. Even the rocks themselves shimmered.

Miranda's skin tingled as she laid her pack at her side. "It's simple, but amazing."

Everywhere she looked was another small, but perfect, detail—a single pink flower growing from a crack in a rock, the light dancing on the clear water below.

"She always said she could think more clearly here. Understand what needed to be done," Carl said.

The crisp air buzzed through Miranda. She imagined Beda right here with them, silent, back straight, legs folded into lotus.

As if confirming her image, Carl said, "Your mother would sit here for hours, just being." He closed his eyes. "Let the vibrations from the falls run through you."

The slab warmed Miranda's legs, and the steady rhythm of falling water wrapped around her. She leaned back, turning her face up to the warm sun, her eyes closed. *Are you here, Mom? Can you see us?* She searched for a change in the air, still the energetic buzz. She listened for a whisper in her mind. No whispers from Beda. She opened her eyes again. Her chest tightened. *Are you really gone?*

"She was the strongest person I have ever known," Carl whispered. "She made hard choices, but she loved you both very much."

Monrovia sniffled. "I wish I knew her for longer."

"I do too," Carl said.

Miranda took a deep breath of crisp air. What would Beda think about when she came here? Was this where she decided she had to save Earth? Why did she think that was her job?

A light tickle brushed Miranda's hand. A large yellow-and-black butterfly rested on the back. She fought the impulse to shake it off.

Is this my sign? It fluttered over to the crystal-clear pool.

"Maybe she knows we're here," said Monrovia.

"I don't know." Carl patted her hand. "Our Beda might be gone."

Monrovia let out a sob. The sound released Miranda's own pent-up tears. She cried openly, like she'd wanted to during Beda's funeral, but hadn't because all of Samsara was watching.

"I'm so thankful to have you girls." Carl took both their hands and held them to his chest.

Miranda considered his tear-stained face. Who was this man who never stopped loving the woman who abandoned him and their daughter, raising their other daughter in a strangled Earth clinging to life? He would be justified in hating Beda, Miranda knew that. Justified if he filled Monrovia's heart with hatred against her mother. But he must have held out a silent hope they would all be a family again one day. Because when she finally returned, he had opened his home—and maybe his heart—to her.

"I wish we still had her, but the three of us can make a family." Carl squeezed their hands.

A rush of warmth filled Miranda, and she wanted more than anything to know this man as her father. She tugged her hand away and threw her arms around Carl's neck, burying her face in his shoulder, hugging him tight. He hugged her back, and another pair of arms wrapped around too—Monrovia joining in. Miranda relaxed into the closeness as they held each other, enjoying the gentle vibrations of the waterfall, the warmth of the slab. It was so peaceful. An unfamiliar and overwhelming feeling of safety settled on her.

The gentle vibrations grew stronger until a few small pebbles rolled off the edge of the slab.

Monrovia sat up. "Is that normal?"

The warmth slipped away as Carl straightened. The ground rumbled. Unmistakable.

Carl swept his head left, then right. The crack of breaking glass split the quiet.

"Get to the trees!" he yelled.

They bolted off the rock.

Monrovia was quickest, with Miranda right behind her. A deafening boom dropped them all to their knees. The land churned under her feet, and Miranda wrapped her arms around the trunk of a tree to keep from falling.

"Hold on!" Carl yelled, and she did.

The ground buckled and shook as if trying to knock her loose. Something shattered against the ledge where they had been sitting. Miranda craned her neck to look back. Her jaw dropped as squares of pastel glass rained from the sky, smashing along the stone and into the pool below. She squeezed her eyes shut. *That wasn't glass. If I look in the water, I'll see it's just quartz from the mountain.*

She opened her eyes again and zeroed in on her pack dangling from a tree branch at the edge of the rock. Her safety, her security, hanging by a thread. She let go of the tree and lunged for the pack.

"Miranda, get back here!" Carl shouted, high pitched and strained.

Shards of brightly colored glass littered the stone. She reached for her pack. A shadow darkened the water below. Chills raced down her arms. Her fingers curled around the strap, and she tugged her bag free.

"Miranda!" Carl shouted again.

The shadow grew larger. She glanced up and her heart stopped. A familiar curve of carved stone. *No, it can't be.* A piece of a small bridge bore down on her. She clutched her pack and bounded back to the trees, clenching the trunk again.

The curved concrete arch of the foot bridge Miranda crossed daily during her work commute in Bubble City came into full view, falling fast as if from a great height. It smashed into Beda's rock, splitting concrete and stone in every direction. Miranda turned her face away from the shrapnel.

After what seemed like minutes, the ground settled, no more rumbling.

"Is it over?" Monrovia asked.

Miranda kept her head down, afraid to see only a jagged open space where Beda's rock should be, and pieces of that bridge in the water below. *It's ok, look, you were hallucinating.* She slowly stood, her hands shaking as she secured the pack on her shoulders. The slab where they had gathered just a few minutes before stood half its size with an edge now jagged and raw.

Carl's cheeks flashed red as he fumed at Miranda. "What were you thinking? Going after that bag? Nothing in there is worth your life."

Miranda tightened the pack against her back. It was the only security she had, but she didn't expect him to understand. She shrugged. "Sorry."

Monrovia stared into the forest, apparently dazed.

Carl huffed. "Landslide. There may have been an earthquake." His face darkened, and he looked away, into the woods. "Boulders will be loose, and it may start again. We have to get out of here."

Landslide. Of course. Miranda stepped toward the edge, peering down into the water. Her blood ran cold. Shattered glass, pink, blue, and green, and the curve of the familiar bridge winked up at her, unmistakable. "Can you guys come look at this?"

"Get away from there! It's not stable," Carl said.

Miranda inched cautiously back. "You saw what broke the rock, right?" Did he believe it was a landslide, or was he trying to convince himself?

Carl turned away mumbling, "I'm not sure." More loud booms echoed. "That sounded close. Come on." He hurried through the trees in a stooped posture, as if such a position offered him better protection.

Miranda weaved her way along the path behind him. They made it to the cushioned carpet of an eerily unchanged forest. Sunlight painted patches on the ground and wind whistled between the branches. Miranda played back what she'd just seen: squares of pink, blue, and green glass from the bridge in Bubble City tumbling like marbles from a child's hand. Then the whole bridge behind it. How? Earth was gone.

And Carl saw it, even though he wouldn't admit it.

Unless. Unless it wasn't the bridge at all.

I didn't dream it. It was real.

Carl stopped on the trail, bent over with his hands on his knees, heaving. Monrovia put her hand on his back. He straightened up, showing a pained expression, but did not speak.

"Did you see what fell?" she asked Monrovia.

"No. I was covering my head," she said.

"I saw it clearly. The foot bridge from Bubble City fell from the sky and shattered Beda's rock." Saying those words gave her a mix of satisfaction at having aired the truth, but also turned her stomach. But if she ignored what she saw any longer, she'd have to punch a tree. "I crossed that bridge every day to get to work. It fell from Earth."

"Do you hear yourself? That is not possible," Monrovia said.

"I know, but it happened."

"It was a landslide, like Dad said, probably caused by an earthquake."

Miranda glared at Carl. *He's trying to pretend he didn't see it.* "Tell me what you saw."

Carl opened his mouth, but no words came out. He had been watching her on the rock.

Monrovia filled the silence by saying she felt the ground shake and saw something smash into Beda's rock.

So, her head wasn't buried.

To Miranda's growing irritation, Monrovia did not say what the *something* was that she saw. Carl nodded in agreement, adding nothing.

Heat rose to Miranda's cheeks. "Pieces of the bridge and glass are in the water."

Monrovia shook her head. "That's not possible. It must have been stone sheared off the mountain by tremors."

"And quartz," Carl looked sick as he said the words.

Miranda's legs softened, and she found she didn't have the strength to stand. She dropped to the ground and put her head in her hands, then faced Carl again, hot tears streaking her cheeks. "You saw it. It was a bridge. Tell her."

His hands shook, and his face was ashen.

"It was an earthquake," Monrovia said. "We should expect after-shocks."

Miranda's hands were now tight fists. "Earthquakes don't fall from the sky."

"Objects from planets that are recent history don't fall from the sky either." Monrovia's lips formed a tight line.

Miranda wanted to run deep into the forest, away from Monrovia's piercing stare.

"Girls!" Dark shadows rimmed Carl's eyes—shadows that had not been there that morning. "Please, it does not help to fight." Monrovia stormed ahead, and Miranda struggled to calm her breathing.

Whether Monrovia wanted to face the truth, pieces of Bubble City had smashed into Nibiru, and Miranda had to find out why—and if it could happen again.

CHAPTER 5

TIGHT GRASP

Miranda plodded among the roots growing over the trail, in part because of the waning light, but mostly to let Monrovia get a good lead. Soon, her stomping feet were far ahead. The stillness and growing darkness made Miranda shiver.

"Carl?" He should have been close behind her. The trees seemed to lean in, stretching their limbs to catch—or keep—her. "Carl?" she called again, quieter so as not to disturb the stillness.

She backtracked until the outline of a dark shape framed the trail. The hairs on the back of her neck stood on end. "Carl?" Soon, the profile of slumped shoulders became clear. He sat on a fallen log. "I thought you were behind me. What are you doing? It's getting dark."

He held his head, and his shoulders heaved.

Should I leave him alone?

He looked up with puffy, red eyes. "It was Beda's special place."

Miranda had never seen him in a state like this before. *What would Monrovia do?*

Miranda laid a hand on his shoulder. It shook as he unleashed fresh tears.

"It should have always been there for the two of you. A place for you to go to remember her. It should have been the grave we couldn't give her." He choked out a loud sob.

Miranda searched for something comforting to say but seeing him like this erased coherent thought. His eyes widened as if a sudden and terrible theory grabbed him.

"Did we do something wrong, Randa?"

Miranda's stomach sank to her feet. She sat down heavily on the boulder next to him, wished she needed him to explain more, didn't immediately know what he was asking. Yes, Alois tortured Earth, but why had they expected to stop him?

To hear Carl say it. She had tried to push her own anxieties aside, to pretend she could be happy in this new world, but now Carl voiced her deepest fear: they had made a terrible mistake and there would be consequences.

"I don't think Alois is gone," Miranda said. It came out as an accusation, but she didn't blame Carl. *Tell me I'm wrong.* "He's punishing us." She whispered so quietly he may not have heard, but his lips straightened into a tight line which said that he had.

He softened his mouth and gently laid his hand on hers. "Please don't worry about that. There must be plausible explanations for what happened. We just need more information."

"What if this happens again?" Miranda said, her stomach clenched. *More things falling from Earth.*

"No." Carl shook his head. "Whatever happened was a freak occurrence."

His eyes were so kind, his face lined with worry. He had stopped thinking of his own pain. Miranda's worry consumed him now. She wanted to wipe it away, to believe it was over, and they would find another cause, but what other explanation could there be?

Carl squeezed her hand. "We need to move while there's still light."

Miranda hauled herself up from the log. Each step along the trail was a chore, but she easily kept up with Carl as he moved along. When they stepped out of the forest, the moon hung over the river and a tent shaped shadow plagued the beach.

As they got closer, Monrovia called out, "I was too tired to make a fire. There are some cans of beans over there." She motioned to a pile near the tent.

Carl opened two cans and handed one to Miranda. She found a spoon and ate a mouthful of cold beans, then another. She'd eaten worse. The spoon rattled against the sides as she scraped up more. None of them wanted to talk. Monrovia went to bed first. Miranda ate slowly, waiting for Carl to turn in. She needed to clear her head, to be alone, but Carl seemed to find excuses not to go to bed.

Finally, Miranda said, "I need to sit up for a little while. Get my head straight."

Carl furrowed his brow.

"I promise not to go any closer to the river." Miranda tried a weak smile, but it felt like a too-tight jacket, and she dropped it.

He nodded and disappeared behind the folds of the tent.

***

A crisp wind blew off the mountain, rattling the tree branches. Miranda sat cross-legged on a rock on the beach, like Carl earlier today and Beda so many times before. She had hated it when Beda sat perfectly quiet for hours, but now she understood, during those times, Beda could have been anywhere.

Miranda knew who to ask to find out what they were up against. And she knew she'd have to stretch herself beyond comfort to find them. She slowed her breath, filling her belly on the inhale and sucking her stomach to her spine on the exhale, emptying herself.

Kirasu, if you're out there, speak to me.

She cleared her mind and focused on the strange melodies that followed Kirasu, keeping her eyes closed. Minutes stacked as the river rushed in a rhythm over the rocks. An owl hooted in the distance. Her hands rested, heavy on her knees.

Kirasu, show yourself and meet me.

Wings flapped above her. She ducked and watched a dark owl fly low over the water.

Tell me if it's him.

She fidgeted and waited. The damp night air closed in with a chill and returned her pleas with silence. She sat until her butt prickled and her back ached. Finally, she broke her position, pulling her legs in close to her body, hugged them tight, and rocked.

What did we do?

Tears fell quickly, and she heaved sobs under the moon's soft glow—the same moon that watched over her as she sat at Bear Rock with Nathan. She longed to feel his arms around her like that night. She wouldn't run this time.

"Nathan, I believed we were helping you. And Beda—Mom." She touched her lips, looking out over the cold water. *Did you die for nothing?*

The beans in her stomach congealed to one large rock as a wave of helplessness washed over her, taking her back to floating driftless in space, lost, looking for Beda and Monrovia. *Where would you be, Nathan, if we had died out there?* But Earth was already trapped in the black hole by that time, souls waiting to be reset.

Maybe it needed to start new, maybe we never should have intervened.

The muted ripple told her the river was deeper in this spot. She'd clung to the barbed wire not far from here. She shook off the chill of the air, and the memory, and climbed down from the rock. If Alois was back, he'd have to be stopped, but being damp on a hard rock apparently wouldn't help her get answers. The dank air fell away inside the tent. She settled into her sleeping bag and let her tired muscles shut off her brain.

As she drifted through the interim between the focus and the dream, Miranda floated in darkness, looking out at pinpricks of light. A distant shriek rattled her core. Soft drums rolled in around her and the high whine of a violin broke through. A song was forming.

Miranda spun around in the darkness, searching for the source of the music, or the voices, but only colors and instrumental sounds wrapped around her...

"Kirasu!"

The lyrics cut through and the words were precise.

> Not realizing who she'd become
> She blended into what was perceived
> She was quick to imitate
> A master of mimicry
> Made to consume, implicitly

"What do you mean? Is that me?"

> The last gasp is a tight grasp
> Shattering the home you've outgrown
> Surrender to the threshold
> You're a crush proof hero.

Nathan's body crumpling under the force of an unseen hand came back to her. "No!" she sobbed as the song played on. Something grabbed hold of her shoulders and shook her.

"Miranda." Carl's voice pierced her dream. "Wake up."

The music faded and the red tent walls came into focus. Carl's face hovered above hers. She threw her arms around his neck and sobbed.

"You were screaming and crying in your dream." He held her tightly.

"I saw Nathan crushed again." She didn't tell him about the music. It was too hard to explain.

"You're safe here," Carl said, releasing her. "Try to get some more sleep. You're going to need it tomorrow."

Miranda lay back and tried to settle her racing heart as she listened to Carl's and Monrovia's rhythmic breaths, the dream playing over and over until the first rays of dawn slipped into the tent.

CHAPTER 6

FATEFUL RIDE

A cold mist hung between the trees, blanketing Miranda's footfalls. Her rushed breakfast of handfuls of granola sat like a lump in her stomach. Carl wanted to move fast, so they'd packed up quickly right after dawn.

He had mumbled some excuse about wanting to get back to Samsara, but Miranda suspected they were not hurrying *to* a place so much as hurrying *from* a place. The carefree, effortless joy he showed upon first entering the forest had evaporated. His shoulders slumped as he marched forward, not looking back to see if they were keeping pace. Miranda kept up with the two seasoned hikers, despite her tender shin, as they tromped over roots and loose rocks in the unnaturally hushed forest.

"The animals aren't moving like before," she said.

"We're making too much noise moving fast," Monrovia said. "They are staying out of our way."

As if to illustrate the point, a flock of birds fluttered out of a tree, disappearing into the blue.

"No damage here either. That's a good sign," Monrovia said.

She was right. No chunks of concrete or other debris, not even a tree newly felled. Miranda felt the briefest flutter of hope. Losing Beda's special place hurt, and the violence of the way it was taken would leave a scar, but if that was their punishment for getting in Alois' way, she could live with it. A not so tiny part of her even believed they deserved it.

"Hopefully he's done with us," Miranda said.

"He?" Monrovia stopped in her tracks and whipped her head around with a quizzical stare that morphed to a glare so menacing, Miranda braced for a hit.

"No stopping," Carl grunted.

Miranda let Alois' name stay on her tongue and gave Monrovia some extra space.

The sun had burned off the mist by the time they made it to the field of high grass. Sweat beaded on Miranda's forehead. They only had to cross the field to get to the call station. She expected the ride back to Samsara would be silent. And what would it be like in the apartment now, with Carl brooding and Monrovia vigilant for signs of Miranda's instability?

I can pitch a tent in the park.

Miranda stared at her feet, lost in thought, but stopped short of walking directly into Monrovia's outstretched arm.

She seemed frozen, unable to move or talk, as did Carl. They were staring at the field. Miranda peered through an opening in the trees. Twisted heaps of steel, pieces of broken concrete, and shards of glass crushed the tall grass. Bile crept up Miranda's throat.

Of course, destroying Beda's rock wasn't enough for him. He wants more.

A twisted 'Z' caught her eye. The lettering was familiar. She scanned the ground for the missing T and E in the tower's name. Monrovia had seen that tower too, in Bubble City. Irrefutable evidence.

Miranda trudged into the mess with Carl shouting after her to be careful.

She yanked the mangled letter free and held it up. It was heavy. She had to hold it with two hands. "Do you recognize this?" she asked Monrovia, her heart thudding against her chest.

"No," Monrovia fired back.

"This Z is from ZTE tower, a building near the coffee shop," Miranda said.

Carl looked like he might lose his breakfast in the bushes.

"This building is from Bubble City," Miranda said.

Monrovia balled her hands into tight fists. "No." Her voice shook. "We destroyed Earth when we collapsed the black hole. That is not from Earth."

"But you've seen the building!" Miranda shook the Z.

"It can't be," Monrovia snapped back.

Heat rose to Miranda's cheeks. "Carl, look at what's in this field. Steel beams, concrete. Buildings on Nibiru aren't even made from these materials."

Carl stared at the rubble, not speaking.

Miranda laid the heavy letter back down, clanging against the steel beam, echoing in the stillness. None of them spoke. Finally, Carl raised his hands.

"I will take some samples back to the lab for testing."

He stepped into the debris and picked out a few pieces of broken concrete small enough to fit in his pocket. "Watch your step."

Monrovia followed behind him.

Miranda shook her head. He wouldn't confirm what was right in front of his eyes. They were both scared. She studied the sea of twisted metal and rubbed her arms. *I'm scared too.*

***

The explosion of debris had taken out the call box Carl needed to hail a rover.

Ten miles to Samsara.

With each step, Miranda's pack bit into her shoulders and her boots squeezed her feet. She thought about what she could take out and leave but gritted through it instead. Thick stands of trees lined the road like curtains of brown and green, deep shadows cutting ruts between them. Only the occasional mound of broken glass or splintered bricks cluttered the dirt road. As they walked farther, there were no more signs of wreckage.

The sun climbed higher, but the day was too young for afternoon rain. Until then, they would sweat. Worry nagged at Miranda. Alois punishing Miranda, Monrovia, and Carl made a certain kind of sense, but he must understand the other people of Nibiru had played only a minor part. She gnawed on the skin by her thumbnail. All the damage must be behind them.

After walking what may have been three miles with only one brief break, the trees gave way to vibrant, green grass with rolling hills. A flash of light bounced off a shed up ahead. Miranda pointed. "Do you think that's…?"

Carl threw down his pack and rushed to what they all hoped was a working call box.

He might want a ride even more than me.

She let her pack drop off her shoulders and leaned against a low wooden fence imprisoning grazing animals with heads three times the size of Miranda's. They dotted the hills, lazily chewing and flicking away flies with their tails.

Carl hunched in the booth. The distance made his figure small as he seemed to take something apart.

Her feet throbbed.

"Is he messing with wires?" Miranda asked.

"Looks like it," Monrovia said, pointing behind Miranda. "Watch out, that guy might lick you."

Miranda snapped her head around and a large black eyeball stared back, close enough to touch. She screamed and fell backward in the dirt.

"That's just a cow. It's not going to hurt you," Monrovia said.

The creature loomed at the fence. "It's huge."

Carl returned, head hanging. "There's no signal. We should rest and eat."

He slumped to the ground and fished the last bag of granola out of his pack. They passed it around, each shaking out a handful. He paused before taking a deep drink from his water bottle. "We have a long way to go."

Miranda took short sips, conserving. It may be a long time before they find fresh water again. She knew how long she could last. A nose hair-curling stench wafted over from the cows. Miranda choked down the granola.

"Did something chew through the lines?" Monrovia asked.

"Doesn't seem like it. Seems fairly new." Carl's eyebrows knotted together tightly in an expression that was becoming familiar.

Hot rays beat down as they left the ripe air behind them. Sweat rolled down Miranda's spine as she resumed Carl's fast pace. Her boots pinched her feet, and again, she rolled through the list of contents on her back to see what might not be worth keeping. She cinched the straps tighter. They marched for at least an hour without slowing until Carl suddenly threw his hand up and spun around, a crazed smile spreading across his face.

He's cracking up.

"Listen," he said.

Miranda strained to ignore the persistent buzzing of insects surrounding her and concentrate on other potentially useful sounds. She noticed a gentle whir separate from the annoying pests. It was getting louder.

"A rover!" Monrovia shouted.

"Wave your arms!" Carl flailed wildly.

"I don't even see it," Miranda said. Meanwhile, Monrovia was whipping her arms around her head and jumping up and down.

A sleek silver ship crested far-away treetops. Miranda forgot her aching feet. She jumped up and down, shouting. Her feet burned in protest, but she didn't stop.

The rover came closer, straight for them, then cruised right over their heads, not slowing down.

"No!" Miranda dropped her arms, feeling the cost of her exuberance in the weight of her limbs. A guttural cry unleashed from Monrovia that made Miranda flinch, drowning out her bodily protest.

Carl hadn't taken his eyes off the ship and hadn't stopped waving his arms. He waved them harder, shouting, "They're coming back!"

Miranda squinted at the sky as the rover rounded an arc. Her hands tingled. *Are they really coming back for us?*

In seconds, the rover lowered its steps in front of them. A woman in knee-high shiny black boots strode down the stairs. She wore a burgundy cape, an impractical choice for the heat, but one that made it immediately clear she expected to be respected—and indoors.

The woman shielded her eyes from the glare. Her arm was ghostly pale, her skin almost translucent. Despite the heat, Miranda shivered.

"Are you all okay?" the woman asked, squinting at them.

Miranda watched her lips move, but the sound seemed to be only in her head. She glanced at Monrovia to see if she heard it, too. Monrovia's head bowed slightly.

"Senator Cloudlyn, what a surprise to see you out here," Carl said.

The woman he addressed as the senator cocked her head, taking the smallest step closer. "Dr. Ess, is that you?"

Senator. Miranda knew Carl last saw this woman when he asked the Senate's permission to convene a Gathering to destroy Earth. When he'd told the Senate, the black hole was headed to Nibiru. It was more convenient than the complicated truth. Miranda imagined this woman didn't like being lied to.

She snapped her head to Miranda, peering closer. Miranda squirmed on the spot. *Did I say something out loud?*

The senator turned back to Carl. "Why are you out here?"

"We've been camping, but haven't been able to call a rover. Something seems to be wrong with the signals."

Her face tightened. "You've been in the woods?"

"Yes." His jaw clenched. "For three days."

This news activated her. "Come in, all of you. This is my rover. The public network is down." She ushered them into the cool interior of the machine. "And it's worse than that."

Miranda's mind raced as she fell into a large, plush seat.

"There's no food, but you can fill your bottles here." The senator gestured to a silver cistern built into a wooden cabinet. "I'm sure you are thirsty after walking all day."

Carl motioned for their bottles. They each handed them over.

Monrovia perched; her hands clasped tight. "Was there an earthquake in Samsara?" She almost whispered the question.

Miranda's throat clenched. She wanted Monrovia to take it back. No. There's an electrical problem with the signals, nothing more. What they saw could not have happened in the city. He wouldn't.

"Earthquake?" The senator took a deep breath. "I've been surveying the damage caused by…" the senator paused as if searching for the right words. "…what appear to be buildings that fell from the sky."

The words slammed into Miranda's gut like a fist. A wave of nausea followed. Monrovia's face was unchanged, as if she chose not to hear or understand.

Carl swallowed hard, not meeting the senator's gaze. "Not Samsara," he said.

The senator seemed to study their reactions. "Most of Samsara is in ruin."

"Ruin?" Carl whispered.

Miranda's panicked surprise morphed into a need to explain the truth to the senator. She was a leader. She could do something. "The buildings are from Earth. We're being punished."

Senator Cloudlyn turned to Miranda, her dark eyes probing, deep set in a sharp, thin face. Miranda broke the trancing stare and locked eyes with Carl. His silent plea told her she'd misjudged. Do not say more. Carl knew this Senator, Miranda did not. She wanted to claw it back.

"Tell me more," the senator said.

The damage was done.

The dull ache in Miranda's stomach tightened into a hard knot. Monrovia's stare heated her cheek, and she squirmed in the large seat, staring straight at the senator, wishing time would reverse so she could say anything else. But now she had to say more.

"A building smashed in a field. We climbed over it this morning." Miranda shrugged, hoping it might end the questioning.

The senator's dark eyes settled deeper. The stare felt familiar. "And the building was from Earth?"

The voice rattled in her head, tinkling like rain or ice. Miranda shuddered and wanted to stop, but the truth poured out as if she had no control. "From Bubble City."

The senator leaned in closer and hissed in clipped words that fell like sleet, "And you know this from your time on Earth, with your mother?"

Miranda gulped. No one on Nibiru went to Earth, but was it forbidden? Was she supposed to keep her time there a secret? She searched back through the conversations with Carl, but she couldn't remember. This shouldn't be new information for the senator. Miranda sucked in a breath as she looked back up. The senator's body had gone as rigid as ice. Miranda nodded and inched farther back in her chair.

"And who or what, in your opinion, is punishing us?" the senator asked.

Miranda searched for some way out of this. She knew Alois was a complicating factor best left for never. Carl had never mentioned him to the Senate. While her brain scrambled for plausible statements, her mouth dutifully reported, "A man named Alois controlled the black hole."

Miranda's own jaw dropped, and a sharp pinch on her arm told her Monrovia did not approve. She was strapped to the truth now, like a ticking bomb. Surely the senator would have understood if they had told her about Alois before. Once she knew what he had been doing, she would understand why they had to act. It would help them if Miranda explained more. "Alois had trapped Earth in a cycle of torture and planned to reset it, wipe people's memories, make them all start over. He'd done this countless times before. We had to stop him."

The senator sat back in her chair as if blown by a stiff wind. Her eyebrows arched like daggers. "I don't recall being told of an individual capable of manifesting a black hole and manipulating an entire planet. I recall learning Earth was doomed, with no way for it to come out of the vacuum. That we had to help their souls to a better resting place, then stop the black hole from coming for us next." The senator angled her head to Carl while holding the rest of her body stock-still. "Dr. Ess, did you perhaps leave out any details when you presented the Senate with your plan for saving Nibiru?"

Carl opened and closed his mouth several times, but no sound came out.

The senator continued. "I will be direct. It appears you withheld key information from the Senate about the full nature of the calamity facing Earth, and now you have unleashed the force of this entity on Nibiru."

Miranda's chest tightened.

"No, you don't understand—"

Carl squeezed Miranda's hand a touch too tight, not reassuring. His palms were wet.

"We had no choice, we—"

"My mother killed Alois to stop him from coming after us." Monrovia's voice was tight as she cut in, her face streaked in red. "She died to protect us."

Miranda wanted her sister's words to be true, but the evidence...

"You would have me trust we are facing the cold retribution of the universe instead?" the senator said.

Miranda's head spun as she tried to pinpoint where she'd lost control of the conversation.

"There must be a reasonable explanation for what is happening." Carl patted his pockets. "I took some samples from the wreckage we passed earlier. I plan to have them analyzed at the lab."

The senator twisted back to Carl. "Remind us all why we had no choice but to destroy Earth?" She almost hummed the question, leaving no doubt she knew the answer.

"The black hole was coming for Nibiru," Carl mumbled.

The senator focused on Miranda, leaning in close. She smelled like tea and dust. Miranda pulled away, wanting to sink into the chair. She spoke slow and low. "Was the black hole coming for Nibiru?"

Her stare bore into Miranda's mind. She wanted to say yes, to be emphatic. *Yes, Alois was coming for us next.* That would make the woman back off, convince her they had no other option. But a cold energy spilled off the senator, peeling back the layers of Miranda's veneer, rifling through lies, not stopping until she found the truth.

"Well?"

To Miranda's horror, only one word slipped out, "Maybe."

The senator shifted to face Carl. Miranda almost saw the waves of fury rolling off her. Monrovia let out a sob and covered her face.

Miranda's stomach sank. *Why didn't I tell her what she needed to hear?*

"I have a new hypothesis, Dr. Ess. Once your wife and daughter had returned, you manipulated your people to use our sacred gift to complete a heinous act, to destroy a planet you hated. And now its protector has turned its wrath on us."

Miranda jumped. "No!"

Tears streaked Monrovia's face, her hands in fists. "You've got it all wrong. We released Earth from an endless cycle of torture. We saved those souls from torment."

"By ending their world? That is a cruel hero indeed," the senator said. She pushed a button on her chair and a screen rose from the armrest. She tapped furiously, then pushed the button to lower it again.

"We *freed* them," Carl said weakly.

The senator held her hand in the air. "Be still. You will explain it all to the Senate. We will see how charitable they are with liars."

Carl's shoulders sank. Miranda tried to catch his eye, but he would not look her way. She was terrified to speak again. The knots in her stomach tightened, but she had to say something to defend him. "We were trying to help."

"I have heard enough." The senator clipped the end of each word to make the finality clear.

Thick silence hung in the rover as it slowed to a stop. Miranda wanted to slide down the steps and seep into the ground like a dried-up puddle.

CHAPTER 7

CONSPIRACY

As Miranda descended the rover's steps, the stink of burning plastic singed her nostrils. The toxic stench was familiar. Like home. *Not Samsara.*

Concrete and splintered wood, torn fabrics, glass, and steel littered the street. A man seemed lost as he dug through a pile of rubble, aimless, as if he forgot what he was looking for. A string of small colorful flags lay in the mud at his feet. Miranda gripped the rail. *Did we do this?*

A hand clenched her elbow. "Move along." She found her feet again.

Four guards circled Carl. One spoke in a low voice; Miranda stayed close to hear. "Dr. Ess, the Senate requires you to be detained until they convene an emergency trial."

"Now? I've been in the woods for days. Can I go home and shower first?" The full meaning of the guard's order seemed to sink in. Carl shouted, "Trial? What are the charges?"

The senator strode forward. "I suggested conspiracy to cause irreparable harm to the people of Nibiru."

Blood rushed to Miranda's ears as she searched for something to use as a weapon, a large sturdy stick would be ideal. She'd keep a few of them busy to give him a chance to run.

Anguish clouded Carl's face as Miranda settled on broken bricks. She snatched one with a sharp, ragged edge and waited for the right moment to lob it at the tallest guard.

"Can I say goodbye to my daughters first?"

Miranda's heart banged against her chest. Now was her moment. The senator nodded, and Carl stepped to Monrovia. Miranda reared back, ready to fire.

"You can't do this!" Monrovia yelled. "Arrest *her*!" She stabbed a finger at Miranda who let the brick fall and tried to look innocent. "She's the one who worked with Alois. Maybe she's still working with him."

The suggestion hit with the force of a building falling from the sky. Miranda staggered.

She hates me. She thinks it's all my fault.

"Monrovia!" Carl shouted. "Miranda is your *sister*. You cannot say such hateful things."

The senator waved at Monrovia. "We could haul you all in, but on Nibiru we do not incarcerate children, but—" she pointed at Miranda and Monrovia with a long bony finger, "don't leave the city."

Tears streamed down Monrovia's cheeks. As the guards advanced, she clutched Carl's waist. "Don't go."

He buried his face in her hair.

Miranda felt hollowed out. Her arms and legs itched to fight, then run, but Carl wouldn't. How had she messed up so badly? He released Monrovia and reached for Miranda.

He should hate me. This is all my fault. He pulled her close and Miranda moved to wrap her arms around him, but they pulled him away.

A guard said, "Time to go."

"It's not your fault," Carl called as they dragged him to a black rover.

"It is," hissed Monrovia.

The senator flicked her wrist at a guard. "Shadow them. I don't want either of them leaving town."

Miranda lost sight of Carl as they hustled him into a pod and the door closed. The senator's robes fanned out, kicking up dust as she disappeared into her own rover.

Miranda wanted to crawl into a hole and cry until she was empty. It was bad enough that Alois had targeted Nibiru with his wrath, but she'd made it so much worse. Why had she said any of that? Why did she trust that woman would understand?

"I'm glad Beda didn't raise me. I'd hate to be as damaged as you are." Monrovia gave a menacing stare.

Miranda's muscles tensed, poised to deliver a blow. "It's not Beda's fault."

Monrovia let out a sharp laugh. "You're not disputing you are deficient."

How was this the same person who had dressed her wounds just a few days before? Monrovia acted happy to never see her again. "You know I'm not working with Alois," she said.

"Do I? I saw you holding the book."

"Wh-what? I found it under *your* bed."

"But I hadn't used it," Monrovia said.

"Dammit, I am not working with him!" Miranda shouted. "I didn't mean to get Carl in trouble. That wasn't—" She broke off, averting her gaze, but her sister's accusing stare flashed from every surface. Miranda breathed deeply. "I told her the truth about the buildings. She would have figured that out on her own. Telling her about Alois was an accident." *Like I couldn't stop talking.*

Monrovia's cold glare bore into Miranda. "You got my father arrested."

Miranda studied the ground. Glad Monrovia had come out and said it. "He's my father, too."

"I wish he wasn't." Monrovia spat the words like she wished they were acid.

But they burned more than any liquid—this caustic truth. Miranda's throat tightened. The edges of her vision blurred. She struggled for a breath.

"If you aren't Alois' minion, then I think Beda took you to Earth because you are cursed and you made the whole place die."

What if she's right?

She found her breath and curled her fingers into fists. Right didn't matter now. The burn of that scowl made Miranda want to pound it out of her.

Miranda raised her fist and braced to strike. Monrovia's eyes widened, but she stood her ground. Carl's concerned, urging plea loomed in her mind. *Sisters.* Instead of taking a swing, Miranda broke into a sprint, dashing down an alley, into rising smoke from unseen fire. The thud of heavy boots behind her made her run even faster.

Boots crunched gravel behind Miranda. She ran harder. It wasn't Monrovia gaining ground on her, not with those thudding footfalls.

"Stop!" a voice shouted. "I need to keep you two together."

Miranda stole a glance back to see one of the senator's guards huffing toward her. A large hood hid his face, impressive that it stayed up as he ran full speed. From his size, he looked to be in shape. *I won't outrun him.*

She snapped her head forward and skirted around a jumble of splintered wood and shattered bricks. Her heart banged against her chest. She wanted to run until her sides ached and her lungs burned, then run further.

A flower basket tumbled from a rickety balcony, spilling its dirt and small purple flowers in Miranda's path. She lurched over it.

"You're making this harder than it needs to be. Stop running!"

The voice was familiar, but she didn't know why. Miranda ducked into an alley billowing with smoke so thick it hung like a curtain masking everything behind it. She didn't slow down. The smoke would hide her, too.

The vapor stung her eyes. A tattered awning flapped in her face. She flung it aside and smashed face-first into a stack of bricks as tall as herself. Blackness swallowed her vision and her mouth burned. She fell, spitting blood. Her hand flew to her face. Nose in the original position, no major cuts, just a split lip. Her head throbbed. Footsteps pounded closer, as if the sound itself was angry. She shut her lids against the noxious air and crawled. *You can't take me.*

A hand wrapped around her arm and yanked her up. It was a man, or a strong boy. He held her tightly against his side, moving swiftly out of the smoke-filled alley. Her head lolled and her feet slapped uselessly at the ground, like they had given up. She slipped out of his hold and crumpled.

Miranda lay on the spot. He had dragged her out of the alley and now clear skies loomed over her, just beyond the senator's yellow X on his sleeve. Her babysitter. She squinted against the sun to see his face, but he hid in the shadow of his hood.

"Who runs *to* smoke?"

The sudden and intense need to vomit gripped her. She scrambled to her hands and knees and retched until all she had left was clear spit.

He grunted and gave her space. Miranda wiped her mouth with the back of her hand, not caring what he or anyone else thought right now. Her sister hated her because she'd gotten Carl locked up. Carl probably hated her, too. Whatever was happening, she deserved it.

She rolled over and looked up at the sky. Her stomach empty, numbness set in.

The guard ripped at the bottom of his shirt, then crouched beside her, handing her the scrap. She wiped off spit and puke as he flicked off his hood.

"Thanks." For the first time, she clearly saw his face. The ground under her seemed to shift. Nathan's smooth features stared back at her.

Her body tingled, and she itched to throw her arms around him. "How?" He had found his way to her. *But oh my god, I just threw up everywhere.*

She peered closer; he didn't seem happy to see her and the eyes were wrong—brown, not green. Then she remembered this exact person sitting on Carl's couch just a few days ago. She'd fainted and fallen onto the coffee table.

Oren. The impostor.

The differences were obvious now. Nathan would never wear his hair that short, and he would never join the senator's guards.

"You okay?" He pulled her to her feet. "I don't know what's going on between you and your sister, but I'm assigned to watch you both, so I need you to stay together. You understand that?" His clipped words were a demand, not a question.

Miranda nodded, trying to negotiate standing on wobbly legs.

"Are you always a basket case?" he asked.

She had to admit she hadn't left a good impression. "You remember the last time we met?"

"You dented a wooden table with your head. I won't forget that anytime soon."

A giggle rose in Miranda, then another, and another, and soon she doubled over, laughing hysterically. It came on its own, unbidden, and she couldn't say why, even if she wanted to.

Oren moved back, as if afraid her hysteria may be contagious.

His horrified look made her laugh harder, as if her body chose to laugh instead of crumble. Every time she tried to stop; his bewildered face made her laugh even harder. She laughed until her stomach seized, then her laughter turned to tears, just as unexpected and unexplainable, as if her body no longer connected with her mind.

"Don't do that. Someone will think I hurt you." He patted her shoulder. "Come on." He linked his arm through hers, guiding her. "We have to go back to Monrovia."

The mention of her sister's name brought on a fresh round of tears springing from the hole Monrovia's scorn had ripped inside her. Oren cursed under his breath as Miranda leaned on him for help walking.

As they got closer to where she'd run from Monrovia, Miranda sucked in a breath and stood up a little straighter. She did not want Monrovia to see her in such a state.

Oren gripped her arm tightly.

"I can walk now," she said.

His grip tightened. "This is where we left her. Where is she?" His voice gained an octave as he scanned the area.

There were only a few people close by: a stooped older woman, a child with matted hair. A few others who would never be mistaken for Monrovia.

Oren squeezed Miranda's arm. "Where did she go?"

"You're hurting me." Miranda pulled against his grip.

He looked at his hand wrapped tightly around her forearm and dropped it as if her skin caught fire. "I'm sorry. I didn't mean to."

Miranda rubbed her arm, taking comfort in seeing him sweat.

"Fifteen minutes and I already lost one. Where would she go?"

Miranda shrugged and sat down. Her pack kicked up on her shoulders, banging against her head. She muttered and let it fall.

"We're not resting. We have to find your sister."

"*You* have to find my sister," Miranda said.

"I can't lose you, so that means *we* have to find your sister. Get up."

She didn't budge until he offered a hand to help her. After emptying the contents of her stomach on the street followed by the unexpected laugh-cry fest, she didn't have the strength to stand on her own, but she didn't tell him that. She nearly buckled under the weight of her pack. "I need to eat."

"We'll eat after we find your sister." He tugged a length of thin rope from his belt and held it up. "I'm going to tie this to your belt loop," he said the words loudly and slowly, like he doubted she would understand.

"What if I say no?" she asked.

"Then I will restrain your hands first and do it anyway. Would you like to keep access to your hands?"

Miranda heaved a sigh, and he looped the thin rope through and tied it off.

"I don't want to be tied to you either, but I can't find her just to lose you again." He picked a folding knife out of his pocket and took several steps back. He cut the rope and tied the other end to his belt loop.

The same firm jaw. But he held himself differently than Nathan. His shoulders didn't curl and his frame filled out. This boy was confident and well fed. *Such a strange coincidence.* Carl said there were no such thing as coincidences. Everything happens for a reason.

Miranda eyed the knot in her belt loop. "I can still run, but this time I'll be able to drag you."

"Or I can run and drag *you.*" He flashed a bitter smile that made Miranda shiver.

Any notion that he wasn't so bad evaporated in that instant. His eyes flashed with hatred. She took a half step back.

"Where would Monrovia go?" he asked.

"Maybe to our apartment?"

"Sounds reasonable. Let's go." He yanked on the rope to make her change direction.

"You don't need to do that."

He didn't answer.

Miranda trudged along in his wake, picking her way around mounds of debris, for once wishing she could forget

Nathan's face. It was painful to see it reproduced on this idiot.

They came to a street lined with cottage-style houses with small, neat yards. A fragrant blossom decorated the low fences. The memories of spicy noodles and skating smacked her like a stiff hand. That the skating rink was likely a mass of rubble made her lightheaded. She sank to the sidewalk. Oren tugged hard on the rope, jerking her forward and snapping her out of her thoughts.

"Stop doing that!" Miranda said.

He ignored her.

"Why are you being mean for no reason? I haven't done anything to you," Miranda shouted.

Oren turned back. His face was scarlet. "I'm not sure I've ever heard of the senator ordering someone to be arrested. It doesn't happen. You know what that means?"

Miranda fidgeted. "But—"

He threw up a hand, cutting her off. "It means she's certain your father, and probably you, are somehow responsible for all this destruction." He snarled at Miranda. "And you want me to be nice?"

Heat rose to her cheeks, and she ached to tell him, anyone, it wasn't true. Instead, she said, "If we caused this destruction, it wasn't on purpose. We never wanted anything bad to happen to Nibiru, and we'll fix it, somehow." Miranda searched his face for a flicker of understanding, or trust.

Oren barked a laugh, then set her with an icy stare. "Like you fixed Earth?" He tugged the rope and started off again.

Miranda stumbled forward, refusing to let his dig hurt her, but she had to bite her lip to stop the tears. "You let Cloudlyn think for you? You're no better than a robot."

Oren scoffed.

But part of her believed there had to be another way. She craved the chance to go back in time and make a different choice. But what could she do differently? Stop Beda from fighting Alois? Leave Earth and those people trapped at Alois' mercy? Would that have been the right thing to do?

The strangely pristine street funneled them onto a once proud promenade now strewn with debris. Buildings sagged with missing walls and windows. Many had succumbed to a lump of broken remains. She tripped over loose bricks and recovered her footing while the clatter echoed around the empty street. She wanted to dampen the sound, keep it quiet like the funeral before the party. Every street they'd walked down had been as empty as this one.

"Where is everyone?" she asked.

He studied the crumbling buildings, and she thought his lip may have quivered. "We finished rescues on this street. People are at other sites to tend to the wounded or help another way."

He started out again, but slower this time, like he carried more weight. After another few minutes, Carl's building came into view.

Miranda took a breath. Miraculously, in a row of caved-in and buckled structures, Carl's building stood tall with only a few broken windows. "It looks untouched."

Oren spat, his cheeks reddening. "Why should your building be the only one left standing around here?"

A smile spread over Miranda's face, but the lightness she felt at seeing the building was overtaken by a quiver in her stomach. It wasn't fair. Why was their building spared? What was Alois doing? She took off in a run, making Oren scramble to keep pace. She needed to find Monrovia inside, to sit with her on the balcony, to figure out how to make things right together.

Miranda walked through the front doors first, with Oren trailing. A gasp caught in her throat. *No. This is wrong.* She dug the heels of her hands into her eyes, then pulled them away; it didn't help. Where the back half of the building should be raw edges of splintered bamboo and broken glass clawed at the sky, as if searching for their missing pieces.

Chaotic piles of debris rose to the second or third floor, blocking the trees in the park beyond.

She choked down a sob as Oren let loose a sharp laugh. Her hand formed a fist, but she stopped herself from punching him in the stomach. "You're a real jerk."

"You deserve this."

His hatred sent a shiver down her spine.

She yanked the rope hard, pulling him off balance, then made for the stairs. The honey-colored banisters were still smooth under her hand. Clusters of greenery hung from the ceiling, decorating the space with bright green and fresher air. From here, it was possible to pretend everything would be normal when they reached the top.

Oren paused before opening the door to the hallway. Was he thinking the same thing? Did he want to delay leaving this moment of sanity, too? He flung it open and stepped aside to let Miranda go first.

A scream fought to let loose, but Miranda held it back— it would give Oren too much satisfaction. Just beyond Carl's apartment door, the building dropped away in a jagged open yawn. Miranda hugged the wall as she walked closer to the gaping edge. She made it to Carl's door and turned the handle.

Miranda stepped in, leaning against the wall that should have faced the kitchen, but instead of pots and cupboards, trees swayed in a restless wind. She struggled to catch her breath. Only a few steps away, Monrovia dangled her legs over the broken ledge where the balcony should have been.

"Go talk to her," Oren said, with a softer tone than he'd used before.

"You go talk to her." Oren's softer tone was nice, but it wasn't enough for her to cozy up to her sister.

Oren scowled, then moved closer to Monrovia, dragging Miranda with him. "Hey. Senator Cloudlyn told me to watch both of you, so we all have to stay together."

Oren jumped as a dark shape hopped out of Monrovia's lap and ran to Miranda.

"Luna!" Miranda let out a joyful scream. She scooped up Luna's small body and nuzzled her soft fur. "I'm so glad you made it, kitty. You're a fighter." Luna purred.

Something rumbled above them, and a chunk of concrete plummeted down smashing into the rubble below sending up a plume of dust. Another larger rumble shook the building. The muscles in Miranda's legs tightened. She searched the sky. *Are more buildings falling?*

"It's not safe here. We have to leave," Oren said.

Monrovia did not move from her spot. She had not looked at either of them since they came in.

"Rona? We need to go. It's not safe," Miranda tried to sound firm.

Oren pulled Monrovia's arm. She snatched it back. In a hoarse voice, she said, "I'm not leaving. I have nowhere to go."

Miranda wanted to stay mad at her for the horrible things she'd said, but those hollow, defeated words melted her anger.

Oren tried again, this time laying a hand on her shoulder. "This building is falling to pieces. We have to move. There's plenty of food and water at Bushuto Gardens."

Monrovia gruffly shook her head. "Leave."

Oren turned to Miranda and stabbed his finger in the air as if saying 'make her.'

Miranda shuffled as close to the edge as she was willing and sat down. Luna jumped into Monrovia's arms. "You're not going to leave me alone with this jerk, are you?"

Monrovia didn't budge.

"You know I won't stop, right? I won't stop annoying you, but I also won't stop trying to free Carl. I am a horrible person for getting him arrested, but I'll get him out." Miranda leaned closer. "It would probably be a lot easier with your help." Her chest felt lighter as the words slipped across her lips. It was all true, would it be enough?

Monrovia sniffled hard as she turned to Miranda. Her eyes were bloodshot and puffy. She looked lost; her skin drained of color. "You think we can?"

Miranda grabbed onto the glimmer of hope. "Absolutely. I don't know how, yet, but we'll figure it out."

Monrovia tucked Luna close to her side and inched away from the ledge. "Ok." The word came out as a whisper.

Miranda took one look down at the pile of debris. A shiny, round piece of metal winked up at her. Its back plate said 'Harold' and if it was upright, she knew it would look like a trash can on wheels.

This was the only home Monrovia remembered, and its contents had settled into a pile of dust.

Now she's lost everything, too.

The thought left Miranda cold.

How will she ever forgive me? I have to make things right.

Miranda lumbered after Oren and Monrovia, back down the most beautiful set of stairs she'd ever walked on. This would be their last trip. There was nothing here for any of them anymore.

CHAPTER 8

A TWISTED HOPE

Oren paused at the twisted-branch archway that announced Bushuto Gardens. He smoothed his t-shirt, tried to tuck the ripped section into his pants, then let it go again.

Did he really care what people thought? Or was he stalling?

His eyes flit around the white tents set up as makeshift hospitals striping the grass. So many injured. People darted in and out, finding a way to be busy—a way to help. The last time Miranda had seen this many people gather here was for Beda's funeral. Now there was no ceremony, only action.

Miranda stepped through the archway after him. He tugged on the cord connecting them. "If I untie this, will you stay together and here?" He eyed them both, waiting for an answer.

Miranda shrugged, annoyed he hadn't seemed to consider tying Monrovia to them as well.

"Is that a yes?"

The fight drained out of her. Where would she run? She didn't look at Monrovia but warmed as they said "yes" at the same time.

"Okay." Oren's shoulders relaxed, and he untied the knot on his belt. Miranda fumbled with loosening her side because he had tightened it too tight. Oren pulled a knife from a hidden pocket on his shirt and cut the rope so that it dangled to Miranda's mid-thigh.

"Thanks," she said flatly, glaring at this fresh addition to her pants.

He pointed at some long tables. "Food and water are over there. I'm going to see who needs help." As if second-guessing his decision, he turned back and wagged his finger at both of them. "Don't leave. I'll get in a lot of trouble. And stick together."

Miranda beelined for the food. Oren's problems didn't factor into her decision to stay or go, but for now, this was the place with food and water. Monrovia trailed beside her, not talking, not looking at her. Miranda imagined they may have done this as kids. It might have been a game then, when being mad turned into seeing how long you go without talking, but the stakes were so much higher than a kid's game. *She might actually never want to talk to me again.*

Miranda stopped at a long table lined with hastily constructed sandwiches and water in squat brown containers. She scooped up a flat sandwich and a water and tried not to notice that Monrovia had not done the same.

You need to eat. Would Miranda have to say it?

Monrovia stretched out her hand slowly and took a sandwich. She examined it as if it was a foreign object and dropped it into her pocket, then looked past Miranda like she was invisible and wandered away from the table, toward a row of tents.

Miranda shoved half a sandwich in her mouth, chewing furiously as she trailed behind. She pretended to be casually following, but she wanted to stay close, hoping Monrovia would slip up and say something, anything, to her.

"Rona!" The shrill scream shattered the muted hustle of the garden.

Miranda scanned the area to see where it came from. Someone came up from behind, wrapping their arms around Monrovia. Tan's head popped up from behind her. Miranda hadn't seen him since he'd taught her to skate in the jungle. Had that only been last week? The thought made her head swim. He looked tired, but somehow kept his bright smile.

"I was so worried about you," he said to Monrovia. "You hadn't shown up here and I saw your apartment, so I thought you were…" His voice trailed off and his eyes misted. "I'm so glad you're okay, but where the hell have you been?"

Monrovia returned the hug. "We were camping."

So, she can talk. Her tone was forced normal.

Miranda dug the toe of her boot in the dirt, waiting to be acknowledged.

"Of course. The world goes to hell, and you were camping," Tan said. He gave Luna a scratch on the head and she leaned into his hand approvingly.

"It happened out there, too," Monrovia said.

"Oh." He stopped petting the cat and shifted his feet. "Do you know why this happened?"

"No, should we?" Monrovia's eye twitched. Miranda was sure Tan hadn't caught it.

"No, I mean—" He left the thought and leaned in to give Miranda a hug. She awkwardly patted him on the shoulder. "You look banged up."

Miranda licked her swollen lip and wiped her nose. Dried blood there, too. "I got into a fight with a wall."

Tan tilted his head as if asking what that meant, but didn't, and she didn't offer.

"Tan!" a voice yelled.

He called back to a woman standing outside a long, white tent, drying her hands on a formerly white coat. "Coming, Mom! I've been helping her with patients all day." He turned back to Miranda and Monrovia. "Come on, we can use extra hands."

Monrovia gave Luna a kiss on the head, then put her down and walked to the tent.

Miranda's stomach turned at the idea of seeing people's injuries. She searched the beaten down grass for an excuse until Tan grabbed her hand, tugging her along.

He offered a tired smile. "You need those scrapes checked out."

The air in the tent was thick with stifled moans. Miranda wanted to sprint back out and not stop running.

"You brought reinforcements." The woman in the stained lab coat kissed Tan on the top of the head and gestured to Monrovia to wash her hands in the bowl of water set up on a makeshift table. As Miranda eyed the exit the woman seized her head and tilted it back, looking up her nose. Her hands were stiff and her grip tight. *Is this normal?*

"Relax, I'm Doctor Kaur."

Miranda tried to slow her quick, shallow breaths. The doctor pinched her bottom lip and tugged her jaw down to get a good look in her mouth, then moved on to examine the scrapes on her hands. "Anything else?"

"I think I banged my shins up pretty good." Miranda yanked up her pant leg to reveal large bruises with cuts.

The doctor nodded and doused a small rag in a clear liquid and motioned for Miranda to sit on a stool. "Hold this on your lip. It will clean it and make the swelling go down."

Miranda touched the rag to her lip. It immediately stung and throbbed. She sucked in a breath and held it in place. Dr. Kaur filled a syringe and thumped it to knock out the bubbles. Miranda leaned away from the needle.

The doctor smiled. "Not for you." She held it out to Tan. "Cot four, left arm."

He took it, marched to the cot, then kneeled to administer the drug deliberately.

"What can I do to help?" Monrovia asked.

Miranda marveled that something seemed to have clicked back in place for Monrovia. Faced with a job to do, her sister had tucked her emotions away. Miranda wondered when they would show again.

Miranda slumped down. This place did not inspire her to action. It made her want to hide. Even if she hadn't smashed herself into a pile of bricks, she didn't think she'd be volunteering.

"Cot six needs his wound re-dressed. He's bleeding heavily. I gave him a coagulant. Hopefully that helped, but I'm sure he needs a fresh dressing."

Monrovia took the gauze and tape from the doctor, not hesitating as she made her way to the cot. Miranda dabbed at her lip with the rag, content to stay a patient.

Dr. Kaur stood at Monrovia's shoulder and motioned for her to pull down the sheet. She did as instructed and the man moaned as it pulled away.

"He got stuck by a steel pole," the doctor said, "but he's got a chance. Pull the old dressing back and pack this onto the wound, then cover it again. Simple."

A scream ripped through another part of the tent. The doctor shoved a jar into Monrovia's hand and rushed to attend to that victim. Monrovia looked at the wound before her, then locked eyes with Miranda.

Monrovia's face was wide with panic. Miranda searched for the right thing to say but only came up with, "Be gentle."

Monrovia grimaced and yanked at the bandage. The man moaned. She whispered, "Sorry," and ripped the bandage back. He groaned as she smeared the yellow paste onto the puncture wound and covered it again with clean white gauze, taping it into place.

"I did it." Sweat beaded Monrovia's brow. "Are you okay?" she whispered, leaning over the man.

He was quiet again.

Doctor Kaur reappeared to review Monrovia's handy work. "Good job on this. Go wash your hands again."

The doctor turned to Miranda, who wanted to sink into the wall. But before she could disappear, the doctor was in front of her slathering a thick paste onto her bloodied palm. "You'll be as good as new in no time. Wish all my patients were as lucky."

Tan joined them from the far end of the tent. He touched his mom's back. "Mom, you need a break. I'll take over for a while."

Dr. Kaur stroked his cheek and the circles under her eyes seemed to get darker. "Okay, just for a few minutes." She crumpled into a folding chair with a deep sigh.

Her exhaustion was clear, but she also gave the impression she was content and fulfilled by being able to help. Miranda wondered what that must be like. She wanted to talk to her more, to understand her. There was only one thing she could think of asking. "Where were you when it happened?"

Dr. Kaur took in a breath through her nose and looked at the tent ceiling. "I was on the terrace at our house. I had just watered the plants when a massive boom knocked me to my feet. Tan ran out, and that's when the first pieces fell." She looked at the bright sky outside the tent as if she didn't trust it could be real. "A massive gate fell from the sky."

Miranda shuddered, remembering the towering iron gate that protected Bubble City.

"We ran to the basement of the building and stayed there for hours." The doctor's hands shook.

"How long did it go on?" Monrovia asked.

The doctor cocked her head. "How long? Weren't you in it?"

"We were camping," Miranda said. "But it happened there, too."

"I'm not sure how long it lasted here. It came from everywhere. It felt like hours," Dr. Kaur said. "I don't understand what could have caused that."

As Miranda imagined the horror of the city coming down around them, a boy with spiky, black hair glanced in as he walked past the tent. Instantly, she knew his eyes. She remembered zipping through Bubble City on the back of his motorcycle. There was no question it was the same boy. But how could he be here? She threw down the rag, mumbling an excuse about fresh air, and sprinted outside to follow him.

CHAPTER 9

A NEW ENEMY

Miranda caught the boy's arm. He spun around, his expression a patchwork of alarm and confusion. She kept a tight grip and froze. *I'm an idiot. He's a copy.* But he looked so much like Davon, he even wore his hair the same. She searched her mind for what to say and remembered she'd seen this copy before.

"You knocked me down." *Why did I say that?*

He cocked his head. His clear blue eyes sparkling. "I didn't touch you."

"No, the day of the Gathering." Prickles of heat flushed her neck. She hadn't wanted to make a big deal of that, but now she had to explain. "You ran into me with your skateboard." This was stalling until her brain caught up with her impulsive hand.

Recognition sparked. "It was an accident. I said I was sorry."

He tugged at his arm, and she released it, horrified to realize she was still hanging on. But he didn't turn away. She pushed her embarrassment aside to study him. This boy seemed like Davon in a way that Oren had never seemed like Nathan. Yes, his black hair was spiked like Davon, but his nails were also dirty, like he spent his time working on machines. Motorcycles? She'd only known Davon for an afternoon, but even in that short time, it was obvious he loved that deathtrap more than anything else.

"Do you ride motorcycles?"

The boy's eyes widened. "You mean a combustion engine bike?"

"I mean a motorcycle that goes *vroom*." Miranda stabbed at the ground with the toe of her boot. *Wrong. Definitely a copy.*

"How could I? You know we can't have those engines."

Of course, she didn't know, but no need to tell him that.

He checked over his shoulder and turned back with a wicked grin. "But I have dreams where I'm riding one."

A flutter fanned through Miranda's belly. If he stretched his mind, he may be able to tap into memories of Bubble City. He had to be more than a copy. "You rode motorcycles on Earth."

He jumped back as if stung. "I've never been to Earth. Who has?"

She couldn't explain it herself. Maybe he was right, this version had never been to Earth. But he clearly had a connection to the version who had, even if he didn't understand it. Did Oren remember anything from Nathan? Was he ignoring the connection?

The boy studied her through narrowed eyes.

"No one has, forget it. I must be too tired. Sorry I bothered you." Miranda skulked back to the medical tent. Her temples flared and throbbed.

He jogged after her. "My name is Hugo, by the way."

She didn't turn around but gave a half-hearted wave as she walked away.

"Miranda!" Monrovia's voice cut through the quiet. "You can't run off."

She's talking to me.

Did this mean they'd go back to some kind of normal? "I thought I saw someone I knew," Miranda said, holding her splitting head in her hands. Monrovia raised an eyebrow as she looked in Hugo's direction.

"You know people here? Besides us?" Tan said, joining Monrovia's side.

"No, she doesn't," Monrovia said flatly.

"I thought—"

High-pitched pops cut Miranda off, and she jumped.

"Good afternoon, I'm sorry for the fright. We're all on edge. This thing is loud when it starts." Dr. Kaur fiddled with a megaphone from a small platform stage. "Rescue team six asked me to share some updates on the search and rescue mission."

People gathered around the stage and a hushed quiet fell on the crowd.

The microphone picked up her deep breath and the crinkle of the worn paper. She read from notes. "The volunteers combed the southeastern quadrant near Barataria Bay. The recovered bodies are being stored in the gym at the school in Mitte. If you have missing loved ones who may have been in that part of the city, please go there to see if you can identify them."

She paused and took another deep breath. "They are moving to little Thon Buri next. The team reports survivors may still be found, but that window is closing. We must all remain hopeful, but also maintain reasonable expectations." She paused for several seconds. Her shoulders drooped. "Dr. Sophia Roma also has an update for us." She held out the megaphone as Sophia joined her on stage.

Miranda's chest tightened and Monrovia stood up straighter as Carl's trusted lab partner and best friend took the megaphone. Was Sophia going to tell all these people Carl had been arrested?

She'd been part of all the conversations, consulted on every detail of what facts they left out of the official story of why they had to destroy Earth. Would she explain to the crowd that they had to make tough choices, and we all needed to support Carl now? Would she try to convince them it was not his fault, and we need to demand the Senate let him go?

Miranda wiped her palms across her pants and tried to read Sophia's expression as she prepared to speak.

"There is more disturbing news that you should be aware of. We've confirmed reports of another Falling about an hour ago."

Miranda thought back to the shaking and debris that fell when they were in the apartment. *But it can't keep happening. It has to be over.*

"We had hoped the movement was settling debris, but we've confirmed it was new buildings falling. It happened again."

The crowd gasped.

Miranda chewed her thumbnail.

"We all want to understand what is happening, and why, and now we want to know when it will end." Sophia lowered the megaphone slightly, then brought it up again as if she'd made a decision. "I can't answer those questions for you today, but I can tell you that Dr. Ess, my partner at The Interstellar Research Group, has been arrested for conspiracy. Specifically, the Senate has charged him with withholding vital information about the black hole that was purported to be a danger to Nibiru."

The color drained from Monrovia's face, and she stood completely still. "Conspiracy?"

The word crashed down on Miranda like a door slamming in her face. She suddenly found it hard to breathe. *You know we had to free them.* She glanced at Monrovia, who stared straight ahead, expressionless.

"Based on information gathered since he's been in custody, the Senate believes there is a link between Dr. Ess's actions and the buildings falling from the sky."

Miranda balled her hands into fists. Sophia stood calmly on that stage and pinned all this destruction on Carl, acting as if she'd had no role.

Miranda wanted to punch her way through the crowd and snatch her off the stage by her hair. Instead, she planted her feet and dug her fingernails into her palms, because everything she said was true. If Carl had refused to lead the Gathering, Beda never would have had enough strength to stop Alois. If he had been allowed to continue with experiments on Earth, he would not have attacked Nibiru. Maybe. Miranda's stomach churned.

More gasps and murmurs circulated.

"Many of us here lost the people dearest to our hearts," Sophia went on. "I just left the hospital where my husband is fighting for his life."

Miranda sucked in a breath. *Oren's dad.* He hadn't said anything about that. *No wonder he hates me.*

Sophia wiped away tears. "But I needed to tell you myself that I believe Dr. Ess is responsible." She backed away and handed the megaphone to Dr. Kaur, who took it, her mouth hanging open. The doctor laid it down as if it might be contagious and stepped away.

"We trusted him!" a man shouted.

A woman from the crowd jumped on stage, snatching up the megaphone. "He lied to us, and now thousands of people are dead."

Miranda's urge to fight overtook her need to retch. *Alois is doing this, not Carl.*

Monrovia dropped to her knees in the dirt. Miranda hovered over her, wanting to scoop her up and get her out of there.

A man joined the stage and spoke into the megaphone. "Please, be logical. What would Dr. Ess gain from using his position to harm us? It doesn't make sense."

Another person jerked the megaphone out of his hand. "He may not have known what would happen, but if he lied to the Senate, he betrayed us."

An older woman near Miranda yelled, "If Earth would have survived, if we hadn't intervened, that explains why we are being attacked. We severed the balance, and we are being punished. But it's Carl Ess who should be punished!"

Miranda dug deeper half-moons into her palm. They should be angry at Alois, not Carl, but they'd never even heard of Alois.

"*He* must be punished!" a voice cried out, and a chorus of agreement surfed the crowd.

Miranda's head pounded; her thoughts jumbled. She glanced down to find Monrovia curled into a ball, covering her ears.

"He was not working alone," someone yelled. "Find the others!"

Miranda jolted upright. The others? Her heart skipped a beat. She knew what people were like—people everywhere craved the simple solution. Her urge to fight crystallized into a need to run. She would get much farther, faster on her own, but what would they do to Monrovia?

"Come on." She yanked Monrovia's arm to pull her up. "We're getting out of here."

Monrovia looked up with red, puffy eyes. "Oren said not to leave."

"We're not staying here."

She blinked, as if confused. "But the Senator said—"

"This crowd wants our blood," Miranda whispered harshly. "We need to move."

Monrovia did not budge.

"We need Lau," Miranda said, because if there was someone who could help them, someone who could stand up for Carl to the Senate, and maybe even stop Alois, it was Lau. "She can talk to the Senate. Come on."

Tan appeared at Miranda's elbow. "Go to Tunica Park."

She jumped back at the voice, so close to her ear.

"Slip out quietly, and I'll bring you some provisions." He tapped his foot. "Go before this crowd gets really hostile."

Monrovia hauled herself up slowly, as if her limbs were too heavy to hold. Tan slipped into the crowd, heading in the tent's direction.

Miranda turned and walked right into Oren, his arms crossed, and his mouth set in a scowl.

"Glad you didn't leave. The senators are bringing you both in for questioning.

CHAPTER 10

CO-CONSPIRATORS

Cold fear shot through Miranda, and, in one quick move, she grabbed a fistful of dirt and flung it at Oren's eyes. He stumbled back, yelping and wiping his face.

It wasn't enough. She had to bring him down. "Sorry about this." She rammed her shoulder into his stomach full force, dropping him to his knees.

Monrovia gaped at Oren, lying coughing in the dirt.

Miranda yanked her up by the strap on her pack. "Run, now!"

She kept hold of the strap and took off. Monrovia stumbled, but Miranda held tight. Then they were both running, gaining speed as they hit the street, not looking back. Miranda's side ached, but she pushed herself harder.

"In here." Monrovia tugged her into the archway of a building that still had most of its walls.

Miranda slid down the wall, huffing. *Finally free.* Knocking Oren to the ground hadn't been how she wanted to do it. *But if it's him or me...*

Monrovia leaned with her hands on her knees, breathing hard. She flipped her head up, staring at Miranda with a look close to pure hatred. "That was the stupidest thing we could have done. You beat up a Senator's guard, and we ran! Now one hundred percent of those people think we are co-conspirators." Her glare pierced Miranda. "Are you up to something I don't know about? Should I flag them down and turn you in myself?"

"I saved you." Miranda clenched her teeth to hold back other words. "Why did you come with me, anyway?"

"Because you dragged me by my pack strap." A vein in Monrovia's neck throbbed with an unhealthy intensity.

"You could have stopped running," Miranda mumbled. Had she been dragging her sister? "I didn't want to beat up Oren, but he wasn't going to let us leave."

Monrovia stared at the ceiling as if counting the cracks. "The senators won't pull our fingernails out. They only want to talk to us."

"You think we should sit in some stuffy room and answer the same question two hundred times while more buildings fall and Carl gets the blame? We need to find Lau. She can stop him."

Monrovia bristled. "Alois is dead. Beda killed him."

This dogged refusal to see the facts utterly drained Miranda. She wiped the sides of her face. "Rona, you know this has to be Alois."

"But Beda…"

Neither of them wanted to say it out loud. If Beda had not killed Alois, what had she died for? "Lau must have answers. If we let them take us more people will be hurt. We need to get to her."

Monrovia's head nodded so slightly Miranda almost missed it.

"Agreed?"

Monrovia's eye twitched as she watched the open doorway.

An undisturbed pile of brick dust lay at Miranda's foot. She stabbed her finger through its middle, dragging red strokes. Her sister's lips were a tight line and her hands stayed folded stiffly in her lap.

"Are you going to stay mad at me forever?" Miranda wanted to punch the wall.

Monrovia kept her eyes on the doorway.

"This whole place is a scam. I told the senator the truth. That's supposed to be what you do here. Trust each other, tell the truth. I thought that's what makes you better than people on Earth." A dry laugh fell out like a cough. "But you all are no better than we were. You just had a nicer place to live."

Monrovia motioned: *stop*, and Miranda heard the boots clomping close. She sprang to her feet but stayed in a crouch and snatched up her pack. Miranda tugged the edge of Monrovia's shirt to ask her to follow as she tiptoed deeper into the shadow. She had to admit she wanted her sister by her side. The idea of tackling this alone made her legs go weak.

Monrovia crept after her. Footfalls crashed, closing in.

In the back of the building the ceiling had caved in, probably days before, leaving a jumble of debris and a jagged edge exposing the floor above. Maybe it was strong enough to hold them.

Miranda scrambled up the splintered wood and planted one foot on a windowsill. She caught a piece of bamboo jutting out from the broken floor above and kicked off, pulling herself to the second floor. "Come on," she whispered as she lay on her belly and stretched her arms out.

Monrovia hesitated for one beat longer than Miranda could take. Sweat beaded her brow. She waved her outstretched hand. Finally, Monrovia climbed up the debris and hauled herself up.

The footsteps were louder now. Miranda crawled toward the darkness and saw Monrovia do the same. Flashlight beams played on the wall. *They're here. Be still.*

Boots shuffled through the debris. Monrovia moved another inch, and an unmistakable creek ripped through the quiet. A ray of light shot up, landing near them.

"What was that?"

"Not sure."

Miranda held her breath, willing herself invisible. *Is Monrovia trying to give us away?*

The beams overshot them, landing on the ceiling.

"There's a survivor!" The shout came from outside.

The light raced to the floor and the boots crashed back the way they had come, out into the street.

"There's someone alive. I need all hands!"

Miranda strained to pick Oren's voice out of the yelling guards' tones. She hadn't hit him very hard. He'd be fine, right?

The call was answered from all directions. Debris crashed around.

Miranda whispered, "Now's our chance."

"I want to help save that person," Monrovia said.

"We'll save more people by stopping Alois," Miranda lowered herself lightly down. She waited. *Is she with me?*

Monrovia climbed down and they crept out through a gaping hole in the back wall. The sun was setting, the light gray day giving way to charcoal. They were on a side street now. The bustle of the rescue clanged behind them.

"This way." Monrovia dragged her into the open street.

"We have to stay hidden," Miranda hissed, yanking her into a clump of bushes.

Monrovia pointed across the street. "That's the way to Tunica Park."

"Fine." Miranda slinked out of her hiding place and hurried down the sidewalk. "Stay close to the shadows and away from rover lights." As soon as she said the words, a searchlight blazed down the middle of the road, making broad sweeps that lit up the buildings along the side. "Dive!"

They both hid behind a thick group of bushes. *She's with me.*

The rover's lights continued past, sweeping in broad strokes.

"Hey." Impulsively, Miranda gripped Monrovia's hand. "You know I didn't mean to get Carl arrested, right? I would never do anything to hurt either of you."

Monrovia shrugged and pulled her hand away. "Let's get to the park."

The shadows blanketed them as they crept down the street. Miranda clung to the hope that Monrovia may not hate her after all.

CHAPTER 11

THE LAST TRAIN

Clumps of trees darkened rolling hills of wet grass. The tallest hill rose from the center, its peak crowned with stands of banana trees sticking up like unruly hairs.

"How do we find Tan?" Miranda asked.

"Let's start there." Monrovia pointed at the peak with the spiky strands.

From the hilltop, they took in the randomness of the destruction playing out in the streets beyond this quiet oasis. One street had houses flattened, but on another nearby, houses stood seemingly untouched. And of course, there was the park where they stood, a refuge of green, spared.

"Hey! Over here," a voice called from the darkness.

Miranda dropped to her belly.

"Tan? Is that you?" Monrovia whispered.

A leaf danced at the edge of Miranda's vision. She stood again, squinting as she made her way to one of the thick patches of banana trees. "Are you in there?"

Tan popped his head out from between two leaves like a lizard with a leafy frill. Miranda burst out laughing; it felt good.

"Shush!" He grabbed her hand and pulled her into the leaves. She fell, still laughing, into the dirt.

Monrovia crawled in behind her. "Did you check for spiders?"

"I thought you loved spiders," Miranda said.

"Never said I wanted to live in their house."

Tan sat under the canopy and crossed his arms, looking stern. "I recall telling you to leave *quietly*. Remember that? Not to get the entire Senate guard on your tail."

Miranda shrugged. "Oren wasn't going to let us leave."

"Yeah, remind me to stay on your good side." Tan rummaged in his bag and brought out two sandwiches. "Provisions, as promised."

Miranda snatched a sandwich and bit through the rice paper. "Thank you so much," she said, bits of food flying from her mouth. "This is so good." She slurped some water.

Tan cleared his throat. "The things that woman said on stage—were they true?"

Monrovia squeezed the bread in her hand. "*That woman* used to be Dad's best friend."

"Did he really lie to the Senate?" Tan asked softly.

More bread flew out of her mouth, but Miranda didn't care. "You don't even know about Alois, but he's the bad guy here, not Carl."

Tan raised an eyebrow. "And where is this Alois now?"

"We killed him in the Gathering," Monrovia said.

"W-w-e did what?" Tan sputtered.

"But we really didn't," Miranda mumbled.

Tan shook his head. "You guys left out a lot of fine print when you asked Nibiru to support the Gathering." He rubbed his arms and sat up straighter.

A rhythmic low rumble filled the air.

"What's that?" Tan's voice pitched toward panic.

The rumble was familiar, but out of place. "Is it a train?"

"We don't have trains here." Monrovia peeked through the leaves. "Where is it coming from?"

The rumble grew louder, coming closer. Miranda snatched up her pack and broke the cover of the leaves. "Over there." She pointed left. "No, there."

Metal screeched on metal as a light broke through the shadow, hurtling at them.

"Run!" Miranda dove out of the trees, clutching her pack and rolling as far as she could from the sounds of grinding metal.

Showers of sparks lit up the darkness.

A deafening boom shook the ground, and Miranda covered her ears as three cars of a rusted, gray commuter train sailed past her, tearing up the grass, obliterating trees and shrubs.

The train roared into the street at the base of the hill, sending up a hail of metal and glass. Miranda's body shook. *Alive.* She swallowed and it was like she'd eaten pins. *Screaming?*

She hauled herself up and stumbled through the darkness, the vibrations of chaos still hanging in the air. "Monrovia? Where are you? Monrovia, answer me! Tan?"

"Here," Monrovia answered. "I'm okay."

Miranda collapsed near the voice.

Tan dropped beside them. "What was that?"

The rumble of the train still reverberated through Miranda's cells. "A train from Earth," she whispered, her mouth dry.

"Could there be others?" Tan asked.

Miranda put her hand to the ground, checking for vibrations. It was calm. "No more for now."

"I'm shaking so bad," Tan said. "But why did the death train drop *clothes* on us?"

"What?" Miranda and Monrovia called out in unison.

Something soft landed on Miranda's head. She held it up to the weak moonlight to try to get a better look. "A shredded shirt? Are those flowers?"

"Let me see that." Monrovia snatched the fabric from her hand. "That's my scarf. There should be another."

"You brought silk scarves camping?"

"There's more over here," Tan said. "Is this a skirt?"

Snapping twigs marked Monrovia's crawl to Tan. "These are my clothes."

Miranda rooted around in the dark, hunting for soft fabrics in the dirt. Her hand landed on a canvas strap. "I found your pack." She raised it triumphantly as a cloud uncovered the moon.

"It's shredded," Monrovia said, just as the wreck let loose a long whine of sagging metal that ended with a puff of dust.

Miranda dropped the useless pack, slumping down. "You can put whatever is salvageable in my bag. She combed the damp grass for more cotton and tossed clothes into a pile.

"I found a book, but it's cut in half," Tan said.

"It's broken?" Monrovia's voice sounded strained, just as Miranda asked, "A book?"

Miranda's stomach clenched as she imagined the worn brown cover with gold lettering. It couldn't be *that* book. Why would her sister have brought it? She shivered despite the warm air as she turned to Monrovia. "Is that what I think it is?"

Monrovia inhaled deeply. "I brought it just in case we needed it."

"But you were so sure that Beda killed him," Miranda said.

"Well, it's trashed." Tan threw down the piece.

Lights danced over the wreckage at the bottom of the hill.

"Guards!" Tan hissed. "Come on." He ran through the dark, and Miranda and Monrovia followed. But the lights stayed focused on the hulking wreck.

Tan slowed as they reached the far edge of the park. He crouched in a dark corner. "My hands are still shaking. What now?"

"We're going to find the person who might be able to end this and help my dad," Monrovia said. She sounded resolute.

"Yes! Where are they? Let's go." Tan jumped to his feet.

"She's in Kona on the other side of Terrapin Pass. We need to transport to get to her fast," Monrovia said.

Miranda imagined that Tan's mouth was hanging open, but it was too dark in this spot to be sure. Beda and Monrovia had taught her how to tap into her connection to the universe to move through space—it's how she'd made it off Earth. At one time, almost everyone on Nibiru used the skill, but only a few practiced it now. Beda and Lau were two of the few, and they passed that knowledge down.

Miranda's stomach churned at the memory of burning blood and each cell being stretched and squeezed. She had been happy to leave transporting behind. But with the rover network knocked out, there was no other way. It would take weeks to walk to Lau's village.

"Transport? Like poof to some other place? You can do that?"

"When we have to," Monrovia said. "I'm not sure if you've ever seen someone transport, Tan, but I've been told it can be unsettling."

He made a noise between a grunt and a groan.

"You ready?" Monrovia asked.

Miranda wondered who the question was directed to, but she folded her legs into lotus position and rested the backs of her hands on her knees. She cleared her mind and focused on the sagging porch and unpainted floorboards of the Inn. "Ready."

Monrovia's low toned chant floated to her, and she joined in, letting the vibrations radiate from her throat and travel through her limbs. Sweat dripped down the side of her face. Any minute now, her fingers and toes would heat up. She focused harder, recreating every detail from the porch at the Inn. The burn should have started. How long had she been trying? Her butt ached. She chanted more intently, wiping out everything but the tone's vibrations.

Something pinged her arm.

Okay, this must be it.

She readied herself for the painful journey. Another ping on her arm.

"Miranda," her sister whispered.

She cracked open one eye and fell back when Monrovia's face was inches from her own.

"It isn't working." Monrovia said.

"Maybe if we try longer."

"No, we should have already moved. Something was blocking me. Maybe it can't work with Alois gone."

"Or all this debris is blocking the energy flow," Miranda offered.

"Look, uh, I know a guy with a plane," Tan said.

"*Of course* you know a guy." Monrovia laughed.

"I saw him at the gardens earlier today. I can find him in the morning. If his plane is still in one piece, I'm sure he'll help."

Flashlights lit up a line along the trees at the top of the hill, seeming to search beyond the wreckage.

Miranda jumped to her feet and slung her pack over her shoulder. "Thanks Tan, we'll meet you back here in the morning."

She and Monrovia ran quietly through the park, away from the grinding, groaning metal and flashlights, back to a street with buildings drooping like cooked noodles. Miranda pointed out a building with a mostly intact front. They both darted for it.

In the doorway, Miranda motioned for her sister to hang back as she searched the bottom floor. Empty—not even a rat.

Miranda collapsed into a dark, dusty corner while Monrovia sunk into shadows at the opposite end of the room.

"Was it a coincidence we were right in the path of that train?" Monrovia asked softly.

Miranda pulled her hood up and settled into the dust. She didn't want to say her real answer. "I don't know."

Soft sobs floated through the night as she closed her eyes and pretended not to hear. She needed quiet. She needed space.

CHAPTER 12

AN ALLY

Dawn's pink lightened the horizon, and the air smelled like wet grass. Miranda had settled in one tree, Monrovia in another. They were back in the park, waiting with good vantage. They had already agreed, if Tan came with more than one person, they would stay hidden.

Miranda picked at a piece of bark. Monrovia had made another dig this morning about her getting Carl arrested. The jabs would likely keep coming. The rough bark dug under her fingernails. When she chose this tree, she had climbed as high as she could stand, but Monrovia had climbed higher. She peeled back a second chunk of bark. It stung as it worked its way farther under her fingernail.

Dark clouds had steadily rolled in since first light, and now the first crack of thunder shook out the rain. Large drops fell as Monrovia yelled something. Miranda couldn't hear and held her tongue out to the raindrops instead of calling back.

By the time Tan appeared, with one person by his side, Miranda's butt was numb and her back ached. She squinted to see the newcomer's face, but a floppy hood obscured it. Tan's hands danced in the air. He may have been telling the stranger about the train.

The rain stopped as suddenly as it had started, and the sun squeezed the droplets into steam. Sweat ran down Miranda's brow. Tan's friend jerked back the hood, showing black, spiky hair.

Him?

Miranda scanned the park for movement. After making sure there were no guards waiting to swoop in, she signaled Monrovia with a thumbs-up, but then noticed her sister was already halfway down her tree.

As Miranda's feet hit the soft leaves, she gave the ground an appreciative pat, then dug under a nearby bush for her pack, savoring its familiar hug as she strapped it on.

Monrovia whistled low.

Tan spun around at the noise. "Where were you?"

Miranda gestured to the tree and Tan cocked his head. "Never can be too careful." She eyed the newcomer and thought, *Davon, motorcycle,* but she remembered here he had another name. So, he didn't have a motorcycle on Nibiru, but he had a plane. Interesting.

"Hugo, right?" Miranda extended her hand, and he shook it.

"That was normal." He winked.

Tan raised an eyebrow. "You know each other?"

"We've had a few run-ins." Hugo smiled.

She hoped he would leave it at that. She wanted to preserve the slim chance Tan might think she was normal.

Monrovia flipped her thick, white hair down shaking out leaves and tossed it back again in a dramatic show. Hugo's jaw slackened as she walked closer. The chances of him helping them seemed to increase with each of Monrovia's steps.

She leaned in. "Monrovia, nice to meet you." She took his outstretched hand. "You were at Bushuto Gardens yesterday. I saw Miranda talking to you."

He squeaked out, "Yeah, she thought I was someone else."

Miranda chewed her thumbnail. That was two chances he had to tell everyone how crazy she'd acted, and he hadn't taken either opportunity. He might be alright.

"Tan tells me you need to get to Kona. Something about seeing a woman who knows why this happened to us?"

Monrovia nodded, not taking her eyes off him.

"She'll know how to stop it," Miranda said.

"That's good enough for me." Hugo grinned at Monrovia. "I have a two-seater glider, but you two can squeeze into the back seat. She can sit at your feet." He motioned dismissively to Miranda.

Might be a jerk, after all.

"Great," Monrovia said. "Where is the plane?"

"It's by the river in Tikal."

"Is that a different town?" Miranda asked.

She waited for an answer, but Hugo was too busy staring at Monrovia, who was consumed with pretending not to notice. Miranda was about to ask again just to break up their charade when Tan stepped in.

"It's a neighborhood," he said, pulling collapsible boxes out of his bag. "And here, I brought water and more sandwiches."

Monrovia picked up a sandwich and walked beside Hugo. "You're young to own a plane, aren't you?" She nibbled the crust.

Miranda looked for a bush to hurl in but settled on eating instead. She and Tan trailed behind them, close enough to eavesdrop.

"My dad and I built it together. He always has a project going, and I liked to hang out with him and watch him work," Hugo said.

Bread almost choked her as Miranda shoved half of her sandwich in her mouth. She recovered and smacked loudly just to see if she could get Monrovia to turn around and sneer at her.

Ignored.

"And where is he now?" Monrovia asked.

Miranda smacked louder and caught Tan rolling his eyes.

"He passed last year."

Miranda stopped angry chewing.

"I'm so sorry," Monrovia said.

Hugo shrugged. "He would have loved to help you. He always helped people."

Monrovia stopped and took a deep breath. "Our dad is Carl Ess."

Hugo whipped around; his gentle demeanor evaporated, replaced by a sharp sneer. "Is he responsible for this?"

Monrovia held up her hands as if asking him to hold on. "No, but leading the Gathering to destroy Earth may have set off a chain of..." She sent a pleading glance in Miranda's direction.

Miranda gulped and said, "Unintended consequences. And Lau, the woman in Kona, is the key to stopping it." She kicked the ground and decided it was the right time to come clean. "Also, not sure if Tan mentioned, but we're kind of on the run from the Senate guards."

Hugo glared at Tan. "No, he left that out."

Tan rubbed his neck and looked at his shoes.

"You need to tell the Senate about this woman," Hugo said.

"Senator Cloudlyn hasn't been in a listening mood," Monrovia said.

Hugo shook his head. "You girls might be trouble."

"You are not wrong there," Tan said.

"You said it yourself that if your dad was here, he would help us. We're trying to stop whatever is happening. Come on, will you help us?" Monrovia said.

Hugo looked at the sky. Was he hoping for permission? "Okay."

"Great. Then before we go any farther, Monrovia and I need a disguise." Miranda fished in her pack for the scarves she'd collected when the train shredded Monrovia's bag. She passed a scarf to Monrovia and tied another around her head and face. Monrovia secured hers too, leaving only her eyes visible.

Tan squeezed Hugo's shoulder. "Thanks for helping. My mom needs me back at the gardens."

Monrovia gave Tan a quick hug. "We'll see you soon."

Miranda peered out from the small slit. The world seemed narrowed; her vision more focused. Get to the plane. Find Lau. Anything else was a distraction.

CHAPTER 13

FRACTURED

Miranda checked over her shoulder with almost every step, picking her way through smashed cinder blocks and broken glass, waiting for Oren to jump out with a team and take them down quickly. She wouldn't even see it coming, except she would, because she was watching and listening. But with each step, no team of angry senate guards—no Oren.

Hugo scampered over piles of debris, almost running to his plane. Monrovia stayed close behind him. He was adventurous—like Davon.

Davon and Hugo had so many similarities. *Not fair,* she thought as he paused to take in the destruction. "The hanger isn't too much farther, but—" He wiped his face. "It would be a miracle if it's in one piece."

"We'll figure out another way to Kona if we have to." Miranda shuffled her throbbing feet in the direction he pointed. There had to be other ways to get to Lau, but none came to mind.

After trudging through more mess, each step a possible broken ankle, Hugo stopped at the edge of a street that gave way to a steep drop. "I don't believe it," he mumbled.

"What?" Monrovia asked as she and Miranda caught up.

Hugo's mouth hung open. "Look."

A cluster of pristine streets stretched before them at the bottom of the hill. Leafy trees, sparkling roofs, not a brick out of place. A group of fully intact larger buildings edged a twinkling blue river. A warm wind brushed Miranda's cheek, and she closed her eyes, whispering *thank you* to who, or whatever, was responsible for this miracle.

Monrovia whispered. "It's so peaceful. But where is everybody?"

"Probably out helping the rescue effort," Hugo said.

As they climbed down the hill, the debris thinned and gave way to grass, then a smooth street.

"The hangar is over here." Hugo led them to a sprawling, green warehouse that faced the water. He keyed a code into the lock. "Grab that other handle."

Miranda yanked the simple black knob and the massive door creaked and rolled back. A perfect plane waited inside, poised for adventure. Hugo ran to it and brushed his hand along a stretch of its side.

"This is *Icarus*." His voice cracked. "My dad spent years working every job he could to pay for the parts. We built it together. I started flying two years ago. I've only had a few solo flights, but today is clear, nothing to worry about."

Miranda's palms and feet sweat.

He stroked the side. "My dad loved this plane. I can't believe it's spotless."

"Let's hope it stays that way," Miranda whispered.

He lugged two lassos off the wall and looped one around a long, slender wing, letting the slack pool on the ground. "Take this and walk it to the middle of the wing." He waved the lasso at Miranda.

She shivered, remembering the ropes Alois had her create in her mind and how they had disintegrated when she needed them most. She took this one, decidedly solid in her hands, and did as he asked.

He popped open the glass bubble that protected the cockpit and motioned for them both to come closer. "When I move these brakes." He directed their eyes to a set of bright-orange weights resting in front of the wheels. "Then you two use the ropes to guide it through the doors. I'll steer."

"Straight out to the street?" Monrovia asked.

"That's our runway." He grinned. "Point the nose that way." He gestured away from the crumbled city. "We need a smooth stretch for takeoff. Ready?" He didn't wait for a reply but yanked back one of the orange weights, and, running to the small back tire, yanked that one away too. The glider rolled forward, and he jumped into the cockpit.

"It's so light!" Miranda marveled as she tugged the plane to the doors.

"That's because it doesn't have an engine!" Hugo beamed. "Amazing, right?"

Miranda's stomach turned as she led the wing around to aim the nose down the street.

"Jump in! Monrovia, you first."

She climbed into the passenger seat and motioned for Miranda's pack. She wrestled it into place under the seat as the plane continued to roll. "How does it fly with no engine?"

Miranda hoisted herself into the cockpit and wedged between Monrovia's knees. "I wouldn't ask that question."

Hugo twisted back in his seat. "This plane uses thermodynamics." His eyes sparkled as he said the word. "We are going to fly like the birds. Settled?"

"Squished, yes," Monrovia said.

Hugo guided the glass bubble back into position, clamping it closed.

Miranda clocked their slow roll down the street. "How do we get in the air?" She ran her cold, wet palms along her pants.

Hugo flipped a switch and black blades glided out of the nose of the plane. They whirred furiously, moving the glider forward. "There is a small motor to power a propeller."

"Do we really have to do this?" Miranda whispered as it picked up speed.

Monrovia patted her head. "We'll be fine. I'm sure."

Miranda wished her sister hadn't added the last part. They picked up speed, and her stomach lurched as they climbed into the air. She gripped her cramped knees until her knuckles were white. They leveled out and Hugo flipped the switch again, and the gentle whir of the propellor stopped.

"What are you doing?" Miranda said.

Hugo laughed. "Relax. The propellor is just for take-off. Now, we sail."

Miranda leaned her head back against Monrovia's knees, not because she wanted to, but because her head had nowhere else to go. For a few minutes the plane glided smoothly, and her heartbeat slowed—then the plane dipped.

Miranda jerked up and hit her head on the back of Hugo's seat. "What happened?"

"We hit a downdraft. Nothing to worry about. We're riding the air currents, just like a bird. Some drafts go up, some go down." His voice was calm.

Miranda tried to breathe evenly. "I don't like sudden movements when I can't get away." She leaned back on Monrovia again.

A low rumble echoed above them.

"Thunder?" Monrovia asked.

Hugo didn't answer, but Miranda heard him tapping instruments. The rumbling increased, and the plane shot up. "An updraft," Hugo explained. "Guess we're going to have a little storm."

Miranda kept her eyes trained on the clouds. Several sensors on the dashboard beeped at once.

"That doesn't make sense." Hugo peered up at the clouds while he tapped at the blinking light. "It's sensing something large, potential collision." He checked the clouds again.

A glint of light—a reflection—broke through.

Slack-jawed, Miranda searched for the words. She pointed up. "Move!"

Hugo leaned hard to the left and the glider bent in that direction.

The top of a building crested the clouds. It was falling fast. Hugo snapped at the controls and the propeller whirred into action. He steered hard as a wall of steel and glass cut through the air, plummeting down. The right wing tilted down, sucked in by a mini cyclone.

"Pull up!" Miranda yelled.

"I'm trying!" Hugo leaned on the joystick, but the current had control, twisting them until the glider flipped upside down. The propeller whirred and whined but couldn't break the suction. Miranda pressed against the glass, hoping the latches would hold, and watched the building fall below them.

Monrovia squeezed Miranda's shoulder.

"When the building hits, there will be a burst of upward air." Hugo's voice rose, and his words came out fast. "We'll have a few seconds to surf out on that updraft before there's another spiral."

Miranda wished he sounded more confident. The ground raced up at them.

Monrovia's grip tightened and her lips moved as if she was reciting a chant or a prayer. Miranda needed a deep breath, but her lungs only allowed shallow snatches. Her blood rushed to her throbbing head.

"Brace yourselves. Updraft coming in three, two…,"

A thunderous boom drowned out Hugo's voice. The plume from impact shot them higher and a loose confederation of steel and glinting mirrors hung in the air for several seconds, suspended, before gravity claimed it to the ground. Hugo jammed the controls and the glider spun back upright as they sailed out of the vortex. Miranda slammed down on Monrovia.

She shouted, "You did it!"

The sensor blinked and beeped again. Hugo gripped the joystick, pushing them forward. "No celebrations yet."

Miranda squished back at Monrovia's feet and squinted at the cloud above them. An outline, a shape. "Something else is coming. Not a building this time. It seems clear." She had an uncomfortable sensation of familiarity.

"Left or right?" he yelled.

Miranda froze. "It's coming on the right."

He pitched the plane a sharp left. The glinting edge of a large, rounded object whistled inches from the glider's long, thin wing.

"Just missed us." He steadied the plane buffeted by the downdraft.

Miranda's stomach sank as she watched the object fall fast. "It's not clear. It's tinted blue to look like the sky. What is below us?"

"Looks like Bushuto Gardens," Monrovia said.

"That's the dome from Bubble City, or part of it, at least."

Dust and debris rocketed into the air.

A tear slid down Miranda's cheek. "It will seal them in."

"Hang on!" Hugo rolled the glider over and under the currents of air until the waves calmed and the frantic sensor stopped beeping. He craned his neck, peering down. "You know where that thing came from?"

As the dust cleared, Miranda saw people, dark spots from up here, running around inside, banging on the walls of their new prison. "They made it to be indestructible." She wiped her cheek. "I hope Tan isn't trapped."

Monrovia's hand flew to her mouth. "They'll run out of oxygen."

"Let's put it down and help," Hugo said.

Other small figures rushed to the dome. Miranda's heart hung heavy. "The best way we can help is by getting to Lau."

"But people are trapped," he said.

"Miranda is right. It doesn't need to be us," Monrovia said. "There are a lot of smart people down there who can figure out how to get supplies and oxygen in. We need to find Lau and see what she can do to stop all of this."

Hugo sighed heavily. "Okay, we stay on course." He steered the nose toward Kona.

A rush of adrenaline surged through Miranda. *Lau, you better have a plan to stop Alois.*

CHAPTER 14

UNINVITED

Clouds rushed past the window, and Miranda tried not to think about the ground, so far below, as they glided in silence. "How much longer?" Sweat beaded on her forehead.

"About a half hour," Hugo said. "Are you warm back there? I can crack the vents."

"Roasting," Monrovia said.

He fiddled with a few things at the front, and cool blasts circulated around them. "Seems like weird timing, two big things falling just as we're in the air."

"A strange coincidence, I guess," Hugo said after a long silence.

An icy shiver ran down Miranda's spine. *And he doesn't know about the train.* She couldn't bear to say the words out loud, but it was hard to ignore they were being targeted. But Alois was so powerful. If he wanted them dead—

The plane dipped, cutting off her thoughts. Miranda gripped the sides of Hugo's seat. "What's happening?"

"Don't worry, that's only the draft over the mountain," he said. The glider rose again. "Almost there. Next problem is to find somewhere safe to land."

The glider banked, lodging her stomach in her throat. She gripped Monrovia's arm and squeezed.

"Almost there," Monrovia said.

Miranda pictured the wraparound porch of the inn, the faded red paint. The last time she'd been there, Lau had all but accused her of condemning Monrovia and Beda to the black hole to save herself. Miranda had left in a huff, waiting on that porch for the rover that would take her to the father she had no memory of. It had only been a few weeks since she took that first ride across Nibiru. It seemed like a different lifetime. And now—Carl. Lying to the Senate had been Lau's idea. She had better have a great plan now—she owed it to Carl.

Miranda chewed her lip.

They sailed through white wisps, gliding lower along the mountain's slope.

"We cleared it," Hugo said. "Is that the town?"

"It doesn't look right," Monrovia said.

"I don't see a road."

Miranda bumped her forehead on the window, craning for a closer look.

"Why is everything the same color?" Hugo asked.

A familiar monochrome sea blanketed bushes, treetops, even some roofs. Miranda's mouth dried. "Can this thing land in sand?"

"It would be hard to take off again."

"Keep going. There must be somewhere safe to land. We can hike in," Miranda said.

"Why sand?" Monrovia muttered.

They glided low over a thin line of trees that separated the town from a green field.

"This looks good." Hugo flipped a switch. The plane slowed and he aimed down, leaning back on the control.

The green field rushed up. Miranda shut her eyes and squeezed Monrovia's arm tighter.

"Ouch!" Monrovia jerked her arm away, but Miranda held tight. "You're cutting off the circulation," she complained as they bounced to the ground and skittered to a stop.

Miranda cracked one eye and released her sister's arm. "Are we down?"

Hugo beamed. "We're down!"

He popped the latches on the glass bubble and hopped out, offering a hand to Monrovia. She freed her legs and climbed out. Miranda extracted herself from the floorboard and climbed down the side with no help offered.

She stretched her aching limbs. "I appreciate the ride, but I never want to get into that thing again."

"Were you planning to walk home?" he asked.

Miranda buried her face in her hands, shaking her head.

"Once we convince Lau to testify for Carl, we have to get back. I will not miss his trial," Monrovia said.

"So that's your plan? What if she says no?" Miranda said.

Monrovia blinked. "She can't."

"I won't abandon you out here when we don't know what you are walking into." Hugo climbed into the cockpit and flipped some levers and came out again, latching the sides. "I guess it's through the woods?" He strode to the tree line.

Miranda sighed and followed. They crossed the field and stepped into the cool shade of the trees. Pine straw littered the forest floor. They each paused, as if scared to take another step.

"It's silent," Monrovia said.

Miranda scanned the forest between the skinny pine trunks. No movement—even the air hung still, as if waiting for permission to move.

Hugo rolled his shoulders like he was trying to shake something off. "It's cold and too quiet."

"Hurry," Monrovia said.

They shuffled through the dense trees, snapping twigs and crunching leaves underfoot.

Miranda shivered under a heavy gaze. Something watching, waiting. She peered between the trunks. "Shh," she said. They kept going. "Stop!" she whispered as loud as she dared.

Hugo and Monrovia both froze in their steps.

Two yellow eyes stared out from a shadow, locked on Hugo, but he didn't seem to have seen them yet.

Miranda dropped to a squat. "Down!" she whispered.

Monrovia sank. "What are we doing?"

Hugo turned to the shadow and a pounding rush of fangs and claws sprang forward. A skinny, snarling wolf pinned him to the dirt in seconds.

Miranda tucked her head and vaulted her body into the matted gray fur, knocking it off balance. It fell on its back but quickly recovered its fighting stance. Her brain shut off as she tasted blood and felt her muscles rippling in her limbs. She locked eyes with its hungry glare. Cool desert wind brushed her body. She remembered stars twinkling around Bear Rock. It's where she had stared this wolf down before. She had no doubt.

He bent his skinny front haunches, eyes fixed on her. Hugo rolled away.

Move along, old friend. She looked deeply into his eyes and willed him to walk away. The wolf shook its shoulders. His howl vibrated through Miranda from the inside out, but she stayed firmly on her hands and knees. The wolf charged past her, storming into the trees.

She fell to her side.

"What the hell was that?" Hugo screamed.

Monrovia yanked him up. "Let's go." They all ran, full speed, for daylight.

Once they cleared the shadow of the woods, Hugo seized Miranda by the arms. "What did you do? Was I really attacked by a wolf?"

The sun bounced off the sand, blinding Miranda. She raised her arms in front of her chest and brought them both down on his hands, breaking his hold. She calmly stepped back. "Yes, that was a wolf."

"And you tackled it?" He spat out the words like he couldn't believe himself. "Then it wandered off? What the hell happened?" He rubbed his neck and looked closer at Miranda. "Who are you?"

"Somebody who saved your butt." She trudged through the shin-deep sand.

Monrovia took two long strides to catch up with her. "You've done that before. You did that on Earth. Nathan told me."

"Earth? Who is Nathan?" Hugo asked.

"That was the same wolf," Miranda said.

"Nathan is a wolf?"

They both ignored Hugo.

"But if it's from Earth, it can't be here."

"Nothing makes sense right now," Miranda said.

Dead leaves poked through the wash of beige. The last visible reminder of small trees swallowed whole.

"Is this place usually covered in sand?" Hugo asked, huffing.

"No," Miranda and Monrovia answered in unison.

As they came into the village, waves of sand streamed from broken windows and lay piled in doorways. It had washed through like water, tearing roofs from walls, and walls from foundations.

"There were animals here. It was green before." Monrovia shook her head.

"This one had to be bigger than any I've ever seen," Miranda said.

"One what?" Monrovia asked.

"The sandstorm. One came through our village when I was small. Beda and I huddled on the floor for hours. It shook the house. We didn't have any windows, but the sand came through every crack. It was everywhere. We were lucky. The people in the lean-tos drowned in sand."

Monrovia clutched her chest. "Do you think that happened to the people here?"

"Sometimes it comes in like a tsunami, sometimes like a tornado."

Hugo walked up a set of steps that had lost their house. "I hope they got out in time."

"No wonder we couldn't get through to Lau. So much confusion here." Monrovia wrinkled her brow and sped up her slog through the sand.

Cold dread settled in Miranda's stomach. "I still can't feel her."

***

The inn sagged, a faded beacon at the end of the road. Miranda trudged through the knee-deep morass fixated on a strip of railing, the only marker of where the steps should be. Her palms sweat as she gripped it and jumped onto what should have been the porch. Would Lau agree to testify for Carl? Would that even help?

Her feet connected with a buried solid surface. Three feet of sand held the door open. Miranda climbed over the pile to get inside. Her heart banged against her chest. Helping Carl mattered, but she really needed Lau to stop Alois. Was she already fighting him?

Monrovia bolted past her. "Lau! Lau Chen! It's Monrovia. Are you here?" She raced through the living room, disappearing down the back hall. "All the windows are busted," she called back.

"Lau," Miranda yelled. A shiver rushed through her as the words *I'm here* rattled in her brain.

Hugo rubbed his arms. "She wouldn't hide from you, would she? She must not be here. If we leave now, we can make it back before dark."

Miranda held out her hand, motioning for him to be quiet.

Monrovia came back down the hall shaking her head.

"I think she's here though," Miranda said. They all looked up the sand-covered stairs to the second floor.

"Was this place always so creepy?" Hugo asked, as they made their way to the stairs.

"Before it was a ghost town full of sand, you mean?" Monrovia stepped on the bottom stair, and it released a loud groan. They all jumped. "Just get up fast!"

Miranda and Hugo clambered to keep up with Monrovia and not get left in the dark. Closed doors lined the upstairs hallway.

"It sure is creepy now," Hugo said.

"Lau? Lau Chen, are you here? It's Miranda."

Her heart banged in her ears. If Lau was okay, she would be downstairs fighting the sand with her favorite weapon— a broom. But instead of helping her do that, they were creeping on tiptoe, afraid of what they might find.

Monrovia pushed open the door at the top of the stairs. "Broken window, lots of sand. Next room." She calmly shut it.

Miranda grasped the banister to keep from falling as a wave of cold sweat rolled down her face.

"You okay?"

She wiped her brow and made it to the top landing. "Sure, no problem." Her scalp prickled as she trailed Monrovia, peeking over her shoulder as she opened each door. Empty.

Monrovia paused at the last door.

"Open it," Miranda said from behind her.

Monrovia shook her head. Miranda saw the color had drained from her face.

"You open it," she said.

"Wh—" but instead of arguing in the dark hall, Miranda reached out, her hand shaking, and turned the knob. It popped open.

A four-poster bed filled the back wall. White curtains draped down from its canopy. They were gathered back at the sides, making a soft frame for the image of Lau lying in the middle with sheets piled around her slight body. Lanterns flickered on both side tables.

"Lau!" Miranda swallowed hard and walked to one side of the bed. Monrovia moved to the other.

Miranda reached for Lau's hand but stopped short of picking it up. Her thin, gray skin looked as if any movement would be too rough. She rested her hand on top of Lau's instead.

"Lau?" Miranda whispered. "What happened?"

Lau's eyelids fluttered but did not open.

Monrovia breathed, "Are you still with us?"

Lau's hand was cold, but her chest rose and fell ever so slightly.

"She's in terrible shape. We have to get her to a hospital."

"She looks like she'll break if we pick her up," Miranda said.

"Hugo, could you fly her out?" Monrovia asked.

"Getting her to the glider would be hard. But if we can do that, then yeah," he said. "But I don't think I can get her there safely in the dark. We'll need to wait for first light."

Lau sputtered a small dry cough and croaked out, "No move."

"You want to stay here?" Miranda asked. She looked frantically from Monrovia to Hugo, but she knew there was no way they could leave Lau here, even if she was now moving her head in the smallest way to show that she meant to stay. "Lau, you… you're really…hurt." *Hurt* didn't quite cover it. She was… dying?

"You need a doctor. Okay? We've got to get you to a doctor."

Lau inched the tiniest movement, which seemed to shudder more life out of her.

Miranda leaned closer, gripping her hand, feeling how almost waxy her skin had become. "What happened?" Her voice shook.

"S…sorry." Lau's left eyelid fluttered, as if saying the word had taken every bit of strength she had.

Miranda bit the inside of her cheek and asked, "Sorry for what, Lau?" even though she was afraid of the answer.

Lau opened both bloodshot eyes. "Lie." Her eyes closed.

"What did she say?"

Miranda ignored Monrovia and squeezed Lau's hand. "What lie?" she asked, her voice quiet, trying not to breathe in case she missed Lau's next words.

Lau wrinkled her forehead. "Carl… lie."

Miranda loosened her grip on Lau's hand. "The Senate arrested him." Did she already know? "We came to bring you back so you could testify for him."

"Wi…" Lau's body shook with a raspy cough as she wheezed out, "Ssh."

Monrovia cocked her head. "Wish?"

But Lau did not add more. After several minutes, she said, "Can't hold it anymore."

"Can't hold what?" A heaviness dragged Miranda's shoulders.

"Falling," she wheezed.

"What do you mean? Hold it?"

A fit of coughs racked Lau's slight frame. Finally, she gasped out, "Back."

Cold crawled along Miranda's scalp.

A tear slipped down Monrovia's cheek. "Is that what happened to you? You've been holding back the buildings? But how?"

Lau's lips moved but no sound came out.

"Say it again? We couldn't hear." Miranda hovered closer to Lau's cracked lips.

"Alois."

Miranda set her eyes on Monrovia to see her reaction. There was no denying it now.

Monrovia bit her lip. "But Beda already stopped him."

Lau furrowed her brow and pursed her lips. She turned slightly toward Miranda and pushed out a 'K' sound and took a raspy breath. She looked at Miranda. "Find Kaa." She closed her eyes again.

Miranda studied the frail woman in front of her. The woman who was supposed to stand up to the Senate *and* Alois. A cold, hard ball formed in the pit of her stomach. "*Find Kaa?*" What was she trying to say?

"Find Kirasu!" Monrovia yelled, and Miranda jumped back.

Lau's mouth curled up gently.

"You want us to find Kirasu? Can they help us stop whatever is happening?" Miranda said.

Lau stayed silent but did not protest.

"How do we find Kirasu?"

Lau fluttered an eye and brought her lips together. Miranda and Monrovia leaned closer. "out of... woods," she eked out. The corner of her mouth turned up in a way that could have been a smile. Her wrinkled skin hung from her bones. Miranda wanted to look away but couldn't.

"Please, save your strength." Monrovia placed a hand gently on Lau's forehead. "We'll find Kirasu. We'll look in the woods." Lau's chest rose and fell again. "You just rest now," Monrovia said.

Miranda motioned to Monrovia to step away with her. They joined Hugo in the doorway.

"We can't wait until morning," Miranda said. "She needs a doctor."

"I've never flown in the dark." He looked back at Lau. "But we can build a stretcher. How hard can flying in the dark even be?"

A breeze fluttered the curtains around the bed. The air in the room shifted; even Hugo seemed to sense it. There was a release, and a new quiet settled. Miranda and

Monrovia walked back to the bedside. Lau's hand rested on her still chest.

Monrovia drew out two shaky fingers and pressed them against Lau's neck. "She's gone."

Miranda collapsed in the chair by the bed and watched Hugo put his hand to Monrovia's back. Sound seemed to retreat. Miranda stared at Lau's face, a gray pallor already taking hold.

Lau had died trying to stop Alois' destruction. Alois had taken Beda, and now he had taken Lau. A tear fell down Miranda's cheek. Kirasu had put Miranda through terrible visions on Earth, but they had also saved her. Could they face Alois?

Her cheeks burned. She buried her face in her hands and let the tears flow because she could not fix this. She couldn't save Carl, and she couldn't save Nibiru. It was over.

A warm hand gripped her shoulder. "Hey, there's nothing we could have done," Monrovia said.

Lau's hands were now folded across her chest. Monrovia drew the curtains on both sides of the bed. Miranda hauled herself out of the chair and looked at the small, frail woman lying in her coffin, a fourposter, canopied bed in the sagging house she loved that would be her tomb.

"I think this is how she wanted it," Monrovia said.

"If she's been keeping more buildings from falling? What does that mean for us now?" Hugo asked.

His answer came in a hail of distant crashes that dropped Miranda to her knees.

CHAPTER 15

A SPARK

The sun had set, leaving the hallway even darker than before. Miranda fumbled for the banister. Lau's empty stare hung in her mind. How had she been holding back the Falling? Why Kirasu?

"We have to go back to Samsara. People might be hurt." Monrovia's voice was close, but ahead, like she was already on the stairs.

Miranda took a few cautious steps, careful not to bump into her. She contemplated going back for one or both lanterns, but the prospect of seeing Lau's stiff body kept her feeling her way in the dark.

"We probably wouldn't make it over that mountain flying at night," Hugo said. His voice came from farther away. He must already be downstairs.

"What can we even do in Samsara to help?" Miranda stepped down cautiously and added, mumbling, "What can we do anywhere?" Moonlight bounced off the sand as she came to the kitchen. It washed their faces in a sickly blue glow.

Miranda pulled a stool out from the counter and crumbled down onto it, laying her head on the hard, sandy counter. Uncomfortable seemed right.

Monrovia slammed kitchen drawers. "So that's it. We stay here and do nothing?"

A piercing howl ripped through the quiet night.

"It's in here or out there with them," Hugo said. "I vote for here. I need some water." He turned on the sink tap and a stream of sand poured out. "Rude."

"Found them." Monrovia lit two candles with matches she'd found in a drawer. She leaned beside a beautifully ornate white-and-blue vase, resting her hand on it gently. Mystical dragons danced over arched bridges laced through an ornate garden. It had a small silver tap. "I can't believe she's gone." Her voice shuddered.

Hugo handed her a glass, and Monrovia stared at it like it was an unknowable object. He gestured to the cistern. "I think you found the backup water."

"What?"

He took the glass back and turned the tap. A small stream came out.

"I'm sorry about your friend." He took a drink and grimaced. "Sandy. But what do we do now?"

Miranda did not lift her head. Monrovia stayed silent.

"Well, can you tell me who or what Kirasu is?" he asked.

"I'll let you take that one," Monrovia said, nodding toward her—Miranda caught the movement from the corner of her eye.

With great effort, she lifted her head off the counter, sand sticking to the side of her face. "Is Kirasu one person? Probably not. Two people? Maybe. They hang out in space, only it's not really space. They used to sing songs in my head and sometimes talk to me. I don't know how they are supposed to help us now, and the only way to get to them is to transport to the place between, that's the not really space but space place. But we can't transport anymore." Miranda let her head fall back to the counter and mumbled, "They might not even be real."

Hugo screwed his face up tight. "Transport where?"

"Really?" Monrovia ignored Hugo's question. "How about this version? Kirasu saved us in the Gathering by getting us back here safely, and they've been helping us understand what is happening all along with their songs and visions."

Miranda waved her hand dismissively. "And that."

"Are they... *people*?" Hugo asked.

Miranda shrugged. She did not have the energy to explain an enigma.

"Why would they be in the woods on Nibiru?" Monrovia asked. "We should have gotten here sooner. Nothing she said made sense."

Lau's dying words: *Find Kirasu.* It didn't make sense. They wouldn't be here, unless… an idea came fully formed. "They shouldn't be here, unless something was wrong. What if they've been trying to hold back the Falling like Lau and now they need *our* help?"

"How would we help strange beings who communicate through song?" Hugo asked.

"We won't know until we find them," Miranda said, wishing she was as confident as she hoped she sounded. "They helped us in the Gathering. We owe it to them to help them now." She snatched up her pack and headed to the door. A lonely howl rang through the darkness, loud and close, freezing her to her spot.

Hugo caught her arm. "Best to wait until morning unless we want to fight more toothy beasts."

"I don't remember you fighting anything," Miranda said, peering out into the black night.

"I miss Nice Miranda," he said, dropping her arm.

Monrovia held a burning candle. Shadows danced across her face. "We're no good to anyone if we're torn to pieces. And we all need to rest."

"We can't wait. We have to find Kirasu." Miranda couldn't believe they were willing to stall.

"We leave at first light." Monrovia spun around and disappeared down the dark hallway with her flickering candle.

Miranda had to admit waiting for dawn was a better strategy than running into the dark to she didn't know where but spending the night in the house with Lau's body sent cold shivers down her spine. Reluctantly, she unhooked her bedroll, spread it out on the sandy ground, and lay down.

"Will she be okay?" Hugo asked.

"She just needs to be alone. She's used to it," Miranda said, and realized the same was true for herself.

Hugo rooted through a closet and found a few blankets to make a pallet. As he settled down, Miranda pretended she was already asleep, but sleep was far away. How could they help Kirasu? And what if she was wrong? What if they weren't helping Lau? She shivered. What if they didn't want to stop Alois at all? Another howl shattered the silence and Miranda clenched her fists and tried to sleep.

CHAPTER 16

THE STORM

Dawn unfolded in soft pinks and blues. Hills of sand rolled in every direction, incapable of resisting a capricious wind. Unsatisfied with its complete domination, the sand also filled Miranda's boots, rubbing between her toes as she trudged in silence toward the tree line.

She had woken with a sore shoulder from sleeping on her side. It had surprised her she'd slept at all. Last night she'd wanted to leave immediately to find Kirasu, but Monrovia and Hugo—and a few well-timed howls—had convinced her to wait for first light. They'd said another quick goodbye in the morning and left Lau forever.

Monrovia stopped ahead, pouring over something, as Hugo peered over her shoulder. Miranda jogged to catch up and saw they were studying a large piece of paper covered in beautiful pictures.

"It's a paper map!" Hugo touched the corners delicately.

"I've never seen one." Miranda leaned in for a closer look, appreciating the artful lines and colorful splash of green forest and gray sweep of the mountain's slope.

"I found it in Lau's office last night." Monrovia tapped a dark green area that stood between them and the glider. "This is the only part that says 'woods.'"

The green fanned out, widening around the mountain's base. In elegant script, someone had painted the name 'Mir Woods.'

"So, we start there?" Miranda asked.

Monrovia folded the map and nestled it into her pocket. She made for the trees. Miranda didn't move, annoyed that her sister assumed they would follow her. But why was Hugo standing stock-still?

"What if that thing is still in there?" he said, staring at the mass of trees.

Miranda scoffed. "Where else would he be?"

Hugo made a small whining noise as he hustled to catch up.

The sand formed high crested waves between the first line of pine trunks, but only a few steps in, it cleared away. No sand, just dirt and leaves, fallen needles.

Hugo walked beside Monrovia. *Were they whispering?*

This part of the forest looked familiar, or maybe it all looked the same, but Miranda thought they were close to where they came in. She called out to Hugo, "You don't have to come with us. The glider is that way." She pointed deeper into the brown expanse. "You could be back to it in half an hour if you walk straight that way,"

Monrovia took a step away from him. "She's right."

Hugo looked right, in the glider's direction, then left. He closed the gap, standing by Monrovia again. "I might regret this, but I want to come."

Monrovia started walking.

Miranda frowned. *He hesitated.* "We don't need your protection."

He cracked a smile. "That is apparent, but—" he took a few steps and stopped, turning back to Miranda, "—is it okay with you if I stay?"

A broad grin spread across her face. It surprised her how much she liked hearing him ask her permission. "Yeah, I guess."

"Monrovia," he called ahead, "what about you?"

"Absolutely." She spun around. "We might need someone to feed to a wolf."

Hugo grinned. "That's a joke, right?"

Miranda cackled with laughter and jogged past him. "I didn't know she had it in her."

They walked in silence as the sun peeked between leaves swaying in the breeze. Light danced, making spotlights on the forest floor. Miranda played a game of trying to step on the bright patches. It helped her ignore her throbbing feet.

After some time, Hugo broke the silence by plopping onto the ground saying he needed to rest and wondering aloud about the plan for food. The sandy dried noodles and seaweed they'd found in Lau's cupboards had long since worn off.

Monrovia flopped down beside him and waved for Miranda's pack.

Miranda handed it over, wondering what secret Monrovia had stashed inside until she miraculously produced three flat sandwiches. "Tan gave us these and I hid them."

Hugo took his and bit in hungrily. Miranda's stomach growled loudly as she did the same.

"We're going to need a plan when these run out," Monrovia said.

The nutty, dry bread caught in Miranda's throat. She sucked the last drops from her bottle. "And we need water."

Monrovia held up her own empty bottle and gave the trees a stern look. "I'm sure there's a creek around here somewhere."

Monrovia spread out the map, resting stones on the corners to keep it in place against the breeze which was intent on growing into a bothersome wind. She traced her finger along a thin, grayish-blue line. "I bet that's a river."

"Do you think it's far?" Hugo asked.

Miranda choked down the last of her sandwich as a low rumble filled the air. They all looked to Samsara.

"It's thunder." Miranda let her shoulders relax.

Back in the Trash Lands, thunder meant rain, and rain meant a raging river bent to smash and destroy everything in its path. But here, the ground sucked it up, hungry for nourishment and always able to take whatever the sky could give. Here, thunder rolled and rumbled, coming from nowhere and going where it wanted. No need to fear it.

"Sounds like we'll get to fill our bottles after all," she said.

Another booming crack, and the first fat drops of rain fell, then came down all at once. Monrovia hurriedly packed up the map. A crack of lightning split the sky, which had darkened to a stormy gray. Another clap of thunder followed by a flash of lightning. Monrovia yelled something and hopped up, running. Hugo followed. Impossibly, the rain came down harder. Miranda rushed in their direction, but lost sight of them between the trees.

"Rona! Hugo!" She held her hand over her eyes to shield them from the rain. Thunder bounced off the trunks, making the once-quiet forest a drum. "Where are you?"

Sticks cracked; feet thudded. Behind her? Two misshapen gleaming spikes broke through the downpour, coming at her quickly. Adrenaline rushed to her legs, propelling Miranda to throw herself out of the way as a deafening crack ripped through the new dark. A heavy branch smacked the ground where she had been standing and a charging buck bounded past, spurred even faster by the crashing limb.

She stayed down in the wet leaves, trying to calm her thudding heart. *A coincidence. He wasn't after me. He was running from the storm, scared.* She found her footing and her voice to run and shout again. "Hugo! Rona!"

She stumbled and landed on her knees in the mud.

It's only rain, slow down and find them.

She walked, calling their names. Only the rain answered.

I need to get out of the trees.

She wandered toward the mountain, dark against a darker sky. Her pack cut into her shoulders and her stomach protested loudly again.

We were going to find more food. The pitifulness of the thought made her want to cry. *They didn't leave me on purpose. We got separated.*

She tripped on a thick root and fell forward. But instead of being greeted with hard wet ground, she kept falling. She clutched a small root that held for a few seconds until— snap. Her stomach jumped to her throat as she fell farther until her head hit something hard.

Darkness took hold.

CHAPTER 17

THE CABIN

Chirping in the near distance. A sloshing sound as something small darted past. Warmth on her face. A soft, rhythmic gurgle.

Miranda cautiously opened her eyes. Bright sun streamed through a break in the leaves. *Too much.* She rolled out of the blazing beam, testing her muscles and bones.

Still in the forest. Still alone.

A small animal with a bushy tail came close, leading with its nose, curious. She raised a few fingers, and it sprang into the air, twittering as it fled. She shifted and the straps from her pack fell from her shoulders. Stars and lines danced in front of her eyes.

Her head throbbed and her back ached. She slumped forward, dropping her head between her knees. She took a slow breath and realized she sat on a slope. Water gurgled gently nearby. Her tongue lay dry in her mouth.

After several minutes, she raised her head again. No stars.

A glimpse of blue sky cut through the trees and the leaves swayed in a gentle breeze. The forest left no hint of the violent storm the night before. Forests absorb the good with the bad, blending it all with light and shadows.

She spied the source of the gurgle, a stream at the bottom of the ravine. The incline she rested on didn't seem too steep, but the thought of standing left her dizzy. Miranda reached for her pack and noticed a jagged rock about the size of her fist with a dark spot dried to it. She touched the back of her head gingerly and her fingers grazed a knot with a patch of crust. *Dried blood. Need water.*

She scooted down the hill, picking up mud and wet leaves with every inch. Her pack slid off her shoulders and she fumbled with the top to find the cold steel bottle Carl had given her. She filled it with clear water, then fell back against the muddy ground and drank as much as her stomach would hold.

The thudding in her head quieted. She rummaged deeper in the bag for any hidden food. *Monrovia, Hugo.* Did they find shelter? Food? Her fingers netted a small bundle—a hidden pack of granola. She gobbled up the meager contents, licked the bag clean, and rested until her arms and legs felt capable of holding her weight. She clumsily maneuvered into a squat and slowly stood, but when she straightened her knees, she skidded down into shallow, icy water.

Hungry, with a splitting headache, lost, alone, and now wet. Miranda snatched a rock from under the water, not more than a foot deep, threw it hard, and yelled until her head hurt more, for no other reason than no one could stop her.

The rock splashed down, and the ripples faded, unphased, like it never happened. She climbed back onto the bank and added a sore throat to her list of ailments. Upstream or down? She chose upstream, hoping it was the same direction they had been travelling in yesterday. If it even was yesterday that they were last together.

They would be looking for her, right? Screaming their throats raw with worry? She paused, listening to chirping and rustling leaves. No yelling, no frantic search party. *They must be too far away for me to hear.* She shouted, and the effort made her skull throb. Clutching her temples, she had to take a breath before walking again.

Her wet clothes were stiffening from the mud as they dried. She hoped they had found shelter, maybe a cave, and made a fire. They might have even had a nice dinner. She dabbed at the knot on her head and winced.

After some time, the ravine opened. The ground became sturdier, the trees larger, older, many with bright green mosses covering the bases of their trunks. Energy buzzed, and the air seemed to crackle around her. Her head still pounded, but the vibrancy of this place kept her moving. As she walked, she listened for other footsteps, for talking. She leaned against a large tree, letting the rough bark scratch her back, and called out their names again, but not as loudly as before.

Her shouts echoed back at her, bouncing off the wood. *Lost cause.* She emptied her mind and whispered, "Kirasu, point me in the right direction to find you."

A light wind rustled the surrounding leaves, and she whispered the words again. She moved out from the tree with her arms outstretched. The wind picked up and pushed her two steps to the left. It settled again. Was that a sign? She took another few steps and found a worn path lined with stone. *A trail!*

As she moved along, two large trees bent over the path, having grown together to form an arch, like they knew better than to block the way. She walked into their shadow, damp and musty, quiet. The pact between these two trees, holding each other up for eternity, formed a blanket of calm that begged her to rest. She fought the urge to lie down and instead pushed into the day again. A warm breeze blew, as streams of sun broke through. The tree arch beckoned her return, but she pressed ahead, following the trail up a steep hill.

"Rona! Hugo!"

A squirrel skittered up a tree.

The trail lost its definition under heaps of leaves and roots on the hillside. She gripped the bases of small trees and even sunk her fingers into the fresh soil to help her climb, pressing on to the top, slipping and sliding, but determined not to lose ground. *Toe holds, handholds, mud, leaves.*

She made it to the top, gripping a skinny birch trunk while catching her breath. A strange cabin sat tucked into the forest close enough to hit with a stone. It seemed to be constructed from living trees, designed to allow them to continue to grow. Instead of horizontal slats, the walls were made of trees standing as they grew, with branches still leafing out. Tight packed mud and leaves filled the irregular gaps between the trunks.

Kirasu?.

She caught a shallow breath in her throat.

Are they even real people who can walk on the floor?

She stayed crouched in the tree line. *I should leave. Why would they need my help? What can I even do?*

The only paint on the cabin colored a rounded door dark red, like the faded red of the inn. She scrambled onto flatter ground and stood, taking one step, then another.

For Carl. For Lau.

A strong wind came from behind, making her stumble closer. She spun around accusingly, then rolled her shoulders and marched up to the door. Her muscles quivered, head ached, and stomach growled. She hesitated; her hand raised to knock.

What if it's not Kirasu?

She knocked lightly on the rough wood and took several steps back, ready to find the strength to run if she needed to. The door cracked open.

"Hello, Miranda. We are who you seek. And that you are here means Lau is gone."

The words were spoken in stereo, from an utterly black interior. Were they talking in unison? She couldn't see them in the dark.

Miranda nodded. "She died."

The door creaked open wider.

"Please come in. You need food and rest."

Miranda assessed her condition: exhausted, starving, clueless.

I was coming to help them?

She studied the brilliant sky painting the spaces between leaves. *Then why are they here?* She desperately needed rest and food, but more than one part of her brain screamed at her to run.

For Nibiru, she thought as she stepped into darkness, while a more practical section of her brain offered, *for food.*

CHAPTER 18

KIRASU

A small, thin hand wrapped around her wrist, dragging her farther into the strangely cool cabin.

"Forgive us the darkness," the voice said. It belonged to a woman. No, a girl. "Our eyes cannot handle the bright daylight. Here—" Something heavy dragged along the floor, but the sound was muted, as if drawn across dirt. "Have a seat."

The hand guided her and pushed her by her shoulders down into a chair. The strangeness of this encounter, hands on her in the dark, a cabin built of living trees, made her wish she'd stayed face down in the leaves.

They seem safe, in control. *So, they don't need my help. Why would Lau tell me to find them?* Her stomach clenched. *Because they can stop the Falling?*

"Telos, light a fire, so our guest will be more comfortable."

They have names!

"Certainly." The scrape of logs being dragged across dirt filled the small cabin. The voice was meek. Shy? It seemed to belong to another girl.

"Is it safe to light a fire in a tree?" Miranda asked.

"We have a hearth. This is an old home. Those preparations were made long before us." The first voice bounced around the walls as fire caught the logs.

A faint, red glow licked at the wood and, liking what it tasted, grabbed for more, sucking the logs into hungry yellow flames. Pale shadows danced around the room. Miranda squeezed her eyes shut, momentarily dreading what she might see when her eyes adjusted to the light. She squeezed a tight fist. *You can do this. They sound like children.*

As she opened her eyes, the bodies behind the voices came into focus. Two, both small, with large round eyes and slender faces that ended in sharply pointed chins. They were the mirror image of each other, and Miranda realized she could have interacted with either before and not known they were different. Their skin was paper-thin, ghost-white, their hair long and tangled, and their identical loose-fitting dresses hung shapelessly dragging the floor. They weren't *not* people.

The one who had let her in spoke first. "I am Zoi. I found you on Earth." Her voice was low and strong.

"I am Telos." The other one spoke with that softer voice—reluctance? "I pushed you back to Nibiru after the Gathering."

They had seemed so powerful out there, but looked frail and weak here, like the slightest wrong move would break them. "Thank you for saving me and my sister."

"It's true we have grown more accustomed to the place between, but we are not helpless here. We're getting more acclimated every day," Zoi said.

They know what I'm thinking! Miranda tried to retrace her thoughts since she'd come in, but then stopped. Recapping was probably bad.

"Our gift is sporadic. We see some thoughts as a flash, and then they are gone. We really aren't trying to pry," Zoi said.

"Why did Lau tell me to find you?" Miranda asked.

Telos stepped forward. "First, let us address your hunger and thirst, and then we will talk. We have much to discuss."

Zoi stirred the contents of a large black pot that rested on the end of a hook attached to the wall of the hearth. "The gravity here makes us work harder to do everything, walking, standing, takes a lot of work, so we are eating food again, but we are starting small, just broth, but in honor of your visit, I'll add vegetables. The woods hold such bounty, carrot, potato, onion, mushroom, all ready for the picking." She dropped in a few handfuls of vegetables. "I missed eating," she said to the soup.

Telos put a small wooden bowl in front of her. "Broth to warm you while the rest cooks."

The hot liquid burned Miranda's throat but coated her stomach. It had no flavor, mostly hot water, but she was grateful for anything. Telos refilled her bowl. Miranda sipped the contents carefully this time.

"How did you survive out there without food?" she asked.

"A place between is neither here nor there. The rules are different. It's like a physical manifestation of the quiet mind. We only needed to *be* there, not *do* anything."

"It is the quiet that exists between the dimensions," Zoi added.

"Dimensions?" Miranda shivered.

"Earth and Nibiru are versions of each other overlaid with separation, but that separation is being squeezed away," Zoi said.

Miranda gripped the table and leaned back, awash with understanding, like she'd found a lost puzzle piece and clicked it into place. "Versions. Like a copy," Miranda whispered. A vision of Davon becoming Hugo and of Nathan becoming Oren played in her mind.

She bolted upright. "Were the people of Earth copied to make this place, too?"

"The souls of Earth were split to make the people of Nibiru," Zoi said. "Or maybe it was the other way around."

Split. Nathan was part of Oren. Miranda's heart ached and her head reeled. "Where are the souls from Earth now?"

"It hardly matters," Zoi said, her voice tired.

"It matters to me! Once we released them in the Gathering, shouldn't they have come back to their other halves? But they haven't. They're lost." The realization left her cold despite the fire.

Telos patted her shoulder. She jumped because she had not seen her get so close. "We are tired, and we want to go home."

"But aren't you here to stop the Falling?"

Telos clicked her tongue. "Only you can do that."

Miranda's head felt hot, and the walls seemed to close in. "No, not me. That's why Lau sent me to find you."

"Did she say that?"

"Well, not exactly."

"Perhaps she told you to find us because we are watching Alois," Zoi whispered.

The room shifted, and Miranda steadied herself against the table. A wave of sickness rolled over her. No one else could wrought such destruction, but the truth of it weighed her down. No more questions, no more hoping it might not be true. Beda *had* failed. "You've seen him?"

Telos nodded. "Alois is causing the collapse of our home. We believe it is punishment for what you and your mother started," Telos said.

Punishment. The thin soup burned as it came back up her throat.

"Our home is disappearing, but you can fix this," Zoi added.

Miranda swallowed it down. "I can't stop him."

"He may seem unreasonable, but he isn't. We're seeing his temper," Telos said.

"What we're saying is you need to ask forgiveness," Zoi said.

White hot flashes shot up Miranda's neck. "Forgiveness! From him? He ripped my mother apart."

Telos's eyes darkened. "Do you want this world to be ripped apart around you, too?"

Zoi set down a fresh bowl. Miranda wanted to push it away, but a whiff of earthy starch caught her nose and made her mouth water. She lifted the bowl and drank, gobbling up the small spud, soft and buttery, still in its skin. She took another gulp and got carrots.

Zoi held up her hand. "Do not carry all of this weight, my child. Alois can make this right."

"Lau Chen used all her psychic energy in the place between working to prolong the separation, but the task was too great." Telos's gaunt face became even more drawn. "Alois alone has the power to reinstall the barrier between the dimensions, but he needs to hear from you. He needs to understand you are repentant."

But I'm not.

Miranda stared at Telos and munched a woody mushroom. Its complex flavor coated her tongue. The image of Beda thrashing under his power in the black hole filled her mind. Telling Miranda to beg forgiveness from this despot was too much.

"If he restored the dimensions, he would also recreate his suffering on Earth," she said. "I can't do that!"

"He can be brought to reason." Zoi sipped from her own bowl of broth. "And we do not see any other way to stop the destruction of this world."

Miranda twisted the bottom of her shirt around her finger until it hurt. There was never another answer. Alois was *always* the source of the chaos. But to grovel at his feet, to beg forgiveness, as if Beda's sacrifice was a wretched act?

"I can't even get to him. I haven't been able to transport since the Gathering."

"He will come to you," Telos said.

"How can you be so sure? Are you working for him?" Miranda asked.

"We know his habits. And we know what you needed." Telos glanced at the soup.

Miranda's palms sweat, and the room spun again, but this time it did not stop. A woody mushroom floated to the top of the soup.

"What's happening?" Miranda's words were garbled.

Telos came closer. "No need to worry." She guided Miranda to a wooden platform raised just above the ground. "The effect wears off with time." A rough blanket lay on the bare boards. "But you want to lie down now."

Sweat beaded on Miranda's brow, her mouth dry, and a new sound entered her awareness. It seemed different from anything she'd ever heard—and then the sounds became colors wrapping around her. The room got hotter, and Telos's face warped into an hourglass then popped back to the regular shape.

Zoi petted her head. "Shhh, you'll find him and ask forgiveness. Then this nightmare will be over. We will all have a home again."

Bolts of thick yellow stripes danced on the back of Miranda's eyelids. She tried to get up, but then she was floating in a darkness shot through with the pinpricks of stars.

CHAPTER 19

THE CHOICE

A small man with a wiry beard and a dusty, white tunic floated in the darkness before her. Glasses perched at the end of his nose, and a mustache curled around his lip, quivering into a smile. This man was a caricature, tame, bent to lull her, but she knew the giant and terrible thing he could become.

"Miranda, *mon ami.*" Alois leaned back as if in an invisible armchair.

"You killed my mother." Miranda spat the words out, bracing for a violent reaction, but Alois' expression stayed fixed.

"*Non, mon amour.* Your dear mother killed herself while demolishing an entire planet."

"Stop pretending. I already know we didn't destroy Earth. That was just your illusion."

Alois picked at the invisible armrest. "What did you do then? You and your reckless mother?"

"We stopped you! We stopped you from torturing them."

"*Quel ange.*" He twirled his mustache. "And where is Earth now?"

Anger bubbled up in every part of Miranda's body. "You are making it crash into Nibiru!" She wanted to tear him limb from limb, but moving was like swimming in a vat of oil; she barely got closer. "People are dead, and Nibiru is in tatters. Why are you doing this?"

Alois tutted. "*Non, ce n'est pas moi.* You have done this, not me."

"Oh, come on!"

"Your Gathering triggered a great disruption, but it was not the disruption you intended. In your earnestness to undo the suffering of Earth, you triggered the collapse of the buffer between the two worlds, ensuring the two dimensions must collide."

Her head spun, and her confidence evaporated. "Kirasu said you are causing the collapse of a place between and that you can stop it."

Alois leaned back and sighed. "Non, you and your careless mother have destroyed their home and your own. No one can put it back. Natural forces much more powerful than me are at work now."

Miranda's hand shook. It couldn't be true. "No. Splitting a world and its people, making each suffer. The universe did not ask for that kind of experiment." The boldness of truth gripped her, and for the first time since Beda fell back into the black hole, Miranda felt certain what they did was right.

"We stopped you. We freed the souls. That's what we did in the Gathering."

"And yet..." He tugged the long thin tip of his beard while Miranda clawed at the air, fighting to get close enough to wrap her hands around that neck. Alois lounged at a safe distance, ignoring her flailing arms. "If you were so right, why is Nibiru being punished?"

"You are doing it!"

"I truly cannot stop the dissolution of a place between." Alois spoke with a dismissive tone. "This attraction to recreate one world is too strong for me to undo. But you should not presume violence. It is like they are the same. I suspect the two worlds will merge like pouring water into wine. Earth will seamlessly blend in. It will be like the cracks are filled; the missing piece returned."

One world?

Miranda tensed her jaw and steeled her gaze, remembering the buildings smashing into Samsara, the desert sands of the Trash Lands covering Kona. "Earth is pushing through, and it isn't seamless.

He stroked his mustache in silence. His dark eyes stared deeply at her. "I say only that it *could be* seamless, but what will you destroy next if you are not taught a lesson, *ma fleur?*"

His perfunctory confirmation sent an icy chill down her spine. "So you are causing the Falling to make sure we suffer?" Miranda squeezed her fists tight. "People are dying!"

"Human lives are brief."

Stunned, Miranda searched for a sign of hope. "Are you really going to end both worlds to teach us a lesson?"

Alois silently looked out to the stars.

I can't win. He's too strong.

But then Zoi's plea played in her head. *Ask forgiveness.* It would not bring back their home, but it could save Nibiru.

Miranda's shoulders drooped. The fight drained out of her.

A slight smirk played on Alois' face. She looked away into the darkness that stretched beyond worlds and time. *Tell him we went too far.* She remembered people on Earth in the dome searching for something to hold them as they floated helplessly to the top, only to crash down when gravity shifted. A fire burned in her belly. *We didn't go far enough.* She pushed the thought away. *This is for Nibiru.*

Each word seared like a burning coal on her tongue. "If we had not taken Earth from you, you would not be destroying Nibiru. What can I do to make you stop?" She wasn't sure she had the strength to hear the answer.

Alois clapped. The sound was muted, and bile burned the back of her throat.

"You are right to assume I have a price to stop the Falling." He leaned closer. "You and your family led the people of Nibiru to upset the balance of what I created, and I need assurance it won't happen again. Your mother has already paid for this crime, as has Lau Chen, so that leaves you and your sister. My price to stop the Falling is for you and Monrovia to banish yourselves to Europa to live out your days in seclusion."

Miranda's hand flew to her side, protecting her still tender scar, ripped when the banshee had sunk its boney finger into her flesh to stop her from going after Beda. A chill sunk into her bones at the memory of lying on the cold stone floor in the hold of the leader of the banshees, Gyda. Even thinking about the piercing shriek of the banshees and their leader's icy stare made her skin crawl. Gyda with that voice that tinkled like sleet on a windowpane. To spend one day, much less the rest of her life, in that cold stone prison—desolate despair. Miranda's stomach dropped. "Banish us? But what does that solve?"

"You must be punished, and this new world deserves the chance to make its mark without you causing more mayhem."

Miranda took a breath to try to make sense of this. There was one good thing. He'd left out Carl, so he must not know his role.

"Your father's payment is coming," Alois said as if answering her thought.

Miranda's heart sank. "What are you going to do to him?"

He raised an eyebrow. "I will do nothing to him."

Miranda's head spun. *Does he mean the trial?* She focused on Alois again. "You said yourself that you can't stop the worlds from merging. So, even if Monrovia and I disappear, it won't change Nibiru's fate. You'll run out of things to throw at us when Nibiru and Earth fully merge," she said. "I just have to wait."

"*Tellement intelligent.*" Alois chuckled. "But if you remain, I will continue to punish the new world. Or,"—he tapped his chin and regarded Miranda thoughtfully—"perhaps you would be swayed if I agreed to reset Nibiru back to how it was, before the Falling started? I may not be able to bring back the lives lost, but I can restore the place. Your Nibiru would be whole again for only the price of banishment for you and Monrovia."

"You could put it back?" Miranda's stomach flipped.

"It is the same that I did for Earth on occasion."

Miranda imagined the streets of Nibiru restored, flowers blooming in window boxes, trees leafing green again. "But not Monrovia. She can't be punished for this. It was my idea. She gets to stay."

Alois crossed his arms and looked down his nose. "She must pay."

"No." But Miranda knew Monrovia would gladly give up her life to restore Nibiru. She would not hesitate. Miranda looked out to the darkness, wondering how long she would last out there with nothing. Reset Nibiru, like he reset Earth. *And keep resetting it?* "But what about their memories? You wiped people's memories on Earth. Would the people on Nibiru forget the ones they lost?"

"You still believe you know what is best for everyone? Wouldn't it be better for them not to remember their losses, to continue from the moment I restore their home with the lives they have?"

"But it would be like those people they've lost never existed," Miranda said.

Alois leaned forward and banged on the invisible armrest. "And the pain of their absence would also be gone. It does not change the past, only removes the future pain."

Oren would have no memory of his father. She studied her hands to give herself a moment to think, away from Alois' penetrating gaze. Yes, he would stop the Falling, but they would lose so much more. And would he stop there? Would Nibiru be his new experiment? A competing thought popped into her head as clearly as if someone whispered it in her ear. She spoke the words exactly as they came to her head. "But where are the souls?"

It was fast, but Miranda caught the almost imperceptible twitch of his mustache. She rolled her shoulders back, making a tight fist. This was the answer. She had to find the souls and bring them home. That was the way to free Nibiru from his clutches instead of consigning them to his rule. "Why didn't the souls find their other halves when Beda freed them?"

"Who says they did not?"

"No," Miranda said. *I would know if Oren had his missing piece.* "You are holding back. You say Nibiru will be restored, but you aim to keep the souls separated. You want Nibiru as your new playground. Where are the souls, Alois?"

Another wince, barely noticeable. She was getting to him.

His voice boomed: "You have your choice. You can live your days in isolation while Nibiru blooms or you can watch it get torn apart from the Falling. I will give you two days to choose. Now go."

"What happens in two days if I don't go to Europa?" Miranda's mind raced with possibilities.

"Simple. I will destroy Nibiru."

CHAPTER 20

LOST SOULS

The soft rhythmic patter of low whispers and feet shuffling along the dirt floor woke Miranda. Her eyelids were heavy, and her ears felt stuffed with cotton. She strained to make out the voices in the chatter. More than two.

A low firelight lit the cabin. Was it day or night? A cold drop of sweat trickled down the side of her face. She let out a dry cough. The voices became clearer. *Could it be?*

"Rona," she moaned. A warm hand clutched hers, too large to belong to Kirasu.

"We're here, Miranda. Are you okay?" Monrovia's voice wavered. Was she tired or worried?

Miranda's muscles ached. Her head pounded. She blinked hard and tried to push a coherent sentence through the chaos spinning in her brain. "How did you find me?"

"We didn't stop looking. When we came across this cabin..." Her voice trailed off.

"I'm glad you found me," Miranda whispered. A thousand words raced through her mind until one clear idea emerged. "I know how to stop him." She gripped her head as a sharp pain nailed her temples.

"Alois?" Monrovia's voice trembled.

Miranda nodded. "We have to find the souls. He's taken them, hidden them." She forced the words out into the darkness, then fell back against the bare wood, exhausted from the effort, like she was afraid the thought would evaporate.

Zoi and Telos appeared at her bedside. Miranda reached out with her eyes still closed, gripping one of their dresses, trying to bring them down, but she didn't have the strength.

"You drugged me." She dropped the cloth. No way to follow through.

"We're sorry," they said in unison.

"It was the only way to get you in front of him." One of them explained.

Miranda told them about Alois' confession, that he cannot restore the place between, the two worlds will merge, and he cannot stop it.

Hugo leaned closer, his black hair somehow still standing at attention. "Can we trust him?"

"No!" Heat flushed Miranda's cheeks, and a bolt of energy shot through her. She gripped the sides of the wooden platform, but the strength drained out of her just as fast. "But…" She settled back again. "I believe he's telling the truth about not being able to stop this collapse."

Tears welled in Monrovia's eyes. "There has to be some way to save a place between. If we started this, can't we stop it?"

Telos poked the coals of the dying fire with a long stick. "I'm not sure you'd want to, even if you could."

"What?" Hugo coughed out.

Telos stabbed deeper into the coals. "With our home destroyed, your home will be whole again."

Zoi seemed to shrink smaller.

"But that's terrible for you." Hugo lightly touched Telos's small, thin shoulder.

Miranda pulled herself up to rest on her elbows. "Alois will destroy Nibiru with the Falling for as long as he can." *Unless* rested on the tip of her tongue. But she would not tell them about his ultimatum, not yet. "Once the worlds combine, he'll come up with some new way to torture us. We have to bring the souls home. That's the only way the people here will be strong enough to stop him."

The desolate shriek of a bone-bleached banshee scraped at her heart. Her skin prickled from the cold.

Telos pressed her. "Is there something else?"

Miranda shook her head. She owed it to Monrovia to talk to her first about Alois' offer, alone, without prying eyes and ears.

Monrovia took a sharp breath. "He's destroying our world, and it's our fault." She stared past Miranda, quiet again for a moment. Then, she asked, "What does finding the souls solve?"

Miranda's brain cleared as if the fog had been burned off by the sun. "If people here have both halves restored, they'll be strong enough to face him."

"How do we find lost souls?" Hugo asked. "That seems impossible."

"It probably is," Miranda looked at Telos and Zoi, "for us." She leaned forward, crouching on the balls of her feet with her palms planted on the wood. Her muscles, now awake, itched to run. "You must know where they are." Telos would not meet her gaze. "He's keeping the people divided for a reason."

"There are too many potential hiding places," Telos said.

"No one knows a place between better than Kirasu," Miranda said. The fire crackled and popped in response, but neither of them spoke. "Nibiru is the only home any of us have now."

"We will look for the souls," Telos said in an even tone, her shoulders slumped, her eyes dull, "but we must have quiet."

A shot of hope rushed through Miranda. "We'll go outside." She hauled herself onto shaky legs and stepped to the door.

In the bright sunshine, Miranda watched wispy clouds race across the sky. Being back with Monrovia and Hugo, and now with Kirasu, gave her hope that they had a chance against Alois.

Hugo pulled up clumps of grass and watched the sky. "We won't have a storm tonight."

"How did we lose you last night? When I checked, you were behind us and then you completely disappeared," Monrovia said.

Miranda watched the round door of the cabin, waiting for it to open. "I lost sight of you. Where did you end up?"

Monrovia told her about a cave they found. Miranda imagined them huddled together for warmth because it was too wet to make a fire. She touched the back of her head and told them about waking up in the ravine.

The day grew longer while they picked grass and waited. Miranda dug a small hole in the soft ground with her fingers, for no other reason than it kept her mind off Kirasu. What if they couldn't find the souls? They had to.

Nathan, we're bringing you home.

Finally, the cabin door creaked open, and Miranda hopped to her feet watching Telos shuffle toward them wearing a blindfold.

"We did not locate them." Her head hung low. "They are well hidden."

"Why did you stop looking?" Miranda said. "We have to find them."

Zoi ambled out, her whole body slouching. She also wore a blindfold.

"We can't do anything more now," Telos said. "We will try again later."

Miranda balled her hands into fists at her sides. *Nothing more.*

Monrovia clamped a fist and gave Miranda a stern look. "Thank you for trying."

Telos and Zoi both nodded.

"Why are your eyes covered?" Hugo asked.

Telos's hand flew to the blindfold, touching it protectively. "We see too much."

Miranda loosened her fists and took a deep breath, rolling her shoulders. *We will find them.* A twinge of sadness twisted in her gut for these strange creatures, even though they made her face the man who killed her mother. They had to live in chaos. "Do you see two worlds here now?"

They nodded solemnly in unison. "We do."

"What do you see when the Falling happens?" Monrovia asked.

Telos paused, then answered, "We see the image before it comes, like a snapshot of the aftermath."

A squirrel sprang from the ground and latched onto a nearby tree, sinking its small claws into the bark.

Monrovia gasped. "Do you know where it's going to happen?"

"We don't know the places, but we have seen the image of destruction before it strikes. But we don't know how long before," Zoi cautioned.

Miranda's heart pounded in her chest. She remembered Lau, lying thin and frail on the canopied bed. Was this why she'd told them to find Kirasu? They would save so many lives by predicting the Falling. Her palms sweat as a darker thought crept into her mind: with Lau gone, her strategy for saving Carl was also gone. But Senator Cloudlyn would appreciate the immense value in predicting the Falling. The senator might even accept a trade: Kirasu for Carl's release, but only after they find the souls.

Miranda stepped closer to Telos. "Come back to Samsara and tell us where the Falling will strike next. We can get the people out of the way. We can save lives."

Zoi cocked her head, and Miranda frantically tried to clear the idea of a trade from her mind. She stared at the squirrel racing around the tree.

"We may see the image hours, minutes, or seconds before the event happens. This is not a science. It's more of an impression."

"The images might be clearer if you were closer to Samsara," Monrovia suggested.

"We don't want to leave," Zoi said.

"But what good is your gift if you're not using it to save lives?" Miranda pressed. "You can't tell us where it will happen unless you are with us."

Zoi trembled and Telos put her arm around her.

"The world out here is too much for us," Telos said.

"We can find a dark place for you to stay, somewhere as dark as that." Hugo pointed to their cabin.

Zoi sank to the ground. "We cannot live out there." She pointed a thin, bony finger at Miranda. "You were supposed to get him to rebuild our home."

"I'm sorry." Miranda touched Zoi's thin hand. It was cold, almost like marble. "We did not mean to destroy your home."

"Or ours," Monrovia added, sniffling.

"But we need you to help keep people safe," Miranda said. She searched Telos's face for a sign she would give in.

"We cannot see every disaster. I did not see that you would try to remove us from here," Zoi said.

"If you can help us find the souls and tell us when a Falling will happen then we have a chance." Fledgling flutters of hope danced in Miranda's belly.

Zoi's shoulders drooped, and her head lolled.

"On a practical note, how would they get there?" Hugo asked. "I can't fit five people in the glider. Three was pushing it."

Zoi's face brightened. "There is no room. We must stay."

"Can you live with yourself knowing you could have saved people and didn't?" Miranda's flutters twisted.

Zoi's lips remained a tight line.

"Hugo, take them in the glider. Miranda and I will find our own way home," Monrovia said.

"Or take them and come back to get us," Miranda mumbled.

"I can't take anybody anywhere if they don't want to go," Hugo said.

Telos put her hand on her sister's shoulder as if preparing her.

Zoi slumped forward like she was trying to melt into the ground and disappear. She looked up with wild eyes. "We have lived so long. I should be ready, but it is sad to die."

Hugo looked around. "That sounds like a 'no.'"

"Why would you die?" Miranda asked.

"Because we cannot live in your world," Zoi said.

Telos patted Zoi's shoulder. "We will go. We will help."

CHAPTER 21

HIDDEN WORLDS

What was taking so long? Miranda kicked at the dirt with the toe of her boot. Kirasu had been in the cabin getting ready for ages. Did they even own anything?

Finally, Zoi cracked open the door, her large eyes staring accusingly at the outside world. She slammed it shut again and Miranda let out an exasperated groan. But soon they stepped out with their blindfolds secured, and with no bags, because they did not own anything. They held hands.

"There's a steep trail over there." Hugo tapped Zoi's shoulder and bent down in front of her. "Better climb on."

Miranda sighed and passed her pack to Monrovia, letting Telos climb on her back.

Monrovia led the way down the trail, Hugo in the rear. Miranda watched every step. Even though Telos was small, slight even, the extra weight made negotiating the loose stones and wet leaves difficult.

Miranda kept her focus on her feet, trying to put the ultimatum out of her mind, but it kept pushing back. *Restore Nibiru if...*

Each minute that passed without telling Monrovia seemed like a mistake. They would be alone soon enough. She would tell her then.

A piercing screech broke the silence and Miranda froze, bracing for impact. But instead of the white bones of a shrieking banshee, this wail belonged to an owl flapping its wings close enough to graze Monrovia with their soft tips.

She shouted and jumped back. The rest happened so fast that Miranda had no time to react. Monrovia's foot must have slipped. She barreled down the incline at top speed.

"Monrovia!" Miranda dropped Telos and rushed forward, but her sister was sliding too fast. Monrovia's scream shattered the calm of the forest as she fell over the edge of the ravine.

Miranda's heart leapt to her throat as she screamed her name again, but her feet did not stop moving. *No. She had to be ok.* She dropped to her knees at the edge. Monrovia lay sprawled out on the ravine floor.

Hugo caught up to Miranda and firmly clenched her shoulder. "Are you okay?" he called down.

Monrovia whimpered in response and the noise started Miranda's heart again. She scampered down the side of the gully, careful of her foot placement.

At the bottom, she crouched beside Monrovia. No visible blood, and she was conscious. Both good signs. "Can you move?"

Monrovia held her arm up. Her wrist bone stuck out in a very wrong way. "Do you think it's broken?" she said hoarsely.

Miranda flinched and took a short breath through her nose to calm the building nausea. In the Trash Lands, a break like that would have healed itself over time but would never be the same. Bubble City didn't hire rejects. It would have made her a beggar. "I'm sure Tan's mom can fix it."

"You think she tends to outlaws?" Monrovia asked, tearing up. "It hurts and I'm all scraped up."

Long scratches painted Monrovia's back and arms. Miranda gingerly helped her sister up. "Come on. We'll get you to the doctor as fast as we can."

Monrovia stood shakily, leaning on Miranda.

"But really, you're lucky. That was a crazy fall and you're walking away."

"With help."

Hugo met up with them and looped his arm around Monrovia's waist and lifted his water bottle to her lips.

"She's all torn up and… her wrist."

Monrovia drank a little and pulled back. "It hurts." Her face was ashen.

Miranda bit her lip. Monrovia, in so much pain, made her want to find a way to fix it.

"Let's get her up," Hugo said.

Miranda followed his lead, and they clumsily guided her up the ravine wall. When they made it to the trail again, she shook them off and took a few steps on her own. Her collapse was not surprising, but the open tears were.

"Find white willow bark," Zoi said. "Chewing that will dull the pain."

"What does it look like?" Miranda asked, whipping her head from side to side.

"I'll help you." Telos raised her hand and Miranda took the cue to help her up. "Lead me." She gestured away from the trail.

Miranda kept hold of her hand, walking in silence until the trail disappeared behind them.

"How about here?"

Telos perched her blindfold on her thin eyebrows and marched among the trees. "I can have it off for a little while." She said as if answering the question Miranda had only thought of asking. "The one we're looking for is short for a tree with lots of branches; the bottom of the leaf is white."

Telos hopped from stone to root and back to the ground. Occasionally, she reached out to the air as if to test it.

"Do you see something else here?"

She held her temples, blinking slowly, deliberately. "It's nothing." She squinted one eye and marched forward. "I found it."

Telos sank her small fingers into the tree, peeling back long strips of bark. Miranda did the same, and they filled their pockets.

"She'll also need food," Telos said.

Miranda made a gagging sound at the idea of them eating food foraged by Kirasu.

Telos scoured the ground. "Only potato." Almost immediately, she looked up, as if startled by something, and held her hand out again like she was feeling her surroundings.

"What do you see?"

Her stare was oddly blank, like she saw nothing and everything at once. A heavy sigh escaped her small lips. "I see this forest, but also a dusty road with no trees. Small buildings line the side. The sky is dark and something is falling, like snow, but it's not white." She curled her lip. "It's dark, gray."

The forest closed in like an alien world. Miranda reflexively dusted off the ash that rained from the garbage fires burning day and night. *We're in the Trash Lands?* She squinted to see the other world between the trees. Only forest. She touched the bark of the tree closest to her, expecting it to evaporate into the mirage it must be, but her fingers grasped the rough bark. She broke off a piece, staring at it in her hand. *But it isn't real.*

Telos shuddered, clutching her head. "It's easier when I don't focus on it. Seeing it all gives me a terrible headache."

"That's really here? Now?"

She shrugged. "It's what we see. Do we see the future or the past, or the present? It is hard to say."

She stumbled around the forest, then showed Miranda which clump of short, green plants were the heads of potatoes. Miranda dug into the ground, soft from the recent rain, and pulled up a cluster. She expected to hit a layer of sand in the soil, but it wasn't there. She went back in for more. When they had a small stack, Telos tied her blindfold back on, and Miranda scooped her onto her back. She jogged the entire way to Monrovia, Hugo, and Zoi.

They found Monrovia slumped with her head between her legs. She raised her eyes to track them as they came closer. Sweat rolled down her face despite the cool forest air.

Telos put a piece of bark in Monrovia's good hand. "Chew this."

She stuffed it in her mouth.

"Make a fire. She needs to drink it as a tea," Telos said.

Hugo jumped to his feet, crashing into the woods to collect sticks.

"I still have the pot we used when we were camping," Miranda said and thought back to that first night in the woods when Carl cooked chili. It seemed like a lifetime ago.

Hugo came back minutes later with an armful of wood. He dumped it and rigged up several stones and sticks to hold the pot, then got it all roaring.

Miranda dropped in as much willow bark as Telos instructed, then dug in her bag for one of the scarves they used as a disguise on their way out of Samsara.

Monrovia raised her head and spoke in almost a whisper. "It's several more hours to the glider."

Hugo assessed the waning daylight. "We're out of time for today, but it's okay. You should rest."

Miranda crouched at Monrovia's side, positioning the scarf around her, making a nest for her arm to rest in. As she tied it with a tight knot at Monrovia's neck, her sister's shoulders drooped, and she let her head drop again. "Thanks."

Miranda filled her bottle with tea and positioned herself so that her sister could rest her head on her shoulder. She brought it to Monrovia's lips, letting her sip it slowly.

"Hugo, there are potatoes in my pocket."

Monrovia grinned slightly, then motioned for more tea.

"Cook them." Miranda pushed back some hair from Monrovia's forehead. She would not move her for anything.

He awkwardly fished through Miranda's pocket to extract the food and set about steaming the potatoes in the little water they had left.

Monrovia's breathing calmed. The earthy smell of the cooking food made Miranda's stomach growl.

When the first one was ready, Miranda held it, burning hot in her fingers, and let Monrovia nibble on it. When she'd eaten it whole, she straightened up, taking the willow bark tea in her good hand with her eyes wide—an improvement.

Miranda took off her boots and socks and stretched her toes to the fire while she sucked down her own small morsel. A darkness spread through the fire and shaped into Alois' dark eyes, staring at her. She choked and moved back. No one else moved. They looked tired.

Was he watching them? *Two days.* And if she and Monrovia didn't go… She shuddered and tried to keep out the unwanted thought.

Miranda ate another potato and fell back on her sleeping mat. Somehow, she had to get Monrovia to a doctor, get Carl out of jail, one way or another, and stop Alois. *All in two days.*

Or she could give in? But that would mean Alois turning his experiments on to Nibiru. She couldn't let that happen.

Pink sky gave way to just a few stars peeking between the leaves. Monrovia stood, knocking sticks out of the way, clearing a spot to lie down.

"Here." Hugo smoothed his coat out on the ground. "Lie on this."

"I don't need it."

"Well, if you don't sleep on it, no one will, and that would be a shame."

Miranda could practically hear her sister's smile. She groaned. "Just take it." *That bark must really work.*

"Thanks." Monrovia settled down on the coat.

Kirasu sat back-to-back, using each other as a wall. Their frailty here still took some getting used to, but they were altogether different in the place between. What would it take for them to fight?

No one person can stop Alois, he's shown us that. Would Kirasu face him or back down?

"It's quieter hanging out with you guys than I thought it would be," Miranda said. "You were always making music in my head before. What happened to that?"

They both stopped chewing to examine her.

"You liked Kirasu," Zoi said, more of a statement than a question. "We made that music from our consciousness in the place between. Music plays in our heads all the time, but it's hard to share with you now like we did before."

"Because of the collapse," Miranda said.

"Likely," Zoi said.

"What do you need to find the souls?" Miranda asked.

"Quiet and time."

Miranda's jaw tightened. *We don't have much time.* "Can you try again tonight?"

"You lack patience," Telos said.

"I do, especially when a demigod is trying to flatten my world."

"We will see," Telos said.

"Thank you." Miranda rolled over in a huff.

She didn't expect to fall asleep quickly, but within minutes she fell into a dream, floating in the place between. The panic of aimless drifting gripped her. She wanted out, but Alois appeared wearing a tight-fitting black coat with long tails instead of his typical tunic. The tall, shiny black hat was out of place on his wiry, white hair. He looked like an unfit Bubble City partier who missed the dress code. *Ridiculous.* She'd laugh if she wasn't so terrified.

"Get away from me!" Miranda pushed against her suspended state but went nowhere.

Alois bobbed close to her, spinning a cane, which only made him look more absurd. A short bark of a laugh jumped out of her mouth. He grinned in response, showing razor-sharp teeth. Again, she fought to break out, but was held, suspended.

Alois circled her, rounding his cane, laughing hysterically, displaying row upon row of dagger teeth.

A song cut in. He did not react—*he can't hear it?* He seemed to move in slow motion.

> It began so quantumly
> It could expand to anything
> But here we are and what a mess we've made
> Like a child so spastically
> Destroys a book repeatedly
> You tore from me my pages full of wonder
> You plundered
> You successfully diffused responsibility
> Too many paper cuts unpoliced
> Most certainly will bleed
> Don't try to be a hero
> Don't try to be a friend

She froze, confused. *What is it telling me? Accept his deal and disappear forever?* But it had said 'don't be a hero', so did that mean not to accept the deal and find another way?

"Don't try to be a friend..." Alois' body morphed, his arms disappearing, his legs fusing, his clothes falling away. A shark with gaping jaws swam through the darkness straight for her.

The scream caught in Miranda's throat. She flailed, trying to escape, but nothing. The shark came fast. She jerked her arms and legs in close, making one big ball. Her heartbeat banged in her ears. She took a quick breath and tucked her head as the massive mouth closed around her.

CHAPTER 22

STALLED CONFESSION

Miranda dug in her pack for the miracle of clean socks but kept one eye on Zoi as she pulled her blindfold over her eyes. What was Kirasu trying to tell her with that song?

The dream had shaken her, but the clear morning helped calm her nerves.

Her fingers touched stiff fabric. *Where is Alois hiding the souls?* She rooted past to find something soft. Sunlight broke through the trees, playing on a patch of green moss. *Why is this what's real?*

Telos yawned dramatically.

"Did you find the souls?" Miranda asked, even though she could tell by their slow start that nothing must have changed.

Telos and Zoi both shook their heads.

Did you look?

Monrovia gave Hugo's coat a feeble shake and held it out to him. "Thanks for that. It's warmer this morning than I expected." She peeled off a sock with one hand and struggled through turning it inside out. Hugo tried to help, but she waved him away. She stepped into her boots, and he swooped in to tie them before she could protest.

I should have clean socks for both of us.

Monrovia stood and took a few steps down the trail. "We should get moving."

Miranda looked at her naked feet. None of the rest of them had their shoes on yet.

"Feeling better?" Miranda asked.

"Well, my wrist is still broken and everything aches, but hanging out in the woods won't help." A piece of willow bark flapped in her mouth as she talked.

"We should make it to the glider in two hours." Hugo put on his jacket and flipped open a compass. "I'll take Kirasu first, then I'll double back for you two. We can all be in Samsara by the afternoon." He studied the compass. "Should be this way, right?"

"You've had a compass the whole time?" Monrovia said.

"Yeah. I took it out of the glider. Why?"

Monrovia tossed him the map, shaking her head.

"What?" Hugo turned his attention to the map, comparing it to the compass. "Yep, this way."

Miranda dumped a few handfuls of damp dirt on the remnants of the fire and chuckled at Hugo's obliviousness as she cleaned her hands on a pile of leaves.

Monrovia faced the new direction. "Everybody ready?"

Miranda tugged on stiff socks, the cotton crunching around her toes, and wrenched on her boots, now caked in mud, but still sturdy. At least they didn't have holes yet. She slipped on her pack and looked up to find everyone staring at her. Even Kirasu faced her with their covered eyes. "I'm ready." One step made her legs shake with yesterday's fatigue.

Zoi cleared her throat. "Sorry to be a bother again, but we're going to need a ride."

Monrovia held out her good hand and Miranda passed her bag over as Hugo collected Zoi. Her biceps screamed as she hoisted Telos into place. It was going to be a long walk.

***

The sun wasn't yet overhead when they made it to the field. Miranda lowered Telos to the grass, her arms stiff and aching. The glider sparkled in the sun, waiting exactly as they had left it. Hugo raced to it and stroked its flank.

"Everything in order?" Monrovia asked, sucking on her tree bark.

He came around the other side with a giant grin. "Perfect." He let out a squeak of a laugh. "I should take you first so we can get you to a doctor."

Monrovia held up her bark. "I can wait. Get them settled somewhere safe."

"Are you sure?" Hugo cocked his head.

Miranda sighed. "Just take them. She won't change her mind."

"They need to get settled so they can identify the next falling. It's probably hard to concentrate with all this movement."

"That is true," Telos said.

"I'll come right back for you after I settle them."

Miranda hoped she was included in that 'you,' but his eyes were glued on Monrovia.

He popped open the cockpit bubble and beamed at Kirasu. "Jump in!"

Miranda held each of their small, cold hands and guided them to the glider. Hugo lifted them into the backseat. They both fit with room to spare.

"Thanks for doing this," Miranda whispered to them.

Telos wrapped her arms around Zoi and gave a quick nod. "Take us somewhere dark," she said.

Hugo nodded and kicked some tree limbs out of the glider's path.

"We won't melt. Get yourself some food and have a rest, then come back," Monrovia said.

Hugo rocked on his heels, staring at the ground, as if considering the request.

"And bring food for us." Miranda rubbed her stomach in big circles.

"Okay, but I'll be back as soon as I can."

Monrovia took a step closer and put her hand on his arm. "Don't worry, you're gonna do fine." She leaned in and kissed him on the cheek. His face flushed red as she turned away, and Miranda thought he might turn into a puddle of mush as he hopped into the cockpit. He fastened the clamps with a dopey grin.

"I bet he'll find a way to fly twice as fast now," Miranda said.

Monrovia shrugged. "He looked like he needed the confidence."

Miranda chuckled. *Sure, that's it.*

The propeller popped out of the nose as Hugo turned the glider around, using the short grass runway to take off again. The small light plane rose almost silently. They watched it climb above the trees and head to the mountain.

Miranda searched her bag and found an apple for them to share. Quiet settled. She savored that Monrovia had finally stopped blaming her for all the problems, had possibly even stopped hating her for getting Carl arrested. Or this might only be a lull in the storm. But now they were alone. There could be no excuse. *I have to tell her.*

"Do you think…" She floundered for the right words.

"Is there more to that?"

Miranda shrugged off the sarcasm and tried again. "Do you think it's better for someone to forget the person they loved who died or live with the grief?" She needed to make sure Monrovia understood what Alois was offering. A reset.

"Where did that come from?" Monrovia asked.

Miranda shrugged. "Just something I've been thinking about."

"You mean forget like never knew?"

"Like the person was erased."

"Would you want to forget Beda?"

Miranda imagined how much of herself she would not understand if she had no memory of her mother. "No." A sharp pain stabbed her chest. "I didn't understand her when we were together, constantly gave her a hard time. I bet the two of you could have made it work." The words scraped her insides clean, leaving her raw, exposed.

Monrovia squeezed her hand. "She had who she needed. I'm sure you made her work that much harder."

Miranda wiped away a tear and snorted. "I've never thought of that."

"But to your question. Pain makes you understand the world. That is important enough to suffer through. But it's hard."

She had to be saying she would reject Alois' offer, right? "Everything would be different if we had stayed on Nibiru," Miranda said.

"We would have had a normal life and Earth would still be trapped under Alois' thumb."

Miranda lay back watching the clouds grow and change. Why did it always have to be *them* making sacrifices?

Of course, she will reject his deal. Silence collected between them like rain in a bucket.

"Alois said something when I was out there with him." She yanked on a long blade of grass until it popped.

Monrovia pointed to the sky. "I saw a flash!"

Miranda bolted up, inspecting the fluffy clouds. "What?"

An undeniable silver flash glinted in the sky.

"Did you see that?" Monrovia asked.

"It's too soon for Hugo." Miranda snatched up her pack. "Come on." She ran to the tree line then stopped, realizing she was alone. Monrovia stood stock-still, staring at the sky. "Come on!"

She snapped to attention. "What if Hugo got word to someone to come and get us sooner?"

"We don't have a lot of friends right now!" Miranda threw her pack under a bush and found a different one large enough to climb into.

Another flash and Monrovia jetted to the tree line, diving into the large leaves beside Miranda. They had a sight line to the field. Only a few minutes later, a shiny silver pod touched down and its door opened.

Monrovia gasped.

"Don't move. Don't even breathe," Miranda whispered.

CHAPTER 23

IN DEEP

Four guards dressed in black crashed through the quiet. The Senate's yellow 'X' flashed in the sunlight on the arm of each uniform.

"He said they would be here!" yelled a guard.

Miranda's throat clenched. *Hugo?* But, no, he wouldn't! Would he? *Have they caught him?*

"Search the woods!"

She risked exposure by peeking to get a better look at their faces, but she needed to know. *Is Oren with them?* She snuck a quick peek above the leaves and sucked in a breath. Oren brushed his straight hair out of his eyes and stared at their bush. He was dangerously close.

Her heartbeat thudded in her ears.

The first guards pushed farther into the woods. One of them called out, "What if they left?" as he trod past them.

Oren stalked the underbrush, not taking his eyes off the bush, heading right to them. Miranda dug her fingernails into her palm and glanced over at Monrovia. She had folded herself as small as possible. It helped that their clothes were brown with dried mud.

Oren came closer—only a few more steps before he would claim victory. Miranda squeezed her eyes shut.

"I found something!" a guard yelled, but it wasn't Oren.

She snapped her eyes open and watched him whip around, running to the voice. "Yes, that's one of their backpacks," he confirmed.

"They're here, people," a man shouted in a gruff voice. "Find them!"

Oren followed the others deeper into the woods.

Miranda cursed herself for not hiding her pack better, but it was the break they needed. She counted to one hundred after the footsteps had passed, then crawled out of the bush, avoiding dry twigs, but she could not escape the crunching leaves. She looked back. Monrovia had not moved but watched her with wide eyes. Miranda waved for her to follow and prayed that she would. She set off again, crawling as silently as possible, and glanced back. Monrovia was moving now, catching up.

Breathe.

They crouched just beyond the bush. A guard stood with his back to them. He might yell to alert the others, but none of them would get to Miranda before she'd be gone. There was no time to search for her pack. It might be anywhere now. She said a silent goodbye to her bedroll and clothes and mouthed, 'Run.'

She sprinted, glad to have Monrovia at her side.

"There they are!" a voice shouted. "Running to the field!"

Monrovia stumbled over a branch, and Miranda barely slowed as she caught her with one arm. Boots crashed through the forest all around. Monrovia found her feet again, and they dashed ahead, clearing the trees.

Miranda darted to the rover with its waiting open door.

Monrovia lagged. "You want to *take* that?" she yelled.

Miranda jumped up the stairs. The guards were bearing down fast. "Get in!" She caught Monrovia's good arm and yanked her inside, then banged on the walls, looking for a switch or button to close the door.

The fastest guard was covering the distance. He'd be at the rover in seconds. Miranda frantically slapped at the wall. "How does the door close?" The stairs hummed as they retracted, and the door began its slow close. Miranda stared at her hand with dismay. "Did I do that?"

"Uh no," Monrovia said. "I found the switch." She settled in front of a newly exposed panel of buttons and levers.

The guard didn't slow down as he made it to the ship. He gripped the doorframe and heaved himself at the closing door, trying to slip under. Oren was close on his heels. Miranda braced against the floor and kicked both feet out hard. Her boots connected with the guard's face, and he screamed as he fell to the ground.

"Sorry," she mumbled as blood streamed from his nose.

Oren's jaw dropped open. He was close enough to make a last-ditch, desperate effort. Miranda met his eyes and shook her head the slightest 'no.' He paused. She wrenched her legs back as the door vacuum-sealed with a satisfying whoosh.

Wish he hadn't seen that.

"Do you know how to fly this?" she asked Monrovia.

"I've done simulations, but flying this takes two hands, so I'm going to need to talk you through it. Get up here."

Guards banged on the sides of the pod. Miranda's vision narrowed to a pinprick, and her boots seemed stuck to the floor.

"You pull it together and help me get us out of here, or we open the door and face up to Cloudlyn. Up to you." Monrovia drummed her fingers on the board covered with buttons and switches.

Miranda dug the heels of her hands into her eye sockets and willed herself back to the here and now. "I can do this."

I can't do this.

"Sit here and hold that down." Monrovia motioned to a large red button on the left. "At the same time, you push forward on this." She tapped a small lever to the right of the pilot's chair.

The banging on the pod became more intense. A bead of sweat ran down the side of Miranda's face.

"When we're in the air, let go of the button and steer with that." Monrovia touched a squat controller with arrows pointing in every direction.

Miranda's face burned. She wiped her wet palms on her pants as she sat in the chair. Reflective steel stared back at her where a window should be. "I can't see anything."

"Take it straight up, and we'll fix that in a minute," Monrovia said.

"Hold this down?" Miranda's hand shook as she pushed and held the large red button.

"Yes, and I recommend we leave before they figure out some way to keep us here."

"And push this forward?" Miranda leaned on the lever and the ship jumped into the air.

Monrovia fell back into a chair.

Miranda's stomach lodged in her throat. "Oh my god!" She yanked the lever back again, and the pod rushed down.

"Stop!" Monrovia screamed.

Miranda froze. The machine lurched to a stop, hovering.

"Gentle movements. Nothing fast."

"That would have been good to know." Miranda felt, more than saw, Monrovia's eye roll. She held down the button again and gently pushed the lever forward. The pod rose smoothly into the air, but Miranda's stomach still reeled. She scanned the levers and buttons. "Which one of these turns the autopilot back on?"

"Nope."

Miranda stared blankly at her sister.

"They would have programmed the rover to go back to where they started, which is most likely either senate headquarters or the jail. Do you want to go to either of those places?"

"No autopilot, got it." Miranda rolled her shoulders and peered out of the small side window. "But I can't see where I'm going. We may be heading straight to a cliff." The realization made her want to send the pod straight down again.

"Working on it." Monrovia appeared to be petting the ceiling over Miranda's head with her good hand.

"I know there's a mountain around here." Miranda gripped the lever as if a tighter hold would make a difference.

"Just keep going straight up. Slowly."

Miranda froze. Had she been pushing it forward instead of up? An array of instruments swirled in front of her, but they were no more useful to her than a heap of tin.

"Oh," Monrovia tapped an almost imperceptible seam on the pod's ceiling, and it popped open. "I found them." She sounded as calm as if she'd found a misplaced glove. A pair of silver glasses sat in the padded compartment.

Miranda snatched them and put them on, even though she had no idea what they did. The queasiness in her stomach clenched tighter as the walls of the pod melted away. They were just two seats hurtling through the air to the face of a mountain. She jerked the glasses off and the reflective silver walls surrounded her again. "These glasses make the walls disappear," her voice sounded as shaky as she expected.

"Higher please," Monrovia said again in that irritatingly calm voice, like she was instructing Miranda in the fine art of painting porcelain. "Yes, and if you put them back on, you'll be able to see what is out there."

Miranda hastily jammed the glasses back on her face and pushed the pod higher. Her stomach clenched tight. "This is the worst idea of my life."

"You've had worse ideas, but not many." Monrovia put on her own glasses. "I will act as a spotter."

The intense dread that gripped Miranda as a passenger flying over the mountain was magnified by a thousand now that their lives were in her hands.

"Push it a little more, slow and steady." Monrovia's calmness had descended into irritation.

Miranda clung to the sureness in that calm and did as instructed. The pod rose higher into a fluff of cloud. Cold panic clenched her as fog circled the vessel. She looked right, left, and back again. Were they going to hit something she couldn't even see?

"Relax," Monrovia said. "You're doing great. Keep it steady." She hummed a tune and sang.

> When bunnies burrow down,
> and larks go quiet
> that's the time for babies to bed.
> When the sun sets low,
> And frogs start singing
> That's the time for babies to bed.

She kept singing, low and quiet, and Miranda took a breath. The fog cleared, revealing the downslope of the peak. They had cleared the mountain. Miranda loosened her white knuckled grip on the lever.

"Do you remember Beda singing that song when we were little?" Monrovia asked.

Miranda tried to recall or even imagine Beda singing a bedtime song. Instead, she briefly tasted the hot ash of the Trash Lands. "No."

"It's one of the few things I remember from her." Monrovia stared out the window in silence.

With the mountain behind them, there was nothing but open sky. Miranda let her shoulders relax. She wanted to take Monrovia's mind away from how she and Beda had left her behind all those years ago. "I can't believe we could take this thing. Seems like there should have been a password or something to get it into the air."

"There's no password to take control because people don't steal pods on Nibiru." Monrovia clipped the words.

Picked the wrong conversation.

"Oops?" Miranda offered halfheartedly. "They must have Hugo." She chewed the inside of her cheek. The pod dipped. She yelped and grabbed the lever again.

"They had to have been looking for the glider. Which means they also must have gotten to Tan," Monrovia said.

Miranda shuddered. *Everyone who has helped us?* "Do you think they're okay? And Kirasu?" Her chest tightened as she realized that, if Cloudlyn already had Kirasu, she'd lost her bargaining chip.

Something dark sped toward them on the horizon. Miranda raised a shaky finger. "What's that?" The thing came closer, and she breathed a sigh of relief as she made out a large pair of wings. It glided to them and hovered below them for a moment, then flapped away.

Hugo.

"If the Senate is holding all our friends, we have to get them out," Miranda said.

Monrovia pressed her lips into a thin line. "No more trouble."

"Do you realize you are still flying in the police pod you stole? I think springing a few people from jail won't add too much to our trouble list."

"I said no. I don't even know how you got me into this stolen pod. It's like I can't stop helping you." Monrovia watched the sky. "Senator Cloudlyn would probably let me go. You're the one with the ties to Earth. You're the alien."

Miranda snorted. "She may have let you go yesterday, but today, you stole a police rover."

The lever jerked hard to the right.

"What are you doing?" Monrovia shrieked.

"Nothing!" Miranda tightened her grip on the steering control and tried to stay calm. The lever moved again, jerking the pod. She fought to keep it steady.

"Whoa! Don't do that."

The rover tilted.

"Uh, I don't have control anymore."

"The guards must have gotten a message to headquarters." Monrovia's voice rose an octave. "They've disabled the pod."

"Disabled it?" Hot bile crept up Miranda's throat. She swallowed hard to push it back down.

"Pull it right."

Miranda leaned her whole body against the controller that now fought her commands. She brought the pod over a shimmering blue lake ringed with tall pines and other evergreen trees. The pod was falling fast. "Tell me some good news."

Monrovia eyed a red button on the console. "If you push that, a parachute will pop out of the roof and float us safely to the ground."

Miranda's hand shot to the button, but Monrovia slapped it out of the way.

"But don't push it! It will trigger an automatic distress signal that will deliver our current coordinates back to the place where this pod originated."

"That's the *good* news?"

Monrovia tightened her harness, so Miranda did the same. "We're positioned over a lake. Let's hope it's deep enough to keep us from smashing to pieces on the bottom." She knocked on the wall. "This thing should bob back up to the surface. Then we pop the emergency hatch and climb out."

"I can't swim," Miranda squeaked.

"One problem at a time. Impact in five, four...,"

Miranda threw off the glasses and squeezed the sides of the seat while Monrovia called out their descent.

"Three..."

The pod slammed into the water.

The harness bit into Miranda's shoulders as the impact jerked her up, then pressure yanked her down, pressing her against the back of the seat. Bubbles rushed past the windows, and Miranda whimpered as they plowed to the bottom of the dark blue lake.

"We'll go down farther, but that's just the force of the drop," Monrovia shouted over the din of rushing water. "Once we hit equilibrium, we will float back up."

"Your nose." Streaks of red fanned across Monrovia's cheeks. Miranda tried to lift her hand, but the force pinned it down.

"It's nothing, just a bloody nose from the pressure change." There was a pause and a slight bump. "There. Did you feel that?"

The pod paused, then changed direction.

"We're going up," Miranda said. "We're going up," she said again, laughing.

"Good news. It was deep enough."

Bubbles rushed by the window as they came closer to the surface. Finally, the pod broke through, bobbing up and down, riding the crest of the waves.

Monrovia pointed to a ring on the ceiling. "That's the emergency hatch. Open her up."

Miranda yanked on the ring, swinging it open. Blue sky winked back at her. She climbed onto the back of a chair and stuck her head through the opening.

"What do you see?"

A biting wind kicked up sun-sparkled waves that licked the side of the pod. Tall trees lined the lake in every direction. It was serene, untouched, as if she was the first human who had ever laid eyes on this beauty. Where and when had anything this perfect ever existed on the dried-up splinter of rock she lived on for years? Maybe not everything from Nibiru was once Earth. The shoreline stretched a distance much too far to swim, even if she'd known how.

Monrovia tugged at Miranda's shirt as she stepped on the back of her chair. Miranda supported her as she stuck her head out. A gust of wind sent a slosh of water inside the pod, but also inched them closer to shore.

"We need to use this wind." Monrovia sunk back into the darkness of the pod.

"Is there any way to get to the parachute without triggering that message?" Miranda asked.

"We might have to dig it out." Monrovia banged around below. "They built the parachute into the top of the pod." A wave lapped at the side, spilling in more icy water. "Here." She passed a black pouch to Miranda. Inside was the daintiest set of tools she'd ever seen. "Maybe those will help."

"I'll give it a whirl." Miranda climbed out, resting on her belly on the slick roof. The wind's cool bite had her wishing for a jacket.

Monrovia popped her head up out of the latch, a piece of bark dangling from her lips. "It should be somewhere in there." She pointed to a dark section of the pod's interior between the roof and the ceiling inside.

Miranda hung upside down and peered in. The area was about as wide as her hand, with wires and bolts sticking out. She dug into the darkness, scratching her knuckles, fumbling for something clothlike. Nothing.

"Reach more."

She passed the tool pouch back to Monrovia and leaned farther over the edge. The cold water lapped at her legs as she shoved her arm elbow-deep into the small opening. She swept the area until her fingers grazed cloth and wrenched a fistful from the hole. She went back again and again until there was a pile of cloth big enough to use as a sail.

Miranda lowered herself back inside, shivering. Monrovia gathered up a section of fabric and Miranda dumped the rest outside, stretching it along the roof. They both stood precariously on the backs of chairs, holding pieces of the thin fabric, waiting for the wind. Miranda stretched her arms wide as possible to give the wind more chance to catch. After waiting so long that her arms ached, the wind finally billowed out their makeshift sail. The pod moved toward the shore. Miranda held the cloth tight in her hands.

"It's working!" Miranda's heart leapt, and she wanted to sing. *No more cold lake.*

The spray wet their faces as the wind pushed the battered pod close to shore. When they reached the shallows, Miranda helped Monrovia out first. She dropped into the water to gauge the depth and gave a thumbs-up when her feet touched the ground. Miranda fell in beside her, splashing into waist-high water.

She shook her bloodied knuckles at the sky. "We made it!"

"We still have to hide this thing. Can we drag it out?"

Miranda tugged the softened fabric with her full strength. The pod moved barely an inch and that may have been because of a wave. "Are you pulling?"

Monrovia let go. "I was. We can't move it on land."

"Can we sink it?"

"That would trash the lake."

A strong wind ripped the parachute from both their hands and sent the pod bobbing along back into deep water. They watched it sparkle in the sun like a drifting, homing beacon.

"We may as well have sent our coordinates," Miranda said.

"We better move quick, then."

CHAPTER 24

A BITTER CHOICE

As Miranda and Monrovia walked, the tall trees with spiky needles gave way to shorter fat ones with thick branches stretching like tentacles searching the forest. A warm breeze replaced the biting chill at the lake, and a nutty, buttery scent hung in the air.

Almost involuntarily, Miranda stumbled closer to the aroma, her mouth watering and stomach growling.

"Where are you going?"

"Don't you smell it? Someone is cooking." Miranda fell to her knees. "I want to eat all of it." But they were only a few hours' walk from the city. The Senate would have spread the word about Carl's wanted children—and who wouldn't turn in the co-conspirators?

Miranda's stomach growled loudly. She dragged herself back to her feet and slapped her forearm hard. It was an old trick from the Trash Lands: give your brain some other pain to focus on for a while. It never worked.

A bright moon replaced the setting sun as they walked, turning the limbs of broad trunked oaks into shadows in their path. Miranda almost smacked into a hulking branch at eye level. She thought of that first hike in the woods when she'd tripped. Carl had seemed mad at her for it. *What was he doing now?*

"What's the Senate going to do to Carl?"

Monrovia's back straightened, and her tone was matter of fact. "He will have a trial. He's allowed to present witnesses, but I don't know who's left," she added quietly.

Miranda thought of the show trials in Bubble City when they caught someone stealing or staying past curfew. They banished most people from the city for life, which was a death sentence of its own. But if the crime was bad enough, they would carry out a swift private execution. Often with no notice to anyone. She shuddered and asked the question she'd wanted to ask since the moment he was arrested: "Will they kill him?"

Monrovia made a noise somewhere between a cough and a laugh. "We are not barbarians!"

Relief flooded Miranda.

"If he's convicted, he will probably spend the rest of his life in jail."

She chewed her bottom lip. She'd waited too long, but every time she opened her mouth to tell Monrovia about Alois' demand, something else came out instead. The words were too hard to say. What if her sister said yes to being banished forever? What if the reset meant Carl would go free? Miranda shivered, but they couldn't give in to Alois turning Nibiru into his newest lab.

Monrovia slowed and dug another piece of bark out of her pocket. "This is the last of it."

"You need a doctor. Is there some way to send a message to Tan without going to Bushuto Gardens?" Miranda asked.

Monrovia shook her head. "I don't want anyone else mixed up in this."

"I need to talk to you about something."

Monrovia pushed a skinny branch aside and kept walking. It sprang back and slapped Miranda's cheek as her boot sank into fresh mud.

"Ow! Ugghh!" Her shoe made a sloshing sound as she plucked it from the ooze. "Hey, stop for a second."

Monrovia threw up her hand and hissed, "Hush!"

Miranda froze with one foot in the air, straining to hear or see whatever had stopped Monrovia. Then she heard it: a low hum so quiet she would miss it in the city, but, out here, the mechanical sound was different enough from the rustling leaves and hoots.

"Where is it?" Miranda asked as a bright light cut a line through the trees a few steps from Monrovia.

"Are we turning ourselves in?" Monrovia said.

Miranda remembered Senator Cloudlyn's icy stare. "If we're locked up, there will be no one left to stop Alois."

"Then we need to run fast, now." Her voice was even, but her eyes were shot through with fear. The light cut another long line through the thick tree canopy. They ran away from it, hopefully in Samsara's direction.

Monrovia led, constantly slapping small limbs in Miranda's face. They ran faster. As the ground became firm, the hum followed. They jumped over and under logs, searching for somewhere to hide.

Monrovia doubled over.

"You need to rest?"

She nodded, holding up one hand.

Miranda spotted a group of boulders well hidden by a ring of leafy trees. She led Monrovia to them. They tucked under a large rock and prayed the searchlight would pass them.

"Why are they being so quiet? They must have heard us crashing through the woods." Miranda's blood turned cold. "They are looking for a place to land."

"Or at least room to let down the ladder," Monrovia said.

"We can't stay here."

They jumped out from behind the rock.

"Over here!" a man yelled.

What sounded like an army of boots crashed closer. Miranda ran through a stream and scampered up the bank. Monrovia was close on her heels. The forest thinned, and a low-slung rocky wall came into view.

"The edge of the city," Monrovia said.

They hopped the short wall in unison and darted for the side streets. Miranda sneaked a look and watched three guards overtop it.

"They are right on us." She yanked Monrovia onto a backstreet. Crumbling buildings lined both sides, ending with a high wall.

"A dead-end alley?" Monrovia hissed.

"If we're supposed to keep running, we will find a way out." Miranda scoured their surroundings. A small, rusted ladder clung to the side of one of the buildings. "Here!"

She jumped for the first rung, but it was out of reach. She jumped again, her fingers grazing the rusted metal.

Monrovia reached her long arm up and extended the ladder down. "You want this?"

"Go!" Miranda shooed her up the ladder.

She quickly unknotted the makeshift sling and used both hands to scamper up, with Miranda right behind. They made it to the second floor. Monrovia climbed through a broken window. Miranda followed, pulling the ladder back up.

She scanned the small apartment, dusty, with chunks of plaster covering the floor and coating the furniture. A large hole showed the room below. "Find somewhere to hide. They may have seen us."

Monrovia held her wrist close to her chest and ran to a bedroom. Miranda dashed for a closed door and flung it open. A riot of game equipment and coats spilled out. Miranda kicked it back in and pulled the door shut behind her. It was pitch black. She burrowed under the mess, settling in a corner. Miranda's ears pricked at every sound, but she didn't hear crashing boots. The dusty closet was warm, and her hand landed on a soft coat. She draped it over her and closed her eyes for a minute.

A low-pitched moan filled the air. Her skin tingled. She wiped a line of drool from her cheek. Another moan.

"Monrovia?" She cast off the clutter and climbed out of the closet, but the soft coat still clung to her. It had a cheetah pattern and large pockets. She put it on despite the heat.

Another moan rumbled through the crumbling apartment.

"Monrovia? Is that you?"

The light from a bright moon streamed through the broken, dusty windows—just enough to avoid the obvious holes in the floor.

A feeble 'Here' echoed. *Monrovia.*

Miranda sped up her search and found her crouched under a bed up against a wall. She dropped to the floor, eye to eye with her sister. "What's wrong?"

Monrovia held up her wrist a few inches above the floor, her face twisted in pain.

Even in the dim light, Miranda could tell it had doubled in size. She winced and looked away.

"Find Tan," Monrovia said.

Miranda nodded, but worried this was beyond the help of a doctor's apprentice, and if he was trapped in the dome, which seemed most likely, she would waste precious time looking for him. Another moan shuddered through Monrovia.

"Are you out of bark?"

She nodded.

Miranda reached her hand under the bed and wiped several strands away from Monrovia's eye. Sweat beaded her brow. Miranda could not move her in this state. "I'm going to get someone here to help you. Hang in there."

She wished there was another option, but Monrovia needed a doctor. Cloudlyn better be as reasonable as Monrovia made her out to be.

"What are you…" her voice trailed as she took in a shuttered breath.

"I'll find you as soon as I can."

The guards must still be close. Miranda looked around the apartment for something to chuck off the side of the balcony. If she made enough noise, they were bound to come, but she also needed time to get out. She still had to find Kirasu to have any chance to save Carl.

She dragged a heavy armchair through the balcony doorway. One door was missing and the other dangled from its upper hinge at an angle.

She steadied herself, ready to hurl it over the ledge. Surely that would kick up enough dust to get their attention. She hefted the armchair up and almost had it over the rail when a loud pop made her freeze. Another pop and the teetering balcony shook and whined. Miranda dove for the doorway and caught hold of the frame as it broke free and crashed with a roar, rattling the building. She dangled at the side, kicking the wall, searching for a foothold. This was more of a clue than she had wanted to give.

"There she is!" a guard yelled.

Finally, her boot connected with an edge, and she hauled herself inside. *Might have been too effective.*

"They're coming. Let them find you," she called out, then sprinted down the stairs two at a time and squeezed through a hole in the back while guards streamed in from the front.

CHAPTER 25

DAY TWO

The first rays of morning stretched over the quiet streets and dipped into the river. This area had been badly hit by a Falling. They would have asked everyone to leave for their own safety and, being good citizens, it appeared they had all obeyed.

Miranda lay on a patch of grass barely concealed behind a building. She was close to remembering her dream from last night—something important, something… it dangled just beyond her reach.

Luna padded up with a limp, gray thing hanging in her mouth.

"Oh, did you?" Luna had led Miranda to this spot last night after she'd tripped in the dark running from the guards. She'd been a little too successful showing them how to find Monrovia. Hopefully, her sister would understand. What else could she have done? Monrovia needed a doctor. Luna finding her in the aftermath was a silver lining.

The cat dropped the limp thing at her feet and meowed. "Is that a present for me?"

She grinned and flinched as pain shot through her cheek. Luna cocked her head and scooped it up again, trotting away. The side of Miranda's face was one long tender scrape. She picked at the gravel peppering the cuts on her hands. *Got to get this cleaned up.*

She bolted upright. *Day two.* The thought arrived like an unexpected visitor. Alois gave her two days to decide. Turn herself in to him and have Nibiru reset, or watch it be torn to pieces. Today was the second day.

Free Carl, find the souls.

She was no closer to either.

Her stomach growled loudly. Luna popped into view, this time with an empty mouth and a coy air.

Miranda punched the ground in frustration. "How can I stop Alois from destroying everything if I have to find food? This is stupid!"

Luna meowed and took off in a run, then skidded to a stop, looking back.

"Am I supposed to follow you?"

The cat yowled a meow.

Miranda dragged herself up from the spot where she'd slept for a few hours and followed Luna through the streets. She recognized a building left standing, then in a few more steps, another. The cat was leading her back to Bushuto Gardens. Back to the main rescue center, where everyone would recognize her. *I don't have to go.* Her stomach growled so loudly Luna stopped in her tracks and arched her back.

They have food. Dip in and dip out. Ten minutes, that's all. Then find Kirasu. She patted down the faux cheetah-fur coat she'd found in the closet. A slight bulge in an inside pocket had her hopeful there might be something useful to help her hide.

She dug in and pulled out two bandannas. Gray and white, just like she wore to keep the ash out of her mouth in the Trash Lands. Her hands shook as she held them, staring, trying to decide if they were real. *Good sign or bad sign?*

Luna thumped her tail impatiently against the ground. Miranda tied one quickly over her hair and the other around her neck. She flipped up the large collar of the coat and darted her eyes left and right as she followed Luna's silent steps into the garden.

Mist rose off patches of wet grass, stubbornly fighting their destiny as mud. Miranda kept her head low while trying to scan the area. A few guards lounged near a table. She'd keep her distance. No one stopped her as she walked farther in among the tents, fewer now and dirtier. Her chest seized. She was face to face with the dull, scratched plastic of the dome that had protected Bubble City from the death outside, but here, in this once beautiful expanse of green, it seemed like death itself.

Dark shapes moved inside and her dream from the night before slammed back in vivid detail. She was here and Beda was with her. A long line of people waited to enter a tunnel. Beda had told her, "It's coming." *It. Another Falling?*

Get them in the dome, Miranda.

The words from the dream came back to her now, as if Beda had whispered them in her ear. She had said it would protect them. Miranda almost felt the soft tips of Beda's fingers, like when she caressed her cheek in the dream and whispered, *You can do this, Miranda.*

"You look like you could use some help."

Miranda jumped at the voice and the recollection of the dream evaporated. A woman in a dirty, white coat with shadows under her eyes so dark it was like counting the rings of a tree pointed a shaky finger. Would this woman turn her in? She seemed too tired to care, like if she sat, she might never get up.

"I fell." Miranda touched the itchy young scab growing on the side of her face.

"Come on, I'll get you cleaned up." The doctor took a few stiffened paces to a large, white tent and stepped inside.

Miranda walked in behind her. The thick canvas snuffed out the bright morning as it closed behind them. Cots lay empty, some with dirty sheets. Were they waiting or abandoned?

"Do you know Dr. Kaur?" Miranda asked.

"Of course." She looked reflexively at the dome.

Miranda's stomach clenched. "Have you heard anything from them?"

She dabbed at Miranda's face and hands with a cloth dipped in something impossibly cold that somehow also burned with a heat like white lightning. Miranda took a sharp breath.

"Oh yeah, this stings really badly," the doctor said in a voice sucked dry of emotion.

"Do you think they're okay?"

"They figured out how to pump in extra oxygen on the first day, and they had most of the supplies in there, so I expect they are doing all right. The tunnel is coming along."

The image from the dream washed over her. People waiting at the mouth of a tunnel.

Get them in the dome.

She shook herself back into the present. *But she's wrong. We need to get them out of the dome, not in.* "There's a tunnel?" she asked weakly.

The doctor dabbed on a cool ointment. "They're digging it to bring everyone out. It should be ready in another day or so. If you ask me, they might be safer in there than we are out here, but they want to get out. It's natural—they're trapped."

"Maybe we can go back in later, if we need to."

The doctor had a vacant stare as she slathered on more of the thick green goop. "This will help it heal." Last, she cut off a measure of gauze and taped it over the wound. The tape stretched from Miranda's eyebrow to her chin. She stuffed the roll into Miranda's hand. "This is for later. You'll need to change that dressing once more today and once tomorrow. The wound is superficial, so after that I say let it breathe, but you can keep the aloe on at night. You'll be lucky if it doesn't scar." She stared at the gauze in her hand and wrinkled her brow as if she suddenly didn't know what it was.

"What's wrong?" Miranda asked.

The doctor snapped back to attention. "That's something I would have worried about before. Not wanting a patient's face to scar. Hardly seems to matter now."

Miranda looked into her tired eyes and wanted to tell her everything would get better, but it meant all of them joining forces to face a demigod. It meant this tired woman in front of her believing she had that power. She had to find Kirasu. These people had to have their missing piece. All she could eek out was, "It has to get better."

"How?" The woman wiped away tears as she looked away. "I'm sorry. It's been a long day." The bright morning sun beamed through a slit in the flap. "Or long, several days, I guess."

Miranda slid off the table with a new resolve to find the souls. "Thanks for your help."

She stepped into the sunshine and flipped her collar up as she headed to grab supplies, then sneak out.

I have to make it better.

The guards had cleared out. She scooped a canvas bag of water from the stack. She flipped open the top and drained every drop standing there at the table, letting it run down her chin.

"Miranda?"

She spun around, ready to fight or run.

The morning sun framed Hugo's black hair that had gone curly instead of spiky, giving him a halo or a lion's mane. Lines creased his forehead. "What are you doing here?"

Miranda grinned, surprised how happy she was to see him. "What are *you* doing here? They let you out?"

He shrugged. "They asked me some questions and let me go." His face darkened. "But they made me leave the glider. I don't even know where it is—somewhere in the country between here and Kona."

She couldn't help but feel responsible. "I'm really sorry about that." But then Miranda's gut punch gave way to a ray of hope. "Did they let Kirasu go, too?" She looked around, as if she may have missed them. "I'm looking for them."

Hugo stared at the ground. "I didn't see them after they separated us. I think they are still holding them."

Cloudlyn trying to crack them. Miranda leaned down to peer up into his face. "It's not your fault they were taken. It's mine. I'll find them."

Hugo scanned the area franticly, like he just remembered something. "Where's Monrovia?"

"I hope she's with a doctor. I think they took her in last night."

He arched an eyebrow. "But not you?"

She took two sandwiches and another water pouch and stuffed them into the large interior pocket of the impractical coat. She smashed another sandwich into her mouth, taking a large bite and grumbled.

Hugo snagged her sleeve. "We should find a less prominent location to hang out."

She followed Hugo and sloshed to the back of the park. They walked along the dome. It was hard to make out the dark figures through the thick plastic.

"Is Tan in there?" Miranda asked, her heart heavy.

"He was always helping his mom out. The way it landed, her tent would be in there," Hugo said.

She imagined he and his mom stuck in there together, waiting and wondering if they would ever get out. "I'm glad they have each other." And she wondered if what she said was true.

A loudspeaker filled the air with a high-pitched screech that settled to a hum: "Good morning, everyone," a timid voice reported. "We have a recent development in our understanding of the Falling."

Miranda straightened her back.

"We believe a Falling will target the prison today. It's not known what time this will happen, but the Senate is asking for volunteers to help evacuate the prisoners to a safe location. If you are available to help, meet at the steps of the prison in half an hour."

Miranda's stomach flopped. *Alois is targeting Carl.*

"They are using Kirasu to predict the Falling," Hugo said, his face a mix of dread and—was that—hope?

Miranda clenched her jaw. If Cloudlyn knew what Kirasu could do, she'd never let them go. There was no bargaining. This was the only way. "I have to save Carl."

CHAPTER 26

THE FINAL FUNERAL

Hugo cocked his head. "This is our chance to help hundreds of people."

"Yeah, of course." Miranda chewed her lip. "You can help a bunch of people evacuate, but I'm the only one who will help Carl escape."

"But what if Cloudlyn's guards are there?"

Miranda tapped the toe of her boot against the ground and considered the problem. "They'll be distracted, and I'm in disguise." She tugged at the collar of the cheetah print coat.

One corner of his mouth lifted. "We can do better than that. There's a pile of donated clothes in a tent. You blend in with the bushes, and I'll see what I can find."

"Are you telling me to hide in a bush?"

Hugo's smile faded and he nodded slowly. "Yes."

Miranda scanned the path—empty, but she shuffled from the bench to the greenery anyway, pushing her way into the stiff branches. Dew from the large leaves wet her clothes and a powerfully dank whiff of dirt filled her nostrils.

She distinctly heard snickering as Hugo walked away. Had he been joking? She settled back, letting the leaves close around her. *Why am I hiding in another bush?*

Only a minute later, footsteps crunched nearby, and she caught sight of two sets of scuffed black boots, the same boots the senator's guards wore. They lingered. Miranda sunk farther into the green, straining to listen.

"She won't say where the girl is. She might not know."

Miranda's heart beat loudly in her ears. *Monrovia.* She wanted to jump out and ask them if her sister was better, if she saw a doctor, but she stayed concealed. *I have to save Carl.*

"Those weird kids can predict the Falling, so why do we need her?"

Miranda was sure that voice belonged to Oren, even though she could not see him. *Is he trying to make them stop looking for me?*

The first guard mumbled a reply she couldn't make out as they walked farther down the path. Another set of footsteps followed close behind. These were more erratic, like someone running. They stopped and Hugo dropped beside the bush.

He pressed a soft fabric into her hands. "Put this on."

Miranda eyed what seemed to be a skirt with large flowers in bright colors and considered throwing it back at him.

Hugo checked over both shoulders. "It's different from anything you'd wear. Put it on."

She couldn't argue with that as she crawled out of the bush and pulled the skirt over her pants. "This is not a disguise. I just look dumb."

Sweat rolled down the side of his face. "Let's get out of here. I don't want to be picked up again."

She darted through the park after Hugo, staring at the ground. Even after they'd made it to the street, he kept up a quick pace until he ducked into a darkened building.

The room smelled like a damp rag left in the heat too long. A steady drip from the ceiling formed a not-insignificant pond on the floor. Miranda sloshed through it to check they were alone and called Hugo. "Why did we come in here?"

He leaned out the door. "Seeing if we were followed."

"I don't have time for this. Which way to the jail?"

He threw his hands up. "I'm the only one trying to keep you out of jail. No. I'll help them, but it's too dangerous for you to be there."

Miranda took a deep breath to suppress the urge to tackle him. "I'm not asking for your permission. I'm asking for directions." She pushed past him toward the street. "I'll find someone else to ask."

"Why are you so unreasonable?" Hugo called after her. "You are your own worst enemy."

"That's probably true." The day was warming, and her extra clothes made her sweat.

Hugo sighed loudly and stepped in front of her. "Fine. Follow me."

Miranda raised her collar as they wound around piles of rubble and row after row of sagging structures occasionally interrupted by a pristine building. Was it random or did Alois play favorites? She shuddered. A basket of blooming purple flowers hung on a balcony clinging from its last hinge. It creaked as it swayed in the breeze. The need to confess gripped her, and she yanked Hugo's shirt sleeve. Her stomach flipped as he spun around.

"If you could return Nibiru to how it was before the Falling, would you do it?"

His eyes widened. "How is that a question? Of course."

"But what if the people who died in the Falling did not come back, and you'd never remember them? Like Oren would not remember his father. And I don't know how far the forgetting would go. It's possible you wouldn't remember your father either."

Hugo didn't turn away, but his focus shifted like he was overcome by memory. His brow softened, and he slowly shook his head. "No."

"But that's all you had to give up for Nibiru to be restored to how it was." Miranda searched his face.

"But giving up our memories is giving up everything."

She nodded and headed down the street again. *Free Carl and make Kirasu find the lost souls. That's what I have to do. We have to face him.*

"Miranda?"

"What?" She didn't stop walking.

"Do you have something you need to tell me?"

She turned back.

His brow knitted as he clutched his hands.

"No," she said.

He didn't take his eyes off her as he led the way again. "Okay. Well, we're almost there. Are you sure you want to do this? There's a very small chance you won't be arrested."

"I'm willing to take that risk." *I have to.*

***

The street ended at the steps of a large stone building. Treetops perched over the arched roof like floating green clouds. A man in a worn guard's uniform shouted directions to a hastily gathered small crowd of about fifteen. He waved Miranda and Hugo closer. She took a quick sweep of the assembled but didn't see any familiar guards. She didn't see any guards at all besides the man giving direction.

He continued, "We stay together as a group. I'll key the code on the cell door, and you'll escort the prisoner down the stairs and into the transport pod." He gestured to an area of empty ground beside him. "The pod will be here soon. Some may need to be helped down. We appreciate your assistance with this. Our guards are attending to other business. For everyone's safety, it is important to stay together."

Miranda and Hugo fell in line as they shuffled in single file. She was keen to keep her distance in case anyone recognized her.

Hugo leaned in close. "What are you going to do in there?"

"Find Carl."

"And then what?"

She didn't answer, but it was a valid question. Finding Carl wasn't good enough. She had to break him out, and she didn't have a plan for that. As she followed the crowd through the large wooden doors, Miranda brushed her fingers along the curving stem of a flower carved into the wood, so much like the iron roses that climbed the gates at Bubble City. Those gates kept people out, these doors locked them in.

The motley collection of volunteers shuffled down the hall to the stairwell on the right. Miranda peeled off. Hugo turned back and jerked his head, as if telling her to get back in line.

Stay with them, she mouthed as she ducked behind a desk and searched the room for other exits. If she and Carl went through the front door with everyone else, they couldn't avoid loading him onto the pod. She had to find him first and smuggle him out some other way.

Hugo disappeared around a corner with the last of the volunteers, and Miranda scoured the large room for a map of the building. Her eyes landed on it, framed by a doorway. She ran to it. Two stairwells, one on each side. Good. Three floors of cells above her. She examined the markings delineating the cells; about thirty on each floor. She had to move fast.

She slipped up the left stairs and ducked her head to glimpse the first floor—empty. If she'd beaten the group, they'd be coming any minute. She rushed along the corridor, peering into the jail cells.

"Carl!" she whispered as loudly as she dared.

The unexpected scene almost stopped her cold. The cells were small, but each was undeniably nicer than the shack she grew up in. Each had a desk with a lamp and a bed with sheets and a matching blanket. A privacy wall shielded what she guessed was a toilet and a shower. Most of the prisoners perched at the end of their beds with packed bags waiting on their laps. A few looked at her curiously.

He's not here.

She doubled back and made it into the stairwell just as the volunteers trotted onto the floor. It would take them time to escort the prisoners out. She moved more slowly on the level above, careful with her steps on the creaky wood, trying not to look like a maniac to the patient eyes staring at her.

"Pack your things if you haven't already. They are coming to transport you." She used her best official voice while keeping the volume low. None of these calm, hopeful faces belonged to Carl.

She hiked up the ridiculous skirt Hugo made her wear and bounded to the top floor. "Carl!" she whispered again as she peered into the cells. "Hi, pack your things, please," she said to anyone who stared too hard. Some inmates moved to organize. She studied the prisoners. Finally, her eyes settled on a familiar face. A warm and inviting, loving face.

"Carl!"

"Miranda! What are you doing here? Are you okay? What happened to you?"

Miranda's hand flew to the large bandage. "I fell. I'm fine. I'm here to get you out."

"But they are moving all of us."

"No, I'm here to get *you* out."

Carl rubbed his forehead. "Like break out?"

Miranda looked at the panel on the door. "You don't know this code, do you?"

Carl reached for her hand between the bars. "I have to stay with the other prisoners."

"What? No. I'm here to save you."

Carl asked softly. "Miranda, why do you think I'm in here?"

"Because I told the Senator all those stupid things and got you in trouble." Tears rolled down her cheeks. "I'm so sorry."

Carl smiled weakly and clasped her hand. "No. I'm here because *I* chose to lie to the Senate, and *I* put everyone in danger. I'm here because of my own poor judgment, not because of anything you did."

"But you wouldn't be here if I never came back."

His jaw dropped, but he recovered. "This is a small price to pay to have you home."

"But we can be together!" She smashed several buttons on the keypad. "You must have seen them enter the code."

He held her hand through the bars. "I have to answer for my actions. This is where I should be."

"But it's my fault." The tears came hot and fast.

"Don't tell yourself that. I wish I could give you a hug." He stroked her hair. "How is Monrovia?"

"I don't know where she is," Miranda said.

His shoulders drooped. "Find her. You need each other."

Miranda searched his face. His eyes were earnest.

"I love you, Randa. You are good enough."

"Then why won't you come with me?"

Footsteps.

"Time to go. Please take care of yourself and Monrovia." She watched him release her hand as if it was happening to someone else. Time seemed to stop.

Alone.

"Go!"

She bolted to the stairs and crumpled into a heap as the door closed.

A male voice boomed at the other end of the corridor. "Carl Ess?"

"Here, sir."

"They have moved your trial to this afternoon, so you'll stay in town. I'll escort you to your new quarters."

Trial today! Miranda listened to the tones of the code as he punched it in. Carl shuffled out. *That was my chance to save my dad.*

Their footsteps faded into the chaotic shuffle of the volunteers arriving on the floor. Miranda huddled in a corner and sobbed.

CHAPTER 27

BROKEN FUTURE

"Is the floor clear?" a voice echoed down the hallway. "Clearing now."

Heavy footsteps moved in her direction. Miranda wiped a line of snot on her sleeve and scuttled under the overhang of the stairwell.

The door creaked open. "All clear." He shut it quickly again. A cursory check.

She crept back to her spot and crumbled to the floor. *They won't check here again.*

One of the men called out to the other as their voices grew more faint. "Time to get out of here. This thing is supposed to happen soon."

Her legs dragged like they were carved from stone. *I'll stay right here. Let it all fall down around me.* But Carl's kind eyes pleaded with her from the darkness of her mind. She couldn't do that to him. Fresh tears wet her cheeks while Beda's words played back: *You can do this, Miranda.*

"Do what? I can't do anything," she sneered.

Guards slammed doors, yelling at each other as they made their way out. The hum of a transport pod grew louder as it gained altitude. No shuffling feet, no shouting commands. The empty building waited in silent expectation of what was coming.

Miranda itched to pet Luna's soft fur. A rumble rolled above. Dust and bits of wall shook free, raining down on her. Another deep rumble shook more free, and now the sleeves of her coat were dusted. She sneezed and bit her tongue.

This is stupid. I'm not going out like this.

She hauled herself up and climbed down the stairs, listening for boots or voices. Silence all the way to the carvings on the front door. She rested her fingers on the handle, listening. Low voices mumbled close with shouted commands in the distance.

"Clear the area," a gruff voice barked. Boots scraped rock.

Another pod took off. *Was that the last one?* Her pulse quickened as she gripped the knob. *Stay here and get crushed or step out and get picked up by the guards?* She leaned against the heavy door. *Are they gone?* She cracked it. *Looks clear.*

She raced down the steps, running for the dense tree line, then climbed up the thick limb of a large oak, flattening herself against the branch, waiting for guards to spill out from all sides and descend on her. No stomping boots. No shouts of "We got her!" Not even the forest breathed.

Did I make it?

Thick, dark clouds hung guiltily, like they regretted their burden to conceal the looming menace. She caught movement, a flash of a reflection deep in the gray. The Falling was coming, ready to obliterate its target. Was Carl protected from Alois now that they had safely evacuated him? Another flash of steel and glass peeked through the clouds. Chills ran down her arms. This one was big. She jumped to the ground, sprinting for deeper cover.

The massive building whistled like a lonely train on a hot summer night as it dropped, filling the air with its warning to get back. Miranda ducked behind a large trunk as the air exploded with shattering glass. The deeper tones of pulverizing stone shook the ground. She dropped to a ball, covering her head. Creaks and pops and more loud crashes. She tucked herself tighter as shards littered the ground.

Mirrored glass, like the kind in the windows of every nondescript tower in Bubble City. She picked up one of a hundred shards as the air cleared.

The fragment reflected the walls of the jail, buckling and heaving under tons of steel and glass. Stone splintered as the tower sank farther, grinding the prison to dust. Groans and pops punctuated by shatters made Miranda wince as the two buildings collapsed into one chaotic pile.

She dropped the shard in the dirt and peeked around to the front of the tree. Wicked fragments buried deep in the ragged bark up and down its trunk. If Kirasu hadn't been caught, could they have cleared the jail in time? She shuddered at the implication and wiped a line of sweat from her forehead.

But she had one more chance to save him, whether he wanted it or not.

The trial.

He should not suffer for her choices. She pushed off the damp leaves to stand and took off her coat, shaking abundant slivers of glass onto the ground.

Monrovia had pointed out the courthouse on one of their walks before everything had fallen apart. It was close to the jail. Miranda knew if she didn't walk in the wrong direction, it wouldn't take long to get there. She looked for a marker among the trees and chose left, to the heart of town. She made her way along the edge of the tree line, which offered a view of the buildings but still gave cover. The guard hadn't said what time the trial would be, but she was prepared to wait.

A familiar low hum buzzed above her. More than likely, the common network was still knocked out, which meant this pod must belong to a senator or their guards. Maybe it was heading to the trial. She stayed in the trees but kept the pod in sight.

Her jog turned to a run as it flew faster. She tried to match its speed, running until her side split. She doubled over heaving for air, the scar on her side pulsating as the vessel hovered and lowered, next to a round building.

A crowd had gathered. A cold chill raced through Miranda. *Are they here to see Carl punished? My father.*

She wove her way closer, staying in the shadows of the trees, then froze. Monrovia stood apart, higher than the people around her.

She's ok. Miranda's heart fluttered with relief.

What was she standing on? Had they let her out just for this? A thick bandage wrapped her hand and wrist, and her lips locked in a tight line as she faced the vessel. Hugo stood by her side, but Monrovia stood rigid, fixed on the rover door. He may as well have been a thousand miles away.

Miranda wanted to run out and tell Monrovia she was sorry for leaving her in that building at the mercy of the guards. But she stayed hidden. Surprise was her only chance. How could she take Carl if he didn't want to go? She pushed the thought aside. *I'll run in and tackle him and drag him away. It will work because it has to.*

The pod door lowered. Monrovia held her fingers to her lips as the crowd pressed closer.

He's coming out.

Miranda's stomach turned. She stepped closer, careful not to reveal her location, but she needed a better look. She readied herself to spring out.

Carl walked between two guards dressed in black. Helmets covered their faces, and they raised batons as encouragement for the crowd to stay back. Carl's head hung low; his shoulders slumped like a broken man. Each heartbeat hurt in Miranda's chest. Her plan began to feel pathetic. *I can't get him away from them.*

A strange-looking man in the crowd caught Miranda's eye. He looked in her direction and twirled a jaunty mustache. *Did I imagine that?* The crowd shuffled awkwardly as he pushed people out of the way to get closer. Every muscle in her body tensed.

A scream rose, then others. The crowd surged forward. She perched on the balls of her feet. *What's happening?*

An orange streak hurtled through the air. A guard smashed the object away with his baton—and it exploded, raining flames down on the two guards and Carl.

Poised to run, Miranda froze, unable to move, unable to breathe. *This isn't happening.* She sank her fingernails into the bark. *I could sprint right to him.*

A shrill scream rose above the chaos of pushing and shoving. The strange man disappeared into the crowd. Guards swarmed, swatting at their burning colleagues, then at the raging flames on Carl.

Monrovia, still perched above the crowd, gripped the sides of her head, shrieking like she believed the sound alone might save him. Time seemed to have slowed. Someone threw a heavy blanket on top of him. Smoke rose as they tore it back.

Carl lay lifeless.

Miranda's knees weakened, and she slumped against the tree. *Someone attacked him, and I didn't do anything. I didn't even try to help. I stood and watched.* Alois' words haunted her: *Your father's payment is coming.*

Her legs refused to hold her weight and she slid down the rough bark. "Carl didn't deserve this." Hot tears streamed down her cheeks.

A stretcher appeared and several people gently lifted him onto it. A silver pod rushed down, and the guards hurried him inside. It was gone again in seconds.

Miranda stared at the charred ground and blinked hard, begging to open her eyes and see Carl walking out of the pod again. It wasn't real—a waking nightmare. She opened them again, and the black stain gaped back at her. Hugo held Monrovia as her body shook.

Miranda's insides felt hollow, like she'd been scrubbed clean of sensation. Alois hadn't even given her two days before he took away everything.

Hugo helped Monrovia down from the debris pile they had been standing on and wrapped his arm around her as he led her away.

Miranda's legs seemed gummy, like they were never meant for walking, but Carl's face filled her vision. "You need each other," he had said. Monrovia would never forgive her if she knew they could have saved Carl by giving in to Alois.

Miranda forced her feet to move. She had to get to Kirasu. Alois would never stop, he had to *be* stopped.

Kirasu better have found the souls.

CHAPTER 28

INTERROGATION

Miranda stepped out of the cover of shadow and ran past the courthouse, averting her eyes from the still smoking ground. She bit her lip to push back the tears. *We're going to get you, Alois.*

A cluster of official-looking buildings stretched along a walkway, two rectangular hulks leading to a large round structure with a blue glass dome that twinkled in the late morning sun. Miranda's skin tingled. *Kirasu are in there.* It was only a hunch, but she was out of options.

She marched boldly to the domed building. Maybe she could walk right in, act like she belonged, and roam the halls unnoticed until she found them.

"Hey!"

Or maybe not.

"Stop right there."

She turned to the voice and was face to face with Oren, his body pulsing with fury.

She held her hands up in front of her. "Take me to Kirasu."

A vein in his neck throbbed with such ferocity, she wondered if it might explode. "You are not in the position to make demands." In a flash of silver, he secured a pair of cuffs tightly, binding her hands in front.

The metal pinched her wrists, and Miranda breathed deep through her nose to stay calm. "I need to see Kirasu."

"We don't usually detain children, but you are a special circumstance." He clipped each word as if it took extreme self-control.

She bristled. "Child? You're probably only a year older than me."

Oren stood taller. "Senator Cloudlyn has questions for you."

He said it with the intention of making her squirm, but she shrugged it off and pressed him again. "Oren, please, I need to see Kirasu. It's important."

"You will see the senator," he said.

"This isn't about following rules." Was there any way to get through to him? "This is about saving Nibiru."

His eyes flashed. "The last thing we need is more of your help. My father died because of what you started."

She pictured Carl again, smoke rising from his body. "I'm so sorry." His words stung, but she needed him to believe her. "Kirasu can fix this."

His jaw hardened, and he gripped her elbow, jerking her toward the building with the sparkling blue dome. They marched side by side up the wide steps.

If she showed Oren she could be normal, he might let his guard down. And if she gave the senator just enough information, she should be released like the others. Then she'd find Kirasu.

They stepped from the bright, hot day into a cool interior. Thin wooden slats traced the ceiling and plants of all shapes and sizes fought to cover the large windows, giving the expansive room a green tint. It reminded Miranda of the lush greenery hanging from the stairwell in Carl's building. A pain stabbed at her heart.

Is he really gone?

Oren led her to a long, narrow table where a thin man with an even thinner face tinkered with a tablet. "This is Miranda Ess."

He straightened his back, looking at the handcuffs like they were a disease he might catch if he stood too close. "Why did you bring her *here?*"

"The senator told us to bring her to her office when we found her."

The thin-faced man pinched his lips into a tight line and pointedly did not look at Miranda. "Senator Cloudlyn's office? You can't leave her in there alone."

"Fine," Oren said. "I'll stay with her."

The thin-faced man nodded curtly and stepped out from behind his desk, beckoning for them to follow him to a grand, honey-colored staircase. As they climbed, the gaps between each stair seemed to grow large enough for a person to slip through. Miranda stepped carefully while Oren gripped one arm. The thin-faced man shuffled ahead, unlocking a glass door. He pushed it open and moved out of the way. Oren guided her in.

"I will inform the senator she is here."

"Thank you," Oren said, still holding tight to Miranda's arm.

The man closed the door and twisted the key in the lock.

Miranda looked down at Oren's hand. "You can let go of me now."

"You won't do anything crazy? No one is going to hurt you. She just wants to talk."

"I get it. I'll talk to her."

Oren released her but kept his hand close, like he was ready to grab her again if she moved too quickly.

Miranda eyed the glass door, wondering how thick it was, but shook off the idea.

He let his hand fall and stepped back. "You can't expect me to trust you."

She shrugged but had to acknowledge he'd seen her in some of her craziest moments. She took in the room: overflowing bookcases of books with worn spines and faded colors lined the walls. Two overstuffed chairs faced a simple wooden desk while sunlight poured in from a large skylight, warming the room and feeding the plants brimming over hanging baskets, their heart-shaped leaves reaching to the floor. In a different context, it may have been inviting, even relaxing.

She lightly touched a leaf.

"Don't touch that."

She ignored him.

Could she reason with Senator Cloudlyn? She wanted to save Nibiru, too. The cuffs cut into her wrists and Miranda shivered as she remembered the Senator's icy stare. She blinked and saw Monrovia again, holding the sides of her head, screaming. She pinched the leaf and plucked it off the stem.

Oren rushed to the vine, jerking it away. "Stop tearing up the plant!"

A bitter taste coated the back of Miranda's throat.

I can't trust Cloudlyn. Carl was attacked on her watch.

"Sorry." Miranda gripped the small leaf in one hand and lightly brushed the spine of a book with gold lettering. "I've never seen this many books outside of a library."

"Don't touch those either," Oren said in a high-pitched voice. "Wait, they had libraries on Earth?"

Miranda let her cuffed hands fall. "We had a large one in Bubble City." She remembered how Nathan's face had lit up when they went there together for one of Beda's talks. He'd never seemed so at home in a place. She studied Oren. "Do you like libraries?"

He shrugged. "They're fine."

What made this lookalike tick? She gestured to his uniform. "Why did you join?"

"My home is under attack." He answered too quickly. "I want to do what I can to help."

"But you joined before the Falling started," Miranda said.

Oren raised an eyebrow. "Service is important in my family. We understand if you want to live in a good world, you have to work to make it good."

The words sounded like they were straight from Beda's mouth. "So, you're going to arrest the next building that falls?"

"Don't make fun of me. Nibiru was fine before you came."

"Yeah." Miranda fell into the cushy green chair. "You said that already." She brushed a curl from the corner of her vision and stared at the wood-grain lines on the desk. "And I guess it's true."

Oren leaned against the desk and crossed his arms, staring at her like he expected her to magically poof into a rabbit. "Why did you do it?"

She wanted to pretend it didn't matter what he thought. But Nathan's face staring back and hating her hurt every time. She leaned closer. "Earth was trapped in a cycle of suffering that we tried to end. I haven't done any of this on purpose."

Oren tightened his grip on his arms. "And that caused all of this?"

"We didn't know anything would happen here."

His face twisted. The vein on his neck throbbed ferociously. "You didn't think using the energy from one world to destroy another might set off a chain reaction?"

"It didn't even happen. We didn't destroy Earth. We destroyed the buffer between Earth and Nibiru."

He walked to the books, pretending to study their titles. "You destroyed the balance that allowed our world to exist."

"Did you help us in the Gathering?" Miranda asked.

He kept his back turned. After a few minutes, he broke the silence. "My father was on the ground floor of a building that was flattened in the first Falling. They got him out and he spent a day in the hospital, but they couldn't save him. And then, today, what happened to Carl…"

Miranda sunk into the chair. Carl. Flames. Smoke. The bottle sailing through the air. Tears welled up in her eyes. "None of us wanted anything bad to happen to anyone."

He spun around, closing the distance between them in an instant, and clamped onto her shoulders, pushing her against the back of the chair. "So, make it stop!" he shouted in her face, anger radiating from him.

I can give in to Alois and the Falling will stop, and he will reset you and everything else. You will not remember any of it. Then your father will truly be gone, erased along with your pain. Miranda swallowed hard. *Would it be better for you to forget?*

Oren cocked his head. "You have a way to end it." It didn't sound like a question.

She tucked in her legs, wanting to disappear into the chair. Tears streamed down her cheeks. Alois would turn Nibiru into his lab. The souls would stay lost, and Beda's sacrifice would mean nothing. Oren's father's death would be meaningless—and Carl… She shook her head.

The lock turned over. Oren pushed off the chair and stood by the window. The thin-faced man entered with a serving tray and placed it on the desk. He smoothed his vest.

"She's coming up."

It was a warning aimed at Oren, who straightened his uniform by tugging his own vest down. His face became impassive, ready to serve as if he had buttoned up his pain, putting it back in the jar he kept it in, sealing the lid.

The thin-faced man passed Miranda a tissue. "Tea?"

She blew her nose loudly as he poured from a plain white teapot. The tea sparkled in the afternoon light. He passed her a cup on a small plate, turning it so she might grasp the handle. She took it with both handcuffed hands and sipped through the steam.

Senator Cloudlyn stepped in, and the room shrank. She unhooked a clasp at her throat, shaking off a long burgundy cloak with golden epaulets at the shoulders. She hung it on a peg on the wall. Her crisp gray pants and light gray short-sleeved shirt said she was ready for action, but also illustrated she had not yet bothered to get dirty. Her knee-high black boots were shiny and not a hair dared betray the tight grip of her braided, low-slung bun. Miranda shrank farther into the chair.

The Senator nodded to Oren. "Thank you for bringing her in. That will be all for now." She turned to the thin-faced man. "Thank you for the tea, Clyde. We'd like to be alone."

Miranda tried to calm the impulse to dash for the door. The two men disappeared quickly through, and the lock clicked into place.

The Senator stood tall. "Miranda Ess. You made us go to quite a bit of trouble to get you here. Are you worried I will hurt you?"

Miranda hoped her voice sounded brave. "They say you won't."

Light from the skylight caught the Senator's eyes, making them glow. "No." She stepped closer. "We don't do that here. We're different from people on Earth, but our kindness has limits." She leaned in, gripping the arms of the chair, bringing her face close to Miranda's, who shrank back, waiting for the blow. The Senator's eyes flashed. *Is she going to bite me? No, that's crazy. Right?* Her face tightened, then relaxed. She let go of the chair and almost smiled. *What is happening?* Miranda's heart thudded so hard people down the hall must have heard it.

The Senator turned her back and poured herself a cup of tea, clinking a spoon in the cup while she stirred. "You know why the buildings are falling."

Miranda stifled a gasp.

Two days, make your choice.

The Senator turned back, her eyes digging deep. "N-n-no, I don't," Miranda stammered. *Stick to the plan. Cloudlyn can't be trusted. Find Kirasu.*

She took a deep breath and in a light tone said, "Tell me about your time on Earth."

Why is she asking me this? Miranda searched for what to say. "It's not interesting."

The Senator remained silent, demanding an answer.

Just enough information, not too much. "I lived there with Beda. We were poor. I went to school for a while, and then I worked in the city," Miranda mumbled and looked away from the pinched face and sunken cheeks.

"And why did you leave us to go to Earth?" The Senator's eyes flashed. "Did you hate Nibiru so much?"

"No, I was little. I followed Beda, but she didn't know I was coming." *Should I have said that? What does she already know?* Miranda's palms sweat.

"And did you like it there?"

Miranda thought back to stealing water to survive and the incessant gnawing hunger, to waking before dawn to ride the train three hours to Bubble City, and constantly watching her back. But she also remembered Nathan's easy laugh while he baked and the never-ending stars of the desert night. "It was hard," was all Miranda managed to say.

"Beda could have contacted someone here, and we would have figured out a way to bring you back. Did you know that?"

Lau's face filled Miranda's mind, then the sagging red porch, the clucking chickens. Beda always knew who could have brought her home. Miranda's scar ached. "No." She studied the wood grain. "I didn't know about Nibiru then."

The Senator sucked in a short breath. "And tell me, why did your mother go to Earth?"

"Beda wanted to help the people. She saw the black hole coming. A vision or something. But she knew it wasn't a real black hole. She thought if they started living more like people here, it would go away."

The Senator set her cup down carefully on the desk and folded her hands in front of her. "But they didn't change, did they?"

"No."

"I heard even you didn't believe they would change."

Miranda bristled. "If Monrovia already told you all this, then why do you need to talk to me?"

"Oh, no. She's very protective of you." The Senator walked to the window and looked outside, then turned back with a wide grin. "What did you think of Nibiru when you first came?"

The fake smile made Miranda squirm. She remembered Carl's large white couch and Monrovia's soft bed. Carl had welcomed her with open arms. "I liked it."

"Different from Earth, wasn't it?"

"Yes." Miranda wondered where this was going.

The Senator dropped her strained smile, and worry lines buried deep into her forehead.

"Monrovia tells me you did not know what would happen to Nibiru. That you didn't mean to set off this terrible chain of events."

Miranda chewed her lip and tried to read this woman's face. *Could she trust her?*

"I believe Monrovia," she said. "It would not make sense to ruin your new home after you had just detonated your old one. I blame myself, in part. I should have been louder in my opposition to your father's absurd plan. That was a lapse in judgment." She took two long strides to close the distance to Miranda's chair. "That means I am partially to blame, so I must stop this." She leaned into Miranda's face again. "Who is Alois?"

"I—" Miranda couldn't find words. Her cheeks burned. Alois would be happy to tell the Senator about his offer, and she would make Miranda and Monrovia accept. Nibiru would be his to mold and play with. His new experiment. And they would be banished to cold stone.

"Why are you protecting him?" Cloudlyn spat out the words.

"I'm not. He killed Beda."

Cloudlyn cocked her head. "But your mother died in the implosion—explosion—whatever it was. She sacrificed herself to destroy Earth. A strange move for someone who dedicated their life to making it better, I must add." She smoothed her hair. "And Monrovia tells me we did not even succeed, that Earth is still out there."

"Beda died fighting Alois in the black hole he created. She ended the cycle of pain he kept Earth trapped in. We all ended it." Miranda decided to give her a piece of information. "And Beda freed the souls Alois had trapped." She studied the Senator's face for a hint of whether she grasped the significance.

"Why is this Alois so powerful?"

Miranda's shoulders slumped. Cloudlyn didn't care about the souls, only understanding Alois. "I don't know. He says he split Earth and created Nibiru as a copy."

The Senator's jaw fell open. "That is a lie. Our ancestors created Nibiru in the First Gathering."

"Sure." Miranda nodded. "Everyone knows that."

The Senator tapped her fingers against the glass. "I cannot get Kirasu to speak to me about this."

Miranda sat up at the mention of the pair she needed to find so badly. "Are they okay?"

"They can't handle bright light or noise but keeping them in seclusion seems to help. They predicted the Falling on the prison, so that was good." The Senator lowered her eyes. "I'm sorry about your father. Nothing like that should ever happen here. He's in surgery now."

Miranda clenched her fists and looked away, blinking back the tears that threatened to spill over. She did not want to break down in front of this woman. *He has a chance.*

The Senator continued, "Kirasu don't seem useful for much else. Why did you bring them here?"

Was she suggesting that predicting the Falling was not enough? How could she know they could do more? "I brought them to help us protect people."

The Senator clenched her jaw. "That was good." She pushed off the desk she'd been leaning against and walked back to the window. "I've determined that either Kirasu or Alois is behind the Falling, but I don't think it's Kirasu because they helped us avoid tragedy at the prison, which leaves Alois." She faced Miranda as the late afternoon blazed around her, making her a dark spot in the brightness. She crossed her arms. "How do I find him?"

Miranda's palms were now drenched in sweat. "You can't just talk to him."

"Well, you must have talked to him to find out he takes credit for our creation of Nibiru. How did you find him?" she said through tight lips like she was holding back a flood.

Miranda wanted to run, but the Senator would easily block her way to the door. Sliding to the floor like a pile of mush was an option. "We had a book, but it was destroyed."

The Senator's lip curled into the smallest smirk. "That is the exact story your sister told me."

Anger flushed Miranda's cheeks. "Well, it's true, and if you already knew, why did you ask me?"

The Senator crossed her arms tighter across her chest. "You're holding something back. I can see it in your face."

Miranda squirmed under her unblinking gaze.

"You've talked to him *without* the book."

Miranda did not avert her eyes, desperately trying to project calm. "No, I haven't."

"Tell me, child." Her stare pierced into Miranda's heart. "Lives depend on it."

Miranda remained tight-lipped.

"If you are not protecting Alois, who are you protecting? Can your sister talk to him?"

"No. She only ever did it with my help."

"Oh." The Senator stepped closer. "It's Kirasu."

Miranda jerked her head up.

"Don't worry. You didn't tell me. I figured it out on my own. You can rest easy." She whirled on her heel, plucked her cape off the peg, and spun it around her shoulders in a flourish.

"What are you going to do?"

"I'm going to make Kirasu patch me through to Alois. It's not logical for him to destroy this world. We must have something he wants." She opened the door and strode through it in one confident move. "I will find out what it is and give it to him."

Miranda slumped down like the wind had been knocked out of her. Cloudlyn would find Alois and negotiate peace. It wouldn't even give her pause to exile Miranda and Monrovia. She'd see it as a fitting punishment for the trouble they caused.

Light slipped from the room, letting darkness take hold. Lau was gone, Beda was gone, Carl was fighting for his life, and soon, Miranda and Monrovia would be gone too. Wiped from the world along with its memories. No one left to stop Alois. *It's over.*

CHAPTER 29

TRUTH, ASSISTED

The sun had slipped below the horizon when a knock on the door startled Miranda. A key flipped the lock and Oren came inside carrying a tray and set it on the desk. A warm, nutty smell wrenched her stomach. It growled loudly in protest of the wait.

"I guess I was right about you being hungry," he said, scooping rice and vegetables into a bowl.

Miranda raised her handcuffed hands to grab it as he passed it over.

Oren cocked his head. "If I take those off, will you be normal?"

She looked at the shiny cuffs. This might be the last meal she'd ever have, so she wanted to enjoy it. "You don't need to worry about me."

He put the bowl down and fished the key out of his pocket, and with a quick click, the cuffs were off. He handed her the bowl again.

She took it greedily and shoveled rice into her mouth with her fingers. The hot, delicious food worked its way to her stomach. Her last hot meal had been in the woods: the can of beans that Monrovia had warmed over the fire after the first Falling. She didn't count the soup that Kirasu poisoned her with. This meal didn't have a lot of competition. They ate in silence until their bowls were cleaned of every grain of rice.

"We can leave this," Oren said. "Clyde will come back for it. The Senator said you can go anywhere you want, but she requests that you stay in the building."

"She's letting me out of here?"

Oren nodded. His demeanor had changed completely. He was being friendly. "I must say I'm surprised. I didn't think you'd cooperate."

"Cooperate?"

"Senator Cloudlyn said you told her exactly what she needed." He was smiling now.

Miranda's scar throbbed. She pressed it hard and smiled weakly.

"So, do you want to see the others?"

She decided to find the limits of this new, friendly Oren. "Can you take me to Kirasu?"

His smile dropped. "Not them."

It was worth a shot.

Miranda passed him her bowl. "Monrovia and Hugo?"

"Yes. You could even take a shower," Oren said.

She looked at her grimy hands and wondered how much time she had left here.

***

Miranda followed him down the staircase, past the entrance floor to where the stairs ended at a pair of white doors. He pushed them open and led her down a hallway flooded with lights. Her heart banged in her chest. *Monrovia*

225

doesn't even know we're about to be banished. I never told her. Miranda's chest got tight.

Oren paused in a doorway ahead of her. "They are in here."

She found it difficult to move her feet but shuffled forward.

Monrovia sat in a chair with its back to the door, but there was no mistaking her long, white hair. Hugo bounced a small ball against the wall with a paddle and when he saw Miranda, he missed his return stroke. The ball skittered across the floor.

"Miranda!" He ran to her. "I'm so glad you're okay." Then his face fell. "I should have stopped you."

Oren raised an eyebrow, no doubt wondering which misadventure Hugo was referring to.

Did he think she'd been crushed in the prison? "You couldn't have stopped me."

Monrovia stayed in the chair and did not look up from her book.

"Hi Rona," Miranda whispered. "How's your wrist?"

She closed her book and put it on the low wooden table. Her tone was even. "He was in surgery for hours. I waited there, sitting on a bench in the hall. I was sure you'd come. He was your father. You'd come. But you never did."

"I'm sorry." Tears fell down Miranda's cheeks. She wanted to run to Monrovia and hug her until her arms hurt, but her feet wouldn't move.

"Should we go to the hospital now?"

Monrovia slowly shook her head. Her cheeks were also wet with tears. "My father is dead."

Miranda clapped her hand over her mouth to keep in the growing scream. Her stomach clenched and her knees felt weak. Oren put a hand on her shoulder.

"I am sorry for your loss." Senator Cloudlyn's tall shadow filled the room. "But it is perplexing that I just learned you had a chance to prevent it, and so much more unnecessary suffering."

Heat flushed Miranda's cheeks.

"What is she talking about?" Monrovia's voice was tight.

"Oh, you don't know?" Cloudlyn muttered. "I suspected as much."

Monrovia sat taller. "Know what?"

The senator stepped into the lamplight. Deep shadows fell across the hollows of her thin face, the darkness contrasting against her bleached-bone-colored skin. "Will you tell her, or should I?"

Miranda looked away from her ghoulish face and wished she could vaporize and dissipate out of there. She did not raise her head but spoke loud enough for them all to hear. "I tried to tell you. I didn't mean to keep it a secret."

"Keep what a secret?" Monrovia spat the words out.

"Alois will stop the Falling if you and I agree to banish ourselves."

A gasp rolled through the room.

"But we can't do that because if we do, Nibiru will be his new experiment," Miranda pressed on. "He's going to reset Nibiru back to how it was before the Falling, but he will also wipe everyone's memories of the people they lost."

"He did not tell me he would wipe our memories," Cloudlyn interjected.

"It's what he did to Earth," Miranda said.

Monrovia gripped the armrest, her knuckles going white. "You've known this for days and didn't tell me?" Her face turned red.

Miranda could not meet her eyes. This was the worst possible way for her to find out.

"If he would take only me, then I would go. It's not fair for you to be banished. You didn't start this, and none of you want to forget your memories. We have to stop him."

Monrovia jumped out of her chair. "It's over, Miranda," she shouted. "I will find Alois and take his deal, but he might not be satisfied with *half* the bargain. Decide if you will make my sacrifice meaningful or not." She strode across the floor to the Senator. "How do I find him?"

"Kirasu can show you," she breathed.

"You can't let him win. He will mess with Nibiru just like he did Earth. No one will be free!"

"What's the point of free if everyone is dead?" Monrovia shot back.

"No one is making you do anything. Make your own choice." The senator's voice was smooth and calm.

Miranda wanted to choke her.

The room felt stifling, her lungs burned for air. "Am I a prisoner here?"

Senator Cloudlyn answered with a quick, "No."

Miranda turned on her heel and ran. She cleared the stairs two at a time to get to the ground floor and bolted through the large double doors into the hot, sticky night.

CHAPTER 30

FREED

A bolt of lightning split the night, revealing a darkness coiled around the city's edge like a sleeping snake. Miranda's heart raced as she ran blindly to the black ribbon of the river.

The sky shook with a deafening crack of thunder. As she reached the water's edge, the ground shuddered with a force that brought her to her knees.

Not a Falling. She braced for more, but the ground stayed steady. Trembling, she watched the currents clash and twist, churning up a chaotic fight for dominance.

They all hate me. A dull ache reverberated through her body. *They should hate me.*

The moon peeked through clouds whipping across the sky. Beda's words echoed in her mind: *You can do this, Miranda.*

She recoiled as if from a shock. "All I've done is fail, Beda!" she shouted at the sky until her throat was hoarse. *Failed to save Earth, failed to save Nibiru, failed to save the souls*

Alois stole and hid away. She whimpered as hot tears ran down her cheeks. "Where are you?" She longed to hear Beda one more time, to feel her close, but the silence was suffocating. "You ran, too!" she cried out, her voice cracking.

"You couldn't save Earth, and I can't save Nibiru." The black water churned with the promise of stillness. Miranda watched it roil, unable to hold a thought until a memory of Nathan gripped her.

It was the night at Bear Rock. He had held her in a tight hug. *Don't let go.* Warmth spread through her limbs. But she had run from him that night, like always, into the dark. Alone.

His warmth felt real. Maybe she didn't need Kirasu to find him. He'd be with the other souls. Hidden, separated from their other halves. If she could find him...

Show me where you are.

Storm clouds broke into a hard rain that beat down on her face. She leaned forward and dipped her fingers into the cool river.

This place deserves a chance without me. They deserve a future where they can forget it all.

A reckless urge overwhelmed her, and she splashed into the water up to her knees.

"You want me gone, Alois? What about this?" She shouted into the darkness as icy water lapped at her legs. She pounded it, each punch swallowed by its own splash. "If I banish myself here, will you stop making everyone else pay for our mistakes?"

She slipped farther into the frigid black, up to her stomach now.

"I just wanted to be with my family."

A powerful wave pushed her deeper, and the soft sandy bottom dropped away beneath her feet. Panic gripped her, and she flailed her arms to get back to the shore. Water filled her boots, transforming them into anchors that pulled her under. She gulped a hasty breath before her head sank into the bracing depths.

She fumbled with her bootlace, but her fingers couldn't grip. The dark embraced her. Drifting, no sound, no light. Her lungs burned. She probed her mind for a sign of Nathan. *If I succumb to this, will I see you?* Her fingers brushed something like stone, but there was nothing there.

Show me. I can almost see.

In a distant corner of her mind, a singular and familiar shriek echoed. Her skin prickled, and she covered the freshly aching scar on her side and thought of the cold stone cells of Europa. *Are you there?*

A stab of pain shot through her brain. Every cell in her body screamed for oxygen and she kicked frantically.

I'm coming for you, Nathan.

Her vision blurred, and panic gripped her.

No.

Against her will, her mouth opened, spilling out precious air and sucking in water.

As she kicked wildly to knock her boots off, something large bumped into her from below. The memory of Alois as a shark with jagged teeth clinched her. She scrambled to get away, but the creature came at her head on.

Not like this.

She shielded her face with her arms, but the animal swerved, broadsiding her, causing her to fold across its back. She clung to its fin, hoping it wasn't taking her deeper into the abyss.

I should let go—

But her fingers, numb from the cold, would not obey. The creature raced through the water until its sleek broad body broke the surface. Miranda gasped for air, eagerly sucking in every breath between fits of coughing. It paused on the surface, and Miranda kept a tight grip on its fin.

You saved me. The animal raised its head and craned its neck to her, letting loose a high-pitched earsplitting call. Its mouthful of razor-sharp teeth glinted in the moonlight.

Miranda screamed, dropped the fin, and slid back under the water, but the creature used its sturdy tail to scoop her onto its back again. She flailed for the fin, and, once her hand gripped it, she flattened herself against its rough skin.

You saved me, twice.

Its muscles rippled as it swam to shore. Miranda clung to her cold lifeline, terrified to find herself under the waves again. It stalled as it got close to shore.

Can you go closer?

It twitched its sleek body, bigger than her own, toward the shore. The jolt made it harder to hold on, but she kept her grip. It thrust again. Miranda shook her head.

"Closer!"

It let loose another eardrum-shattering howl and Miranda's fingers loosened almost of their own accord. Her heart slammed her chest then her foot that still had a boot on hit the sand. Relief flooded her.

Every other thought was crowded out of her brain but one: *Get out of the water.*

Mustering every bit of energy that still clung to her, she dragged herself out of the waves and climbed onto the beach on all fours, coughing and sputtering. She rolled to her side, sodden clothes clinging to her, and puked up water. She lay there, spent, until her head cleared.

The coarse drag of stone under her fingertips rushed back as a hollow shriek ripped through the still night. Miranda hauled herself up to sitting.

The creature waited in the waves, smooth and green, made of lean muscle. It seemed to want her to stand. She croaked, "Thank you."

I know where they are now.

She dragged herself up and forced up another round of whatever was in her stomach, then wiped her mouth with the back of her hand.

Nathan, I'm coming.

She stumbled back to the Senate and to Kirasu.

CHAPTER 31

A NEW ALLY

Miranda banged on the expansive wooden doors of the darkened Senate building. "Hey! Hey!" she shouted until her lungs burned, and the effort sent her doubling over, coughing.

A light flipped on, and the thin-faced man appeared, looking groggy. Miranda straightened as he opened the door a crack.

His lips pinched into a tight line. "It's you."

She pushed the door open, knocking him aside to enter the dark hall. The countless plants hung like shadows creeping in the dark.

He recovered his footing. "Why are you soaking wet in my lobby?"

"It's raining!" Miranda shouted.

His face screwed to a point. "Why are you screaming?"

She lowered her voice a tinge. "Where is Kirasu?"

The thin-faced man stood taller and tightened the sash on his robe. "That is privileged information."

Miranda summoned what little strength she had and snatched a handful of his robe with one hand as she reared back her other fist, in a move she hoped would be convincing. "I may be little, but trust me, I can lay you out with one punch to that bony head. Now, where is Kirasu?" The exertion made her woozy, like she might crumple to the floor any second, but he didn't need to know that.

He jerked away, but she tugged him closer and reared her fist back farther.

"This will hurt." The words were scarcely out of her mouth before a strong hand wrapped around her wrist.

"Why are you so aggressive?"

She whipped around to see Oren holding her arm and studying her like an experiment with an unexpected outcome.

The thin-faced man managed to free his tangle of robe from her grip. "She's crazy."

Miranda growled at him like she used to at the cowering dogs in the Trash Lands. He yelped and made himself scarce.

Oren released her wrist. "He's just doing his job."

Miranda scoffed. "Why don't you hold your breath until I'm perfect?"

"You look rough." He smirked.

"Is Monrovia still here?"

"I don't know. She went to Kirasu."

"Take me there."

"You shouldn't give in to Alois."

She whipped her head up. His face was so close, his brow stitched. *Worried? Can I trust Oren?* She took a wobbly step back and her leg gave out. She smacked to the ground.

He dropped down beside her. "Are you okay?"

"I'm fine. I need some help to stand."

He cocked his head. "What happened?"

"I may have almost drowned," she mumbled, "but I'm fine."

"You need a doctor." Oren's pitch rose.

"No time. I have to stop Monrovia."

He clenched his jaw and wrapped one arm around her waist to help her walk. She leaned on him as they made their way to the stairwell.

"I told the senator there is no reason for Alois to stop just because we give in to his demands."

Being this close to Oren made her knees even more shaky. It was different now that they seemed on the same side, now that he wasn't trying to arrest her. She could almost pretend… No. She pushed the idea out of her head and offered, "Exactly."

"But Senator Cloudlyn doesn't see another option."

Did he just squeeze her tighter, or was that her imagination? Her cheeks burned. *Fever?*

They passed through the white double doors marking the entrance to the dorms. He stopped in the bright light of the hall. The weight of his contemplation settled in the silence. "Why did you do it?" he asked.

She took in a quick breath and searched his face, trying to think of something to lighten the moment. "You mean go for a swim?"

He raised his left eyebrow at a stern slant.

"It was an accident," she said. "I was standing in the river, then there was no more river bottom, happened really fast."

He pushed her out at arm's length. "You started this. Don't you feel an obligation to fix it?"

Tears welled in her eyes, but she made herself face him, not look away. "Yes, and I will." Saying those words helped her stand taller.

He pulled her closer, and she leaned on him again as they made their way down the long hall ending with a door with no light coming from underneath. He knocked softly then twisted the knob. It wasn't locked. Miranda stepped past him into a cool and utterly black room.

"Monrovia? Is she still here?"

"We tried to stop her."

Was that Zoi?

Miranda's heart ached, and her voice cracked. "You did?"

A warm hand gently grasped her own, too large to belong to Telos or Zoi.

"We tried to stop her. We believe Alois is damaged. He's not thinking clearly," Zoi said.

Miranda's pulse quickened.

"You don't trust that he'll stop the Falling even if they both leave," Oren said.

"We were wondering when you would speak, child. You are hurting, too," Telos said.

Oren dropped Miranda's hand. She reached for him again, wanting to keep hold of the firm realness of his grip, but stopped herself. This was about Monrovia.

"We have seen more Fallings. You will go, and it will not stop," Zoi said.

Oren shuffled in the dark. "But then she won't go."

"I have to." The words hung in front of her.

"This is about more than your sister," Telos said.

"Yes, I know where he's hidden the souls. It's the same place he's keeping Monrovia," Miranda said. Imagining her sister cold and alone in a barren canyon on Europa made her want to demand Kirasu send her there immediately. And now she was sure the souls were hidden there, too, somewhere among the screeching skeletons.

"It's good you found them without us," Zoi said.

Miranda's lungs burned. "It wasn't easy." The memory of the cold, black water seeped into her skin, making her still, slow. "If I can bring the souls home, can we stop him?"

"Alois has become very strong. Stronger than ourselves, stronger than Lau or your mother, and we have not seen the full extent of his power," Telos said. "But uniting the people with their missing piece, granting them that truth; this is Nibiru's best hope."

"But remember that Alois means to smash Nibiru to pieces before the souls can make it home," Zoi said.

Miranda shivered as doubt crept in. "Why can't you go free them? You are stronger than me."

"We cannot face what holds them. You know. We will be too tempted to join their kind," Zoi said.

Miranda pictured Kirasu's almost translucent skin, so similar to the windswept bone of the banshee army guarding Europa. Her scar throbbed where the screeching creature had first sunk its finger into her side, holding her in place.

"But you will not succumb to that. You are very far away," Zoi said.

"I will go, too. You should not have to do this alone," Oren said.

"Have you ever projected, Oren?"

Miranda jumped at the senator's voice, cutting through the darkness. When had she sneaked in?

"No."

"Ever transported to a different planet, or even a different part of this planet?"

"No," he whispered.

"Then you can't do this. There's no time to teach you or to look out for you. I'm sorry." She added the apology as if she might actually mean it.

"But there is another problem," Telos said. "We cannot get you to Europa without Alois knowing."

"Subterfuge may not be required." Cloudlyn cut in. "I believe I have uncovered who this Alois is. I was intrigued by what you said, Miranda, that he claimed to have made Nibiru as a copy of Earth and split the souls in the process, so I did some research. He was happy to take full credit for that same story when Kirasu so graciously brought us together. But one man creating this world, a world that I feel in my bones was created through the good intentions of many. I just can't accept it. So, I sat with my feelings and looked back. Now, I believe Alois is indeed one of our ancestors, one of the group who led the creation of Nibiru.

"If the ancestors knew they split the souls of the people of Earth when they created this place, that knowledge did not make it to our legends. It is an unacceptable outcome, and we must correct it. And if Alois is, as I suspect, an out-of-control ancestor who has somehow amassed great power and learned to cling to life, then we must rein him in."

Is Cloudlyn helping me?

"Monrovia is out there. I need to bring her back, along with the souls," Miranda said.

"And how do you plan to do that?" The Senator clicked her tongue.

Miranda searched her mind for a plan. Her style was to run or smash her way to what she needed, or some combination of both. But there was no way to smash through the thick stone walls of Europa's cells, even if she could sneak past the prowling banshees to get close. And if the souls were hidden on Europa, Alois must have had Gyda's permission. Nothing happened on Europa without her approval.

So, how would Miranda go up against Gyda and her banshee army to release them? She swallowed hard. This was not a smash-and-run situation. She would have to face Gyda. When they had first met, when she'd held Miranda in that frigid stone cell, she had mourned the cycle of rebirth and death trapping Earth. Maybe the leader of the banshees could be reasoned with. But the memory of her hollow black eyes sent a shudder through Miranda.

"From your silence, I deduce you do not have a plan, as I suspected, so let me offer my own. I will give you to Alois," the senator said. A cold chill prickled Miranda's neck. "And while he is celebrating his victory, I will release the souls."

Miranda choked. "And what about Monrovia and me? Sounds like in your plan we'd both stay trapped."

"Kirasu said he sees everything out there, so the alternative is for you to free Monrovia and the souls before he can get to you, and sorry to say, I don't think that's likely.

Which leaves us with cunning. He'll think he has won, but you'll need to keep him sufficiently distracted, giving me time to free them."

"You're saying our only chance is for you to turn me over to him?" She wished she could read Cloudlyn's face in the dark room.

"So you can get to Monrovia, yes. I'm confident you can figure out a plan to escape once you are together. You are very adaptable. Get cleaned up and get some sleep. Tomorrow will be a long day. Kirasu, buy us some time— tell him I'm bringing him what he wants."

The door opened, and the senator slipped out into the bright hall.

Miranda fought to pick up her foot, but it resisted her commands.

"You can't really do that," Oren said.

Her head pounded, and she wanted any other answer to be true. The image of Beda's contorted body came back to her. She gripped the sides of her head. "She's right. I can't fight Alois on my own. This way, if we can't get out, at least Nibiru has a chance, and I'll be with Monrovia."

"You'd give yourself up for Nibiru?" Oren said.

"Always, but the rest of you will have to stop him from following through on that reset."

"We need you here," he said.

His words sent a tingling spark through her body.

Cloudlyn boomed from the hall, "Oren, with me, please."

He bolted from the room.

Alone with Kirasu and her doubts, she remembered twisting under the water, reaching out for Nathan and feeling cold stone where there was none. He had been giving her a sign, telling her where he was. "I believe the souls are trapped in stone, or rock."

"This fits our understanding." The answer came from Telos or Zoi. She couldn't be sure which.

"How does anyone free a soul? And how do they get back here? We can't see or touch them, right?"

"There is a barrier keeping them from coming home to their other half. It must be removed."

"What is the barrier?"

Telos said, "It will reveal itself."

"Have you told Cloudlyn this too?"

"She has not asked," Zoi said.

Miranda shifted her feet along the floor, wishing for some solid direction. "Does everyone on Nibiru have a split soul?"

Telos clicked her tongue. "We cannot know all the people who experience this, but we are convinced it is only a portion of the population."

Miranda suddenly worried that some unknown entity might soon be part of her.

Zoi offered, "It does not affect you."

"Why?" Miranda felt somewhat offended she could not have the thing she might not want.

"If you had a split soul, you would have been blocked from transporting between Earth and Nibiru. You could only move between the two worlds because there was no other you," Telos said.

"So, no other Beda?"

She strained to hear Telos's whispered response. "No."

"Now you must rest," Zoi said.

Miranda's bones weighed heavy in her skin, like Zoi's suggestion was enough to bring her closer to sleep. *No other versions of Beda. All gone.* She shuffled back into the bright hall, dazed, as if in a dream.

CHAPTER 32

REST, RESTORE

Miranda blinked in the bright light, forcing her eyes to adjust. *Can Cloudlyn really bring the souls home? Can I really escape with Monrovia?*

"I'll show you a room where you can spend the night," Oren said.

Shielding her eyes from the light, Miranda padded after him down the hall. "I thought Cloudlyn had called you away?"

He shrugged and opened a plain-white door to reveal a simple bedroom with a small bed, a desk, and a lamp.

"Is this okay? They are all the same." He pointed across the hall. "Hugo is in that one. And Monrovia took the one beside his."

It ranked in the top two best bedrooms she'd ever been offered, but the emptiness made her shiver. "Can I stay in Monrovia's room?"

"You can sleep wherever you want." She followed him past several closed doors. "I think it was this one."

He opened the door to an unmade bed and Monrovia's T-shirt hanging over the back of the chair. Miranda's chest ached. *It should be me out there, not you.* She would sleep with the constant reminder of Monrovia's pain tonight.

"Yes, this is good."

"Showers are at the end of the hall. There are towels in the bathroom." Oren stepped back. "Do you have what you need?"

She sat on the edge of the bed, her bones heavy and weak, fatigue drawing on every inch of her body. *I'm coming for you, sister.*

She wanted to rush back and tell Kirasu to send her to Europa now. But if they were right, Alois would know the moment she got there, and he would take her. Nibiru would lose the leverage gained by letting Cloudlyn turn her in.

Oren leaned in, holding the doorframe with the tips of his fingers. "Are you sure you have to do this?"

A warm rush ran through Miranda. It was becoming harder not to see Nathan each time she looked at him. "Yes."

He pushed off the door frame and disappeared down the hall.

Everyone had been telling Miranda to take a shower and rest. Maybe she should listen.

She kicked off her remaining mud-soaked boot and clomped to the bathroom. Floor to ceiling white tiles sparkled all around. Shower stalls lined one wall, toilet stalls lined another. An expertly folded set of towels rested on a shelf beside a bar of soap, a toothbrush, and a small tube. Next to them, a pair of neatly folded pants and a shirt waited to be worn by the next clean person. The precision made Miranda feel a thousand miles from familiar.

The stench when she peeled off her shirt curled her nose hairs. Tromping around in a mid-calf coat in sub-tropical temperatures didn't lend itself to smelling fresh.

Cold water slapped her skin as she stepped in. *Let Alois take me.* The plan didn't sit well with her. But if Kirasu were right, and he knew everything happening in a place between, then there was no other choice. But how would she get away?

The water quickly warmed as she lathered from the top of her head to the bottoms of her feet. She watched the gray swirl vanish at her toes. Her first proper shower had been a few short weeks ago at Carl's house. These luxuries were easy to get used to, but they were also far from guaranteed. *Would this be the last time?* She lathered again, giving the water a chance to run clean.

The barrier will reveal itself. To Cloudlyn?

The familiar tightness took hold in her stomach.

She turned off the tap and wrapped the towel around her. Soft towel, clean clothes. She half expected to see someone else staring back at her from the mirror, but it was her same familiar face. The soggy bandage peeled off easily as she washed her wound at the sink. No more need for bandages and goopy creams. She'd let it scab and scar.

The pants were soft as she put them on, and the shirt fit perfectly. She settled in to brush her teeth for a long time, enjoying the rough scrape of the bristles.

Back in her room again, she found a comb in a drawer, sat cross-legged on the bed with a towel around her shoulders and picked at the knots. She worked them apart slowly, like Beda used to do when she was small. They would sit on the floor of the cinder-block shack while Beda fussed over this hair she did not understand, so different from her own effortlessly straight, shiny mane. Miranda's butt would hurt from sitting on the hard floor while Beda wrestled her curls into submission.

But this bed was soft under her as she worked through the knots. *We're going to bring them home, Mom.* A small tear rolled down her cheek. *I wish we could bring you home, too.*

Beda's face hung in her mind as Miranda lay back on the pillow and fell into a fitful sleep.

CHAPTER 33

A TWISTED PLAN

A trail of guards followed Cloudlyn. Miranda kept pace.

Does she trust me?

The senator's stiff black shirt crinkled with every step.

Do I trust her?

Miranda wore the same shirt as the senator's guards, its yellow X bright on her sleeve, but she was not a part of their club.

The backs of her ankles rubbed against the heel of the too large boots the thin-faced man found for her.

The guard leading them paused in front of a curtain of roots springing from the top of the tree. This was it, the spot she had watched the people in brown tunics gather to atone. Before the destruction started, they had begged forgiveness at this tree while she sipped tea from the safety of the balcony, wondering if they were right.

Did Alois hear them? Did he care?

She whipped around, begging for a miracle, to see Carl's building restored, but a gaping wound stared back where walls should have been. Which broken floor marked the place where his balcony stood? It didn't matter. The pleas of the monks had fallen on deaf ears.

Cloudlyn had explained on the walk that spending so much time indoors had depleted Kirasu, and they had requested to be moved. They needed to siphon a fraction of nature's vitality to have the strength to send Cloudlyn and Miranda out there.

The guard turned to them. "This is where we left them, Senator. I will assess the situation."

Of course, they picked this tree.

He disappeared into the curtain of thick vines, popping back out a few seconds later. "They are still here."

The Senator stepped forward. "That will be all. We must do the rest alone."

Miranda stepped toward the tree but turned back to look at the people gathered behind her. She had not seen Hugo since she had run from the Senate building, and he was not here now. Oren was the only familiar face in this group of a few guards. He didn't smile. None of them did. Most looked at the ground. *A strange send off. They probably hope I won't come back.*

Oren took a small step closer, away from his rank. "Be careful."

His simple action, those simple words, sent a lightning bolt through her body. She couldn't take her eyes off his face. Not long ago she'd hated him for the way he treated her, thought of him as a cheap imitation. But he was hurting, looking for someone to blame—it was only human. She may have done the same. *Why did he care now?* With some surprise, she found she wanted to grab him and hold on, to tell him she was sorry for all the things she'd done. But instead of giving in to the moment of weakness in front of a group of strangers, she kept her feet rooted and gave him a slight nod.

The senator addressed her guards as a group. "We will be cautious." To Miranda she said, "It's time," and disappeared behind the root wall.

Miranda pulled her eyes away from Oren and made herself turn her back. She parted the gnarled roots, surprisingly malleable despite their thickness. One step brought her inside the bosom of the tree, a warm, wet shadow that smelled of dirt.

Zoi and Telos each lay along thick branches, fragile and small against the sprawling tree. Their nearly translucent skin was a strange contrast to the rough bark. They barely raised their heads to look at Miranda and the senator.

Are they sick? Which one of them said they would die if they came with us?

Miranda breathed in the musty smell. Was this the end for them?

The senator stepped closer. "Send us to him," she commanded.

"Wait!" Miranda threw up her hand, moving closer to the fading figures. "This may be the last time I ever see you. I know at first you didn't want to, but you've given everything to help us, Kirasu, so, thank you."

Telos nodded, and in a raspy voice said, "We have done our part, but you should know, we are not Kirasu."

Miranda whipped her head to Zoi, who held the faintest smile, then back to Telos who looked deeply at Miranda.

"Kirasu is not any one being. It floats on the breeze, waiting in the silent spaces to be considered. It is the stuff a place between is made out of."

Miranda gripped the tree to keep from falling. *What does that mean?*

Telos continued, "We opened ourselves to it, invited it, and learned to let it guide us. It is how we see beyond, see through. We hold space for it in our souls and allow ourselves to be moved by it, defined by it, even possessed by it. You've experienced Kirasu. When you saw visions of Nibiru on Earth and your sister saw Earth here. Kirasu made that bridge for you. You can use it to get through this journey too.

Miranda's head spun with Telos's words. *I can use Kirasu?* Tapping into a cosmic energy force seemed well beyond her abilities, but she had never asked for it before. She pushed the idea aside. No, these strange beings could do that, not her.

"I don't plan to rely on magic," Cloudlyn said flatly.

Zoi raised her head for the first time. "Kirasu is not magic. If you are open to it, it is infinite possibility."

Miranda blinked hard. "If you're not Kirasu, what are we supposed to call you?"

Telos shook her head. "This is unimportant," then she whispered, "good luck" and shut her eyes.

A tingle shot through Miranda's body; was it Kirasu or her mind playing tricks on her?

This is it. I will find Monrovia and Cloudlyn will find the souls— or Alois will win. Her stomach tightened as she waited for the tingling burn.

Beda's voice echoed in Miranda's head: *You can do this. You can bring them home.*

Miranda glanced at the senator. *I won't have to.*

Everything was quiet, no sign of movement.

Is something wrong?

She opened her eyes, expecting to be deep within the curtains of the weeping tree, but empty darkness blanketed the horizon. Helpless, weightless darkness. Cold sank into the pit of her stomach, as if she'd swallowed ice cubes.

Alone?

She twisted to the right, then left. Cloudlyn drifted, suspended. Miranda's tense muscles released—*not alone.* But the reprieve was brief. Cloudlyn settled her gaze on something in the distance.

A high-pitched whistle squeezed Miranda's brain. She grabbed the sides of her head, hoping the pressure might stop it. A bright light rushed at them.

Cloudlyn's face was impassive, watching the white light streak closer. And the closer it came, the shriller the whistle. *Make it stop.* Its earsplitting whine rattled, stripping her thoughts bare. Miranda squeezed her head tighter, hands over her ears, but the sound seemed to come from inside her skull.

And then—it stopped. Only the echo rang in the darkness.

"*Et nous y sommes.*" Alois' smooth voice filled the space between the ringing in Miranda's ears. She clenched her jaw.

"In the last sliver of a place between before the worlds collide." He curled his mustache in his fingers and looked at the senator. "You brought her to me?" Only his head and shoulders bobbed in front of them.

Cloudlyn stiffened. "As agreed. Now you have them both. Stop the Falling and turn back the clock to before the destruction started."

Miranda felt like the air had been knocked out of her. Turn back the clock, *reset.* Cloudlyn had made her own deal with Alois.

Of course she has. I'm an idiot.

But *reset?* They will all forget. Miranda clenched her fists and tried to decide who to tackle first.

"Is that what we agreed to?" he asked.

Miranda searched Cloudlyn's face for a hint of the person who last night called Alois an out-of-control ancestor who must be stopped. Was that for show?

Cloudlyn stiffened even more. "You know it is."

"Things have become more complicated since we last spoke," he said. Alois' head bobbed in front of them. "I could do those things, but I may have had a change of heart."

Miranda sank back. Could she find some way out of here while they fought? But the expansive darkness offered no secret getaway.

The senator seemed to stand taller. "You said you would stop the Falling and set things back to how they were if I brought them both to you. Now you have them. I do not require a consult from your heart." Her voice boomed.

Alois looked up. "But you see, my dove, I am burdened with making the decision that is best for the largest number of people. Sometimes that makes little sense on an individual level. It's something I would expect you to understand."

Cloudlyn delivered a stare that Miranda half expected might turn him to stone.

"This whole episode since the Gathering has given me time to reflect," Alois continued, "and I've realized I was being unfair. Once we split Nibiru from Earth, I only experimented with Earth."

Miranda's stomach sank.

"What would happen if they didn't have adequate rain fall? Or what if it came all at once? And then I observed the effects."

Her pulse quickened, and she couldn't stay silent anymore. "Your experiments destroyed that world." She spat the words at him.

An unsettling twinkle flashed in Alois' eyes. "But I left Nibiru alone," he said.

"I'm giving you what you want." Cloudlyn's voice had a hint of desperation that Miranda did not like.

"There's still some heart there, still some hope, but not the flurry of come-togetherness I expected to see. No, they have revealed that given the same circumstances, the people of Nibiru are no different from the people of Earth,"—he paused and looked at Miranda—"were. It's disappointing, but how could it be surprising? They are just a piece of the same people." As he spoke, the rest of his body materialized, piece by piece. First his torso in that same strange white tunic that he often wore, then arms and legs. He held a small glass box in his hand. "The complication is *moi,* and my goals. Nibiru was created to be a better world, but I want to create the best possible. *Alors*, I am driven to start fresh. It can be better."

"No!" Miranda shouted. "You cannot destroy Nibiru!" She saw Beda again falling back into the black hole. *This is not what she gave her life for.* She clenched her teeth.

"Like Nibiru tried to destroy Earth?" His eyes flickered. "*Mon cher*, you gave me the idea. I never would have thought such an action would have gone unanswered in the universe, but the only retribution has been mine. So, I must thank you and your *chère mère* for opening my eyes. To think, I have achieved almost godlike status, and yet I was holding myself back. But even now I reserve bits of truth, and for what?" He twisted his mustache and leaned closer to the senator. "The complication is also you. You want the girls to escape. You want to stop me. *Non.*"

She does? Miranda waited for Cloudlyn to tell him he was wrong, but she didn't get the chance.

He rolled the glass box around in his hand. "The wisest thing for me to do is to remove all of you from the equation." He tossed the box at them, and, in a fraction of a second, it grew, engulfing them in glass walls.

Miranda slammed down onto a stone floor that morphed into glass at the first touch. Cloudlyn clanged down beside her and scrambled back to her feet, shouting, "You cannot destroy Nibiru!"

Miranda touched the walls of their prison, smooth and clear. "He can and he will, unless we stop him." She knocked on the wall. It gave off a dull sound, not the clear ring she had been expecting from knocking on glass. "Sounds like you had a nice deal worked out with him."

Cloudlyn whipped back a lock of hair and scoffed. "Only the same deal he offered you—I just accepted it. But I was confident you'd find a way out of his prison, but now we both have to. Where are we, anyway?"

The glass box held them suspended in darkness. Cold seeped in around them. Miranda shivered.

"We're in his vision," she said. "We could be anywhere, but I'm sure we're not in a glass box."

"I do not like being at the mercy of someone's whim," Cloudlyn called out in a firm tone. "Alois, you did not create Nibiru alone and you can't create a new world alone, either. You need help, and no one will help you do this." She tapped the glass. "This will not hold us for long," she muttered. "Why isn't he answering?"

The familiar, hollow cold sucked deeper into Miranda's bones. Was this what the people of Earth felt? Trapped by his hand, waiting for his mercy? No choice but to accept eternity separated from their other half, divided and waiting.

Miranda tried her hand. "I know where you trapped the souls, Alois. I have seen the rock."

A piercing shriek filled the cube. She reflexively covered the scar on her side and remembered her first meeting with Gyda—Miranda trapped in her cage. Only freed because Gyda deemed she was working for the Creator. Gyda never shared who the Creator was, only that she did not want to cross that being.

Alois had wanted Miranda to free Beda and Monrovia then. He had made sure she succeeded. Did he know what they would do?

"You've trapped them in stone, surrounded by Gyda's skeletons, and sharp cliffs. I've been there, been trapped there." She waited, only silence. "He won't answer. But, Senator, that's where they are, held in the stone of Europa. Let those images lead you." Miranda imagined the cold cliffs, tried to bring herself there. Her thoughts bounced back at her, hitting her in the face, blocked by the glass.

"We can't transport out of here," Cloudlyn said.

Miranda cocked her fist and punched the glass wall with full force. A flash of white-hot pain filled her brain as her knuckles crunched. She cradled her scraped, bleeding fingers against her stomach.

Cloudlyn sucked in a sharp breath and took a step away from Miranda. "Do you typically approach problems fist first?"

Miranda held out her roughly cut hand. "Maybe there was a better way to find out, but we're already there."

Cloudlyn touched the smooth glass. "And where is that?"

"We are on Europa. I'm sure of it. I've been in these cold caves before. My fist got through to the actual wall." Miranda touched the glass and looked beyond it to the darkness outside. "The souls are here, and Monrovia is too."

"So, what do we do?" Cloudlyn looked uncomfortable with her question.

Miranda sank to the ground and closed her eyes, trying to clear her mind. *I'm here, Nathan. Show me how to get to you.* She tried to stretch her mind, to feel him close, but every corner was cold and wet. A drop of icy condensation dripped into her nose. She opened her eyes and found the senator watching her.

She searched her face—sharp cheekbones, hollow cheeks, pointed chin. Cloudlyn had seemed familiar from the first time Miranda had met her in the pod, when she'd grilled her for information. In this place, it clicked. Kirasu's words came back to her: *Remove the barrier holding the souls.* She'd assumed all the missing souls were trapped, but maybe at least one was in charge here. It was just a hunch, but all she had to go on.

"I need you to call your missing piece," Miranda said.

Cloudlyn's eyebrow arched to a sharp point.

"Do you feel it?" Miranda called the cold to sink deeper. The room filled with a tinkle like ice falling on a frozen pond.

Cloudlyn furrowed her brow. "I have no missing piece."

"No? You don't sense anything familiar here? Don't feel a calling to lead your army?"

"What do you know?"

"It's her, the leader of the banshees, that's also you. I'm sure of it." Miranda imagined Cloudlyn as only the bones beneath her pale skin.

"Call her to us."

Cloudlyn shook her head. "There's no other piece to me." But as she said the words, their glass cell gave way to cold, damp stone. Cloudlyn gripped the wall, closing her eyes. Her body shuddered.

The temperature in the damp room dropped and Miranda had the palpable sense that something was rushing toward them. She shut her eyes tight and pictured Gyda as she had last seen her, tattered flowing dress, hollow black holes where eyes should have been, bleached bone, long matted hair. When Miranda opened her eyes, the thing from her vision hovered near Cloudlyn.

Miranda clutched her arms to keep them from trembling. Gyda, leader of the banshees, ruler of Europa, had found them.

Gyda locked her empty eye sockets on Cloudlyn but spoke to Miranda. "I did not expect to see you again moon daughter, but then I met the other and trusted you would soon follow, and here you are."

The other! Miranda's heart leaped. "Where is Monrovia?"

"She is here." Gyda waved a bony arm to dismiss the question. "She is safe."

Cloudlyn reached out to the shock of matted, white hair clinging to Gyda's skull, but stopped short of touching it. She traced the outline of the creature's tattered gown that flowed in ripples where legs should have been.

"I know you," Cloudlyn whispered the words. Every muscle in her jaw tightened.

Gyda snatched her wrist and touched her bony fingers to the senator's forehead, whose body shook, and her eyes rolled back into her head. After several long seconds,

Cloudlyn shrieked and sank down. A single drop of ice fell from Gyda's face, shattering on the floor.

Miranda rushed to Cloudlyn, lying like a pile of discarded leaves. "What did you do?" She held her limp hand.

"You brought her here to claim me? That was too bold."

Miranda bit her lip and squeezed Cloudlyn's icy hand. Her chest rose with a breath. *She's alive.*

"You'd have this impostor merge with me, take me from my life," Gyda hissed. "This is my domain, where we are tasked with catching the discarded souls that drift from Earth."

What could she say that would get this creature on their side? "Alois is the one in charge here. Not you. He's keeping you on a short leash. But on Nibiru, you can have real power." Her heart sank as she tapped Cloudlyn's back. "She makes the laws on Nibiru."

"This one is a ruler?"

Miranda took in a shaky breath. "Yes."

Gyda's jaw clacked bone against bone. "But it does not matter because Alois is stronger."

It was almost certain that Alois was watching them, but Miranda was out of time, no more hiding. "He's not stronger than the people will be if you let the souls return to their other halves on Nibiru. They need to face him." She looked down at Cloudlyn's limp body. "Aren't you ready to stand up to him, too?"

"I see no reason to change anything about our arrangement." Gyda hovered, watching Cloudlyn.

"He's going to destroy Nibiru. He wants to start again. It's the cycle of pain we thought we ended. Gyda, we need you." Miranda's heart pounded in her chest as she stared into the gaping eye sockets. *We need you.* She clenched her hands to stop them from shaking. "Don't you want to live again?"

Gyda let loose a tittering laugh that bounced off the stone. "In this form, I am immortal."

"But you could be *alive*," Miranda whispered.

Gyda ignored her, but her voice softened. "I assume you want to see your sister?"

"Yes," Miranda said.

"I will have her brought here. You can't get off Europa, so there is no danger in having you together." Gyda sank into the wall and was gone.

CHAPTER 34

THE MISSING PIECE

Lonely minutes ticked by, counted by the constant splashing drip. Cloudlyn's back rose and fell with shallow breaths. *Should I wake her?*

Gyda, the leader of this band of screeching skeletons, had said she would bring Monrovia to her, but it seemed like Miranda had been waiting for hours. But it may have been minutes. Another hollow splash sounded. Miranda hugged her knees to her chest. Alois had everything he wanted now—a shallow breath from Cloudlyn—and more. The lonely drip, drip, shattered Miranda's resolve into a collection of interconnected doubts, like a puzzle missing too many pieces. *How could they get out? How could they stop him?*

The cell had no door, so Miranda watched the walls, waiting for Monrovia. *Will she still be mad at me?* Miranda rubbed her arms, wishing for the cheetah fake-fur coat.

Cloudlyn's eyelids fluttered but did not open, as if she was wrapped in an active dream. What had Gyda done to her?

Miranda leaned over and gently poked her back. "Senator, wake up."

Cloudlyn let out a soft moan but didn't wake.

She would never have been Miranda's first choice of cell mate, but she was better than the interminable hollow drips echoing off the walls. With a heavy sigh, Miranda acknowledged she would not survive a lifetime of solitude. She poked the senator again.

"Wake up."

Cloudlyn took in a deeper ragged breath.

A howling shriek ripped through the quiet, reverberating off the stone. Miranda covered her ears and jumped to her feet, spinning in all directions to find the source of the bone-rattling noise, but then it stopped as suddenly as it had started. A small cough cut through the ringing in her ears, and Miranda saw her sister, crumpled, in the far corner of the damp stone cell.

She ran to her side. "Rona, are you okay?"

Monrovia dragged herself to sitting, still coughing, as she held up a hand requesting time to collect herself. "That thing dragged me fast… sucked in a lot of air."

Miranda searched her face for a sign of where she stood with her. Monrovia wouldn't look her in the eye, but Miranda surrounded her in a tight hug anyway, burying her face in her hair.

"I'm so sorry I didn't tell you about Alois' deal. I should have." Saying the words lifted a weight from her shoulders.

Monrovia pushed away. "Don't ever keep something like that from me again. You have to trust me."

Miranda bit her lip to hold back the tears. "I'm sorry." The distance between them gaped large.

Monrovia looked past her. "Is it over? Will Alois leave Nibiru alone?

"No. He wants to wipe it all away and start again."

"But he said!"

Miranda wanted to scream that's why she hadn't trusted him in the first place, but 'I told you so' didn't seem like the best choice at this moment. Instead, she took her sister's hand. Monrovia didn't pull back. "We have to stop him."

Cloudlyn groaned and rolled over.

Monrovia jumped. "What is she doing here?"

The discarded leader inched back to consciousness.

"Her plan was to give me up to Alois and she would save the souls, but he was on to us."

Monrovia moved beside Cloudlyn and touched her back. "Senator?"

She opened her eyes, blinking against the light. "My head hurts. Why is it so cold? Where am I?"

"Do you remember going to find Alois?" Miranda asked, hoping that this confusion was only temporary.

Cloudlyn held her head as she sat up, her brow furrowed. "How are you both here?"

Miranda nodded to herself. That seemed like a good sign. "Gyda brought Monrovia to us."

"Gyda?" Cloudlyn shuddered, and Miranda noted the sharp edge of her shoulders under her shirt, as if they had only the barest covering of muscle and skin.

Cloudlyn wrapped her arms around herself. "So cold."

Three blankets appeared in the corner. *Gyda's listening.*

Miranda ran to them. They were gray and made from fur and feathers. She tossed one to the senator, one to Monrovia, and wrapped the last one around her own shoulders. It took the chill off.

Miranda leaned against the stone wall, grateful for the barrier the scratchy blanket provided. "Alois has everything he needs now. We can't hang around here any longer. We have to get the souls and stop him."

"But we can't transport out of here. We can't project. This place is psychic lock down. Maybe you didn't notice, but we're trapped," Monrovia said.

Miranda nodded. "Unless Gyda lets us leave."

"And why would she do that?" Monrovia asked.

Cloudlyn shivered. "When I looked at that creature, I was repulsed, but I also needed it. I wanted to hold on and never let go."

"She must have sensed all of that in you, and she didn't like it," Miranda said. Louder, she added, "But Alois is drunk with power. He could decide he didn't need this place anymore and shut it down. Gyda can only be safe if she puts him in check."

"And we're here to help," Cloudlyn said, looking around as if she expected a visitor.

Monrovia's eyes seemed to lose focus. "How can we convince him to go back to the original bargain?"

Miranda slapped the floor. "We can't trust him!" She rubbed her stinging palm and immediately wished she had not lashed out. "But I understand it now. You'd do anything to bring Nibiru back to how it was, but that world is gone. We can rebuild a world where every person matters and where we care for it because it cares for us." She took a deep breath. "We all deserve that."

Monrovia's eyes were wet with tears. "But it hurts."

Miranda turned to Cloudlyn. "You need to call Gyda back. You can give her what she wants to get her on our side."

"It looked through my mind, riffled my memories and emotions like they were a pile of papers. It's so strange. When I look at that thing, I need it—like an itch I can't scratch, but the worst itch I've ever had."

"I bet she feels it, too," Miranda said.

"It might take over if I bring it into me," Cloudlyn said.

"But it's our only chance to stop Alois and bring the souls home," Miranda said.

Cloudlyn looked lost. "I never would have imagined my missing piece would be a resurrected skeleton." She examined her bony wrist, then crossed her legs, resting her ankles on her knees in a lotus position. "I will give it what it wants."

CHAPTER 35

CONVERGENCE

Tingles surged through Miranda as she watched Cloudlyn locked in meditation. She took her own lotus position and felt for the souls in this fortress of rock. Her mind returned to the glass box. She pushed beyond it, bumping up against cold stone gathering moss in the dark. She reached for Nathan, searching for a sign, a scent—*if you are here, show me*—until a skin-puckering scrape ripped through the quiet shattering her tenuous connection.

Gyda appeared before them, her matted hair flowing behind her, her finger bones outstretched, ready to rip into anything. "You dare drag me here against my will, in my house!" she shouted.

Cloudlyn stood, dusting off her pants, meeting Gyda eye to eye. Cloudlyn did not acknowledge the anger radiating from the banshee.

"It's inevitable that we come together. I see no reason to delay it." She snatched Gyda's arm. "I can hear your thoughts. I know you want to stop him. You are worried that he's too strong and he will come for you next. You are right to be worried. Join us. Come home."

Gyda cocked her head. "You want to free the souls and put him in the glass cage?"

"Yes."

"It can't hold him," she said.

"But what can?"

"We will find the thing."

Hope flooded Miranda.

"So, you'll join us?"

Gyda moved closer to the senator. "I dropped your flesh to be more like my army." She stroked Cloudlyn's hand, then wrenched her arm from Cloudlyn's grip. "You are a ruler there?"

The senator nodded, but her knuckles were white.

"I will gain your flesh to be like your army."

Gyda raised her arms in front of her body, and Cloudlyn mirrored her action.

"You are ready to be one again?"

Cloudlyn nodded.

Miranda covered her eyes and wished for Cloudlyn there was another way.

They intertwined their fingers, flesh with bone and touched wrist to elbow. Gyda leaned her head forward. Cloudlyn did the same until their foreheads touched. The air shifted in the room and the chill sank deep.

Miranda cinched the blanket tighter around her shoulders and huddled close to Monrovia, farther from the spectacle. A mist rose from the floor, thickening as it circled them. Cloudlyn's lips moved in a constant state, but no sound made it past their circle.

Light flashed from the vapor; another burst and two screams ripped through the air, coalescing as one howl. The room darkened, and the dull rattle of bones clanked to the floor. Miranda buried her face in Monrovia's shoulder, afraid of what she might see.

Monrovia shook her arm. "Look."

Reluctantly, Miranda raised her eyes. The mist had faded, and a gossamer rag floated down, settling over a pile of bones.

Cloudlyn took a deep breath and rubbed her arms while she surveyed the pile at her feet. Her sharp cheek bones cut even sharper, her thin hands even thinner. She helped each of the girls to their feet, and Miranda shivered with more than cold. Was this Gyda before them or Cloudlyn? Or some new combination?

"It's time to free them." The voice danced like a snowflake on an icy wind.

CHAPTER 36

TRAPPED

The stone cell wall melted back under Cloudlyn's fingers, forming a hole large enough to walk through.

Miranda shivered as she and Monrovia followed this new version of Cloudlyn into a vast hall. Black walls shimmered as if made from some type of reflective rock, but a closer look showed they may have been covered in a thin layer of ice. Jagged, long icicles clung to the ceiling by the thousands, ready to break free when called. They glowed a pale blue from within. The ghostly light made the sparkles in the walls shine like stars.

Cloudlyn marched with long strides through the empty hall. This new being, the combination of Gyda and Cloudlyn, would obviously want to rule Nibiru, but Miranda hoped that did not mean bringing Gyda's banshee army. Rather than wait for a nasty surprise, Miranda took a gulp and asked.

Cloudlyn laughed. Or was that Gyda? "I don't think they would want to come, and they still have a mission here."

"What is their mission?" Monrovia asked.

"When people meet their ends, most have a destination. But there are those who do not decide in time. Those souls can become lost, boundless and unmoored. We find them and give them a place to rest."

Miranda shuddered as she thought of the snarling skeletons just outside the door. "Those things don't seem to be resting."

Cloudlyn cocked her head. "Banshees are born from a select group. Some lost souls are not ready for rest."

"Why make them at all?" Monrovia asked.

Cloudlyn looked past them, losing focus on the moment as if remembering. "Out here, alone, it's a good idea to have your own army." They were looking at Cloudlyn, but these were Gyda's words. "They will continue to shepherd those who find their way here." She rubbed her arm as if feeling it for the first time.

Miranda pushed aside her worry of allying with someone who would condemn a soul to an eternity as her soldier. Instead, she leaned into the potent buzz, taking hold. *We're so close.* "What will happen when you release them?"

"The souls know the way to their missing piece. They will go home. Hopefully, we can quietly free them and face Alois on Nibiru with the restored people on our side."

This seemed more like Cloudlyn talking. Miranda wondered where the senator ended and Gyda began, but suspected it wasn't possible to define clearly anymore, like pouring milk into soup: the creation was forever altered, and no one piece was original.

Cloudlyn paused at a pair of looming obsidian doors etched with carvings that claws could have carved. She pulled her fingers back and laid her icy hand on Miranda's head, lightly petting her. "I saw you were strong when you first came here, Moon Daughter. You were so afraid but would not give up. She was looking for you," she said to Monrovia. "I can see many things, but I did not anticipate that you would free me from my own prison."

Miranda looked into those eyes, so much like Cloudlyn's, but darker now.

"What if Alois tries to stop us?" Monrovia asked.

A cold chill ran down Miranda's spine. Telos's words played in her head. Alois was too strong for them, too strong for Lau Chen. Her heart twisted. He was too strong for Beda. But this new Cloudlyn was different, carved from frozen bone. *She can't fail.*

Cloudlyn's pale hand hovered over an intricately carved handle that Miranda hoped was not bone. "If Alois dares to show his face, we fight." She pressed down, swinging the door open.

A screaming wind whipped past craggy rocks as a line of gaped mouth creatures flew straight for them. Miranda planted her feet, bracing for impact.

Cloudlyn raised her hand. "Soldiers, it is I, your leader."

The banshees stopped in mid-air, floating in their spot. A bone-rattling shriek bounced off the canyon walls, and Cloudlyn took a deep breath, as if inviting the shrill cry to fill her.

"It is time to take them home," Cloudlyn shouted. "Help me free them."

Miranda's body hummed with their frantic energy. Cloudlyn raised her arms above her head and unleashed a guttural yowl that sent the skeletons swooping at top speed in all directions. They converged on the canyon cliffs as a tornado of bleached bone and matted hair.

We're so close, Nathan.

The ground shook. Miranda's heart leapt. *This is it. The rock will burst open, and they will be free.* But instead of splitting rock, the air filled with the sounds of crunching bones as soldier after soldier plummeted to the ground. Miranda searched for the cause. Were they colliding in the chaos? Cloudlyn held her arms firm, not slowing her guttural chant. A shrieking skeleton plunged straight down, crashing at her feet as if thrown with great force.

The flutter in Miranda's stomach evaporated as fear took hold. "He's here. They can't get past."

Another banshee smashed to the ground in front of them and Cloudlyn broke her chant, fury flashing in her eyes. "Are you a coward?" She shouted at the wind. "Hiding in the shadows to stop the inevitable? This is my world, Alois. You cannot stop this."

A shimmer rippled along the canyon wall. Miranda squinted to see better. The sheen became opaque in front of her eyes and coiled round and round until it filled the belly of the canyon. Scales grew out of smooth skin, and a diamond-shaped head took form.

"Your illusions do not scare us, Alois," Miranda shouted, hoping that saying the words would make them true.

"Soldiers!" Cloudlyn shouted. "Attack formation."

The banshee army flew from all corners to form a wall in front of their leader. But the serpent lashed out with its head, striking toward the three of them with dripping fangs. Miranda struggled to lift a boulder to hurl at it. Monrovia jerked her behind Cloudlyn before she could try to lob it at the serpent.

"We have to hide," Monrovia said, darting her head left to right.

Can't lose focus, so close. Miranda wrenched her arm from her sister's grip. "Where are they?"

Cloudlyn pointed to a large crack in the towering canyon wall, big enough for a person to climb into. "Trapped in the rock." The giant snake slithered back and forth in front of the fracture, batting away banshees who dared to dive closer.

Kirasu's words came back to her: *You must remove the barrier.* She still thought of them as Kirasu, even though she knew now that it was bigger than the pair of strange, frail twins.

Monrovia clung to her arm again and Miranda fought to pull away.

"Don't go out there," Monrovia pled with eyes full of fear.

She didn't have to say the rest. *Don't leave me alone.* Her pleading eyes were a pinprick almost draining Miranda's resolve. They hadn't talked about losing Carl, but she understood. Monrovia was begging not to be left alone in this world, and if Miranda ran to that giant snake—but what was the alternative?

Skeletons dove at the serpent, and it swatted them out of the air. The wind from its massive tail buffeted her back.

She covered Monrovia's hand with her own. "I'm sorry." And she truly was. Sorry they lost Beda and Carl. Sorry that Nibiru was in shambles. But if she didn't follow through now, Alois would win and Nibiru's suffering would continue. "Freeing the souls is our only chance." She yanked her arm away and broke into a run.

Beda's words echoed in her memory: *You can do this.*

Maybe she could sneak past and find a way into the fracture without confronting this beast head on? She ran to the crack in the canyon at full speed, hoping the skeletons were enough of a distraction.

A loud whistle filled the air, and her knees softened as a dark shadow spread around her. Her feet no longer seemed to catch the dusty canyon floor and the rock wall stretched farther away, like she was running in a dream. Even the incessant crunch of bone against rock sounded muted, like it was far away.

A gentle but clear note pierced the air and snapped Miranda from her trance just as Monrovia lunged at her, sweeping her to the side as the tail slammed into the spot where she'd just stood. The impact shook the ground, and Miranda's heart pounded as she realized how close she had come to being crushed.

Miranda shook her head to clear it and focus on the one coherent note.

Monrovia scrambled back to her feet. "Come on!"

The sky darkened again as the tail rose for a second try. Miranda raced behind Monrovia to the gap in the wall. The sound came from there. The beast aimed at them, moving to strike with its colossal head. Monrovia dove into the narrow crack in the cliff, and Miranda pitched herself inside just as the creature slammed its body against the rock.

They both lost their footing and dropped to their knees. Miranda fought to catch her breath and crawled to her sister. She clutched the sides of her face. "You saved my life."

"I had to," Monrovia huffed. "What happened to you? You froze out there. You almost let it crush you."

Miranda shivered. "I thought I was running, but everything slowed." She stepped deeper into the darkness of the cave to find the source of the music that pulled her from the trance. "Are you here?" She strained to see.

"I don't think the souls will answer you back," Monrovia said.

"Not them," Miranda whispered.

"Yes, child, we are here," Telos and Zoi said in unison.

"But you said you couldn't be here."

"We discussed it further and determined some things are worth the sacrifice."

The giant snake smashed its tail against the canyon wall, again dropping them to their knees.

"Tell me how to free them," Miranda said.

"They are buried in the nooks and crannies of these rocks, held with a spell that Alois is not letting Gyda break."

Another loud crunch and Miranda winced. It may have been four or five of the banshee army being crushed at once.

"Her soldiers can't hold him off," Miranda said.

"We must work together to release them. It's Nibiru's only hope," Telos said.

Hearing that they cared about Nibiru's fate gave Miranda a jolt.

"Connect with Kirasu, feel it, let it guide you," Zoi said.

They rumbled out a guttural chant Miranda didn't even pretend to imitate with notes so low she wondered how such deep sounds came from their tiny frames.

Monrovia kept one hand on the rock and raised her other palm out. Miranda mimicked her movements and let out whatever sounds would come, not trying to understand, but feeling them instead. A rush of energy moved through her as the air shifted and seemed to steal her breath. A soft breeze whistled by her ear.

"What was that?" she asked.

Monrovia's eyes were closed, and Telos and Zoi continued their chant. Miranda straightened up again, pulling energy from the vibrations. *Nathan, we've come for you.* In her mind, she searched for a sign. Bones splintered and shattered against the outside wall as another crashing boom shook them. A wisp fluttered past, cool on Miranda's cheek on its way out the entrance. She felt rather than knew what they were doing was working.

The snake's screech echoed off the cliffs as a thud loosened the surrounding rock. A flurry of wisps rushed by on their way out and up, as if the tumbling stones shook them free. It sparked an idea, and Miranda ran to the entrance of the narrow passage.

The serpent had given way to an enormous bird with scaly legs, brightly feathered wings, and a long, sharp beak lined with rows of gleaming pointed teeth. Dogged banshees gained an upper hand with this form, diving in and yanking out masses of feathers with their needlelike fingers. The creature squealed in pain.

This was a massive version of the bird-like animals with razor-sharp teeth and a skin crawling screech she'd encountered on her first visit to a place between. Those creatures were large, but this thing was twenty times its size. Had they been Alois' visions too?

Miranda swallowed hard and climbed closer to the crack. Alois wasn't giving them the luxury of time. She had to make this go faster.

"What are you...?"

Not waiting for her sister to finish the question, she bolted out into the canyon, sinking her fingers into the first available handholds, pulling herself up. She climbed fast, kicking and punching the rocks. It didn't take long for her hands to become bloody, but freeing any souls made it worth it, and, once the creature saw her, its attack would undoubtedly free more. As long as it missed Miranda and pierced the rock, it would be faster than chanting.

As expected, the giant bird trained its beak to her and let loose a blood-curdling shriek. Miranda clung to the rock as the long, sharp beak barreled in. A banshee swooped in close enough for her to snag a piece of its gown.

"Help me!"

It arched back in a tight circle as the beak zeroed in on her. Miranda climbed higher, but the bird easily stayed in line with her movements. Her knuckles leaked blood, and the ground swayed as she looked down. *Would she survive if she jumped?* A bony arm wrapped around her waist, ripping her from the wall seconds before the gleaming black beak tore a gash into the rock as if it was silk.

A rush of air flowed from the tear, and the bird screeched in fury. Several banshees peeled away from the fight and flew up and out of the canyon as if they were guiding something to safety.

The bony arm gripped her waist tighter, and Miranda leaned back against its sharp body, satisfied that her plan had worked, but there was plenty more to free.

"Take me back." She pointed at the cliff face. "And stay close." She half expected the banshee to release her, letting her fall rather than be ordered around, but it deposited her on the rock as requested.

Banshees had swarmed the creature and were keeping it contained. Miranda continued to climb, kicking and punching along the way, occasionally hearing the soft whistle past her ear that made her keep going. A determined flap of its wings finally scattered the banshees, and Miranda stole a glance back. The creature's beady eyes locked on her. Blood banged in her ears as she scanned the skies for help. A skeleton swooped in, and she held out one arm ready to snatch cold bone. The giant bird toddled closer and, with another resounding flap of its monstrous wing, knocked the banshee into the dirt with a crunch.

She hung on, kicking furiously with one foot to free a few more souls before the sharp beak was on her, poised to pluck her like a juicy worm. She thought of the colorful bird the child had been afraid to touch on the day Monrovia took her skating. That bird's beak was sharp and black like this one. Had any of those things survived these days of Falling? The child? The bird? The strange and beautiful rink tucked into the jungle? As the beast narrowed in on its wriggling treat, one thought pushed out the others: *I'm sorry, Monrovia.*

The teeth closed around her waist, and a breeze whistled past.

You are strong.

Beda? Miranda struggled to turn, but the jaws cut into her sides, immobilizing her. Instead of snapping her in two, they held her with just enough pressure so she could not squirm. She took a shallow breath, and the exhale burned against the vice grip.

Alois took shape before her. His wiry white hair, jutting out from the sides of a tall hat, made him look more like a disheveled eccentric than an evil demigod.

"You've reduced me to base violence. This is not who I am. Why can't you just stop?" Alois pleaded.

"Why can't *you* just stop?" Miranda wheezed the words out, taking shallow breaths back in.

"I don't want to hurt you, but I must perform my experiments. How will humanity improve if not pushed? But you, you will not give up, so I am forced to do something I've never done before."

The jaws clamped, and Miranda clenched her stomach muscles in a pathetic attempt to fight against this.

Telos's voice broke through the pain. "Use Kirasu, Miranda. Think of a place and send yourself there. You can do this."

Kirasu? Is that how we transported?

The jaws crushed down, squeezing out her doubt and the twisted branch archway of Bushuto Gardens flashed in Miranda's mind before it was swallowed up by white hot pain. A firestorm of pinpricks of light streamed at her face, and her cells burned as she died and revived over and over, in a continuous cycle.

CHAPTER 37

UNITED

Miranda's body burned like it was being ripped apart from the inside. She slammed into the dirt in the dark, and the burning stopped. Darkness, but her eyes were open, and she could move. There were no teeth digging into her. She patted her back and stomach—no holes, and she didn't feel any blood. She reached out, feeling her surroundings. Her hands landed on a soft wall. Pieces crumbled, coating her fingers. She smelled it.

Fresh dirt.

She tried to stand but her legs wobbled. She sank to her knees. *Where am I?*

Darkness stretched in front of her. She turned, darkness there too. *A tunnel?*

Her dream came back to her: people lining up to enter a tunnel. Beda had told her to get them in the dome.

She picked a direction and crawled until a patch of light danced on the dirt. She clambered out of the opening and shielded her eyes against the gray day. Bushuto Gardens extended out around her. Medical tents and guards, people milling around. The section of the dome that had trapped so many was still intact; its surface scratched and dented but ready to serve as shelter when needed. Her heart skipped a beat as she scanned the crowd for Monrovia. Would she be here?

She called out for her. A few people watched her with lost or bored expressions. These were not the faces of people reinvigorated by a recent reunion with their missing piece.

What's wrong? Why aren't the souls here? Alois will be right behind me. These people did not look ready to fight.

A strong wind whipped through the garden. It circled Miranda, and its energy vibrated through her. Spontaneous laughter and shouts popped up in the crowd. Her heart drummed in her ears. *It's happening.* A woman near her fell to the ground as if pushed forward by an invisible hand. She stayed in a low crouch, breathing heavy. A new fear gripped Miranda. *Is it hurting them?*

She bent beside her. "Are you okay?"

The woman didn't speak, but stayed on her hands and knees, staring, lost in thought. A man fell forward and someone next to him let loose a surprised shout.

Miranda placed her hand on the woman's back, and her throat tightened. *Did I mess up? Again?*

The woman sat on her heels and looked at Miranda but seemed to see past her. "I understand." She smiled and tears streamed down her face. "We are also Earth."

Shivers ran down Miranda's arm.

A man close by shouted, "I remember!"

"Miranda! You're alive! You're here!"

As Hugo made his way to her, his face changed. He slowed, confused, then dropped to his knees, his body shaking.

Miranda cautiously touched his shoulder.

His arm shot out to the side, and she jumped to dodge the hit. His eyes were closed. He did not seem in control of his movements. His arm fell again, and he raised his head, shaking it, confused. "I met you in Bubble City. I *know* what Bubble City is." He held his head in his hands. "My name was… Davon?"

Tears sprang to Miranda's eyes. "That was your name on Earth. How do you feel?"

He stared into the space in front of him. "I have all of those memories. I was so lost there without my father."

"I guess it will take time to make sense of things."

"It's really gone?"

Miranda sniffled hard. "It's here now. Everything is coming back together."

"Did you bring Monrovia home?"

Miranda's stomach twisted. "We were together, but I don't know where she is now."

Hugo's face darkened. "It's not your fault. It was her choice." His gloom gave way to a goofy grin. "But then, who is that?"

Miranda spun around. A tall girl with long, white hair ran toward them. Miranda caught a sob in her throat. "Rona!"

Miranda ran to her, and they collapsed into a messy hug, which Monrovia broke way too soon. She pushed Miranda back, gripping her shoulders tightly.

"Were you trying to get yourself killed?" Monrovia demanded.

"I needed it to go faster," Miranda said, staring at the ground.

"By using yourself as bait?"

Miranda shrugged.

"You're lucky that thing didn't eat you."

Hugo's eyes widened. "Glad I stayed behind."

"It's happening. He remembers Earth." Miranda let out a huge breath. "How did you get here?"

"I transported back, like we used to. It's like whatever was stopping us is gone now."

Miranda looked at the sky, whispering a silent thank you to, she wasn't sure who, because Monrovia could access Kirasu too. "What about Zoi and Telos?"

"They are holding off Alois, but he won't stay there," Monrovia said.

"No." Miranda looked around at the people laughing and crying around her. "No, he's not done with us."

CHAPTER 38

RESTORED

Miranda searched the crowd, afraid to let hope clench her heart but unable to push it away. Was Oren reunited with Nathan? Would he have Nathan's memories, their memories? *He has to be here.*

The ground rumbled.

"Did you feel that?" Miranda asked.

Monrovia froze, her knees slightly bent, like she was ready to sprint. The ground rolled under Miranda's feet, then slowed and stopped.

As she got her bearings, heads craned up as a familiar crackle rattled from a pod floating above them. Cloudlyn hung onto the door with one hand and gripped a megaphone with the other. Miranda wondered if the crowd noticed the senator's cheeks were more sunken and her bones more pronounced.

"People of Samsara," Cloudlyn boomed. "People of Nibiru. This is a historic day, but it will also be difficult." She paused for the crowd's attention. "The controversial work of Carl and Beda Ess and their children have made me see we were wrong to break Nibiru away from Earth in the first Gathering."

A collective gasp rippled through the crowd. Even Monrovia's hand flew to her chest. Miranda leaned in, hanging onto her every word. Cloudlyn had never even hinted that she believed Nibiru should not have been created.

"Although the Ess family did not plan for it in the beginning, their actions have led to Earth and Nibiru coming together as one. And now many of you have received back a stolen piece of your soul and the memories that went with it. No doubt you are flooded with images of a life on Earth, and with questions, too. It will not be easy, but we must rebuild one world. But there is one who seeks to stop us."

"Who?" a man gripping a skinny gray cat shouted from the crowd.

"He's called Alois, and he's one of our founding ancestors, but he did not move on as the others did," Cloudlyn said.

Miranda watched in awe as the senator commanded the crowd. The combination of Cloudlyn and Gyda made for a formidable leader, and hopefully, a fierce fighter.

"He continued to manipulate Earth and cause much pain. His mind is powerful, and he has complete control over his ability to manifest. This man caused the Falling, and he does not want to stop now. He means to begin his experiments again with our world, to reset us. I believe he will reveal himself soon."

"What can we do against such a being?" a woman yelled.

"With your missing piece restored, we are strong enough to face him together, but we won't fight him with fists. We must focus and send him to a place that can hold him. We must send him to a prison in the jagged rocks of the icy moon, Europa."

For the briefest second, Cloudlyn's flesh seemed to melt away and the skeleton beneath showed through. A shudder made its way through the crowd, and Miranda wondered how these people might react to the full truth about their new leader.

A warm hand landed on her shoulder. "Miranda!"

She spun and her heart jumped into her throat. Oren's eyes flashed green, like Nathan's, and his demeanor was less rigid, more open. But his face held something else, a familiar pain of hungry days and nights, of living alone and wanting to love, wanting to trust, but being afraid. She knew it well, and that pain confirmed she was face to face with a new person, the combination of Oren's sense of duty and Nathan's guarded hope.

Tears ran down her cheeks. He wiped them away and lifted her off her feet into a tight embrace.

"I never thought I'd see you again," he said.

She wrapped her arms around him and buried her head in his chest, not wanting to ruin the moment by talking.

He put her back on her feet and she stared up at him with a lopsided grin. It was as if everything else had stopped. Cloudlyn's speech and the crowd's shouted questions were a muted whir running under the current of electricity coursing through her veins.

He cupped her chin with one hand. "How did you do it?"

"I never gave up," she said. "And I had help from some flying skeletons."

"What?"

Instead of elaborating, she drew him near, her heart pounding in her ears as their lips touched. Her knees quivered, but she didn't pull back. She hadn't even dared to dream this would happen.

He held her close; his lips tasted sweet. In this moment, everything seemed possible.

Her knees wobbled again, but this time it seemed to be more than her nerves. He stumbled and they broke apart. The ground shook violently under their feet.

Cloudlyn shouted into the megaphone for Alois to show himself. Miranda's stomach sank.

A deafening crack boomed, followed by more violent shaking, and they toppled like poorly set dominoes. Panicked screams erupted as the blaring crash exploded into fissures, splitting the ground. The dirt under Oren fell away.

"Oren!" Miranda lunged, just missing his hand. "Nathan!" A cloud of dust enveloped her scream.

"I'm here."

Miranda's muscles seemed to turn to jelly at the sound of his voice, shaky but close. The dust cleared, and he clung to the side of the new fissure, just inside the crack.

She leaned as far over the side as she could without falling and stretched her hand down to him. "Take my hand."

"No." He shook his head. "I'll drag you in. I can climb out."

"Don't tell me no." She leaned farther over the edge, reaching for him, but he was just out of range.

Hands gripped her legs. "I've got you," Monrovia said, just as Hugo laid down beside Miranda, also stretching out his hand.

"I'm anchored. Now come on."

Oren nodded and gripped the loose rock carefully. He climbed closer, almost within reach.

Miranda's palms sweated as he tested the rock for another hand, then another foot hold. Still out of her reach. The ground shook again, so violently this time that he clung desperately with both hands gripping the same rock.

"Do not let go!" Miranda shouted, as if her demand would be enough to keep him steady.

The ground popped and jumped around them.

He locked eyes with her. "I won't." With a sickening snap, his hand hold sheared off. Fear filled his eyes, and, for a split second, he seemed suspended in mid-air before gravity took hold.

"No!" Miranda lurched forward, stretching both arms out, but there was no trace of him.

Someone yanked her back from the edge, scraping her stomach and legs roughly along the jagged rocks. The sharp cuts seemed to belong to another person's skin. She kept her eyes fixed on the fissure. *It can't end like this. It can't.*

The ground rocked and buckled, forcing Miranda away from the edge. A gleaming chrome spike jutted out of the fresh rift, rising fast, as if being pushed by a giant. Half of a building emerged, some of its windows still intact.

"Now they come out of the ground, too? Can this get any worse?" Hugo said.

"You might not want to ask that," Monrovia said.

There, dangling from a ledge, was Oren. Miranda jumped to her feet. "Oren! Nathan!" She didn't know what to call him, but just knew she'd give anything to have him safe.

The building tottered to one side, scattering the crowd away from its shadow. Oren kicked his feet to gain traction and a better hold. He was so small, so high up. He shouted something, but she couldn't tell what. Blood pounded in her ears. He dragged himself onto a windowsill and disappeared through it.

Panic gripped her as he vanished from sight. *Why would he go in?*

Monrovia gripped her arm. "Where is he?"

Miranda pointed with a shaky finger. "In there." Her mind raced as she tried to think of a way to get to him in the middle of this fissure. But before she could even form a plan, Oren burst open a door at ground level and took a flying leap. Miranda covered her mouth and held her breath until both of his feet landed on solid ground. He stumbled and broke into a full run, waving his hands.

"Move!" he shouted. "It's coming down."

She stayed frozen in her spot until he snatched her hand, yanking her into a run.

The building lurched and creaked, and the seriousness of the situation sank in for Miranda. A loud pop gave her a burst of energy, and her mind caught up with her feet. A series of blasts dropped them to the ground. She looked back and the building was gone, dissolved into a hail of dust as if it had been nothing more than a sandcastle.

He wrapped his arm around her tightly as dust billowed.

"Never do that again," she whispered.

"I hope not to," he said with a half-smile.

Monrovia doubled back to them and laid a hand on Oren's shoulder. "I'm glad you're ok."

Cloudlyn still hung from an open door in her pod. She must have regained her composure, because she shouted into the megaphone. "We *must* stop this tyrant. Alois, you are a coward. Show yourself and face us. Do not hide behind these tricks anymore."

"He's too powerful. We need Telos and Zoi. Maybe they can make him show himself," Miranda said.

Monrovia shook her head. "They're not coming back."

"But we need them."

"We have to figure this out on our own," Monrovia said.

Miranda swallowed hard while fear churned inside her like clouds growing before a storm.

CHAPTER 39

THE ARRIVAL

A roaring explosion split the air. Miranda ducked, covering her head.

"What is that?" Hugo asked.

An impossibly tall and whisper-thin figure stretched along the ground, rippling, and waving like a reed as it spread its shadow across piles of rubble. Its long arms bunched on the ground like wasted fabric.

Miranda craned her neck to see the top of the figure. "Why would he pick a form like this?" He seemed vulnerable, almost comical, not like the threatening snake or giant bird with a razor-sharp beak. Was he trying to get them on his side?

Gasps swelled through the crowd as people clutched each other.

"Pardon, if I could have your attention." The smooth voice trickled down to them, almost gentle. "I come before you today to apologize."

Miranda arched an eyebrow at Monrovia.

"I should have tried harder to preserve your world. All of this," his long thin arms lashed over their heads and people scrambled out of the way, "is because those girls used you to destroy Earth, and now," he waved at the rubble of the building Oren rode out of the hole, "the detritus of Earth is mixing with your world. *Dégoûtante.*" His voice carried the disgust down to their level. "Those girls chose to end your world, but they did not give *you* a choice. I abhor violence, you see, but that is the only language some people understand. But, *mes amis*, it does not have to be this way."

Oren leaned in close. "What is he talking about?"

Miranda hushed him.

"I can reset your world to the way it was before the Falling started. I can give you Nibiru back, as it was."

Heads slowly lifted. Some who were scrambling up a mountain of debris to get away now slowed.

"Tell them what he's leaving out. Tell them he'll make them all forget." Oren's voice sounded panicky.

Miranda's tongue lay dry in her mouth.

"I see now I have your attention. *Bon.*" Alois leaned his paper-thin body over the crowd. Miranda shivered in the cool shadow. "Would you like to have Nibiru back the way it was?"

A small voice peeped up from the group with, "Yes."

"Yes!" Alois straightened, his laugh puffing out his one-dimensional frame. "Of course you would like that very much. And I can do it."

"It's a trick!" Cloudlyn yelled into her megaphone. "He will experiment on us and erase our memories."

Alois tutted. "Yes, it would be truly wicked to restore your world to the way it was and to take away the memory of all this suffering—truly tyrannical." A stiff wind kicked his crooked grin into a snarl.

Cloudlyn leaned into her megaphone. "Earth and Nibiru have come together. You are whole now. Our *world* is whole now. You don't want that to go away, do you? We will rebuild, together. Help me! Concentrate on sending him into the beyond! Send him to cold stone."

Miranda tried to focus on sending him back to Europa. She hoped people were listening to Cloudlyn.

Alois shook his thin head. "I think we've heard enough from her today, haven't we?" As his mustache quivered, Cloudlyn rose from her perch on the side of the pod and sailed through the air. She hovered over the crowd, kicking her arms and legs as if that might help.

"Put me down," she shouted.

A glass box materialized around her, and the people watched as her megaphone clattered soundlessly at her feet. She banged on the glass with both fists, but no sound escaped the box.

Miranda's breath caught in her throat. *Cloudlyn was supposed to stop him.*

Hugo whispered, "What is our plan?"

"Do not fear. I am no monster. Look, she's fine, but—" Alois dabbed at his hairline with a thin finger. "Well, she was giving me a headache. As I was saying, don't you want to put Nibiru back to the way it was before the Falling started? Clean up all this mess?"

A woman took a single step forward. "Will the people we lost in the Falling be returned to us?"

"Mom!" Oren's yell snapped Miranda back to the moment.

Alois cocked his head as he looked at Sophia. "That may just be possible, my dove."

"No!" Miranda gripped Oren's arm, desperate for him to know the truth. "He's lying."

Oren's eyes flashed with anger as he jerked his arm away. "How do you know?"

"He told me."

Oren wiped his brow. "I'm sorry. If there is any way to get him back." A tear fell down his cheek. "I have to go to Mom."

He pulled away and raced to Sophia, who was standing in a sea of huddled bodies.

"What is your price for restoring our home?" a voice from the crowd asked.

"Things are going to get bad if he doesn't get his way," Miranda said.

"It is nothing, really." Alois waved his hand, lashing the swathe of fabric around their heads.

Oren huddled close to his mother, seeming to listen closely.

"Hugo, get the people into the dome."

Hugo's eyes were wild. "And what are you going to do?"

"Create a distraction. Monrovia, are you with me?"

"What are we doing?" she asked.

"Giving people a choice," Miranda said.

Monrovia nodded and followed her to the wall of debris that had been growing since the first Falling.

"You know, these problems started with two girls," Alois said. "I want them gone. I would do it myself, but there are rules, so I need you to use your collective power to banish them. That is all. You do that, and I will restore your world. You'll really be doing yourselves a favor. They cause so much trouble."

Mummers flowed through the crowd.

Miranda crested the top of the jumbled pile. From the high wall, she could see Hugo lead a few people down into the opening of the tunnel. She grabbed Monrovia's hand, pulling her up.

"It's us! That's right, up here." Miranda waved her arms to get their attention. "He's talking about us, and he's right. We led you to help us free Earth from the cycle of pain he started because he wanted to experiment on those people. And now he's ready to experiment with us. He stole your missing pieces and hid them away, but we freed them. He split your world, but we brought it together again."

"You know me, you know my father," Monrovia shouted out at them. "We only wanted to do what was right. But what does this paper man want? What does he get out of putting Nibiru back as it was? If he could even manage such a feat?"

"Yeah, paper man!" Oren shouted from the throng. "What do you get out of it?"

Alois puffed out to a larger size, then deflated again.

"You caused all this destruction!" Oren yelled. Sophia tried to pull him to sit, but he wouldn't back down. "You killed my father!"

Miranda shouted, "And you can't bring his father back. All you can do is wipe his mind, so he doesn't remember him. Is that what you want, Nibiru? Do you want to forget the people you love? Because if you don't, you need to get into the dome!"

A longer line of people disappeared into the tunnel.

Alois' over-sized mustache quivered as it had before he trapped Cloudlyn in the glass. Miranda jerked Monrovia. "Jump" as she bounded back and clung to a jagged piece of concrete. Monrovia panted beside her as a glass box hovered where they had been standing. Miranda swung her leg up and scampered back on top of the pile, hauling Monrovia up beside her.

"You missed!" Miranda yelled.

He looked bored and twitched his flopping mustache again. Glass walls surrounded them both instantly.

"Oops." Miranda reared back and kicked the wall hard and fell back onto the glass bottom.

Monrovia yelped as their cube floated out over people's heads. They pointed up, covering their mouths. Miranda rubbed her shoulder. "That's gonna leave a mark." She looked at the senator floating helplessly in her own cube. "Too bad Cloudlyn can't get us out of his one."

A steady stream of people popped up inside the dome. Each figure under that thick cover gave Miranda hope.

"Brute strength is not getting us out of here." Monrovia folded her legs into lotus position.

"What is your plan?"

"We will ask Beda to help us banish him. Once and for all," Monrovia said.

"If that was possible, I don't think she would have left us waiting this long," Miranda said. "We need them." She motioned to the crowd below, necks craned, mouths opened.

"What the—"

A pod sped close, hovering near their glass cube.

"I'm trying to concentrate," Monrovia said, tight-lipped.

"Is that the senator's pod?"

Monrovia cracked open an eye as it swung around. Hugo and the thin-faced man flipped the normally opaque pod's front to glass. Hugo flailed his arms at the window in an apparent attempt to communicate. Miranda pressed her hands against the glass, straining to read his lips. He repeatedly threw his hands out in front of him.

"What is he trying to tell us?" Miranda asked.

"Dance? I have no idea," Monrovia said.

The pod swung to the side and a bright hot laser shot out.

"Get back!" Miranda yanked Monrovia and they fell to the back corner. "He was telling us to get back." She laughed.

"Sure, real funny. This thing is getting torched by lasers, and we're floating in it."

"Would he have a plan for that?" Miranda asked as the glass cracked. Her heart flew to her throat as the cube tipped. She clawed at the glass, trying for anything to hold on to. Alois' billowing laughter filled her ears as they spilled out onto the people below, shielding themselves from raining glass.

Miranda landed on several people, knocking them all to the ground. Her lungs burned as she struggled to regain her breath. She rolled off her back and stayed on her hands and knees until her head stopped spinning. She looked up to see a group of people staring at her with concerned faces.

"Sorry," she croaked out, realizing they had broken her fall. "Are you okay?"

A large man cracked an even larger grin. "I'll make it."

Monrovia dusted off her shoulders and helped up several of the people.

A palpable resolve coursed through the crowd. Miranda drank it in like cool water. "Thank you." She dashed through the masses and scampered back up the wall.

From the top she taunted Alois. "You can put me in another pretty glass box, but my friends are just going to break it again. And these good people are going to catch me again. Who is going to catch you, Alois?"

A cheer rose from the collective that made Miranda want to cry with happiness.

"Let's send him away!" the large man boomed.

"You've made your decision, then?" The wan figure wavered over the remaining crowd. "You had a choice, and you chose destruction."

In a bright flash, Alois was gone.

"Everyone get to the dome!" Miranda yelled. "He'll be back."

Hugo and the thin-faced man hammered on the senator's glass box.

Miranda climbed down the debris pile, shouting at the crowd. "He's coming back. Get into the dome."

A woman gripped her arm as she ran past. "My son, I can't find my son." Her eyes were shot through with fear. "He's only three."

A man wrapped his arm around her shoulder. He looked broken, with gaunt eyes and stooped shoulders. "He's not here, Stella. That was Earth. Her memories are jumbled," he said, as if in apology.

Hot tears sprang to Miranda's eyes. "I'm sorry."

As he guided the woman toward the tunnel, shattering glass split the quiet. Several guards with hammers had joined Hugo and the thin-faced man. The senator crunched glass under her boots as she stepped out of the box. A cheer went up through the crowd. Cloudlyn yelled, "He's not done with us. Get to the dome."

Many more people sprinted to the tunnel.

Cloudlyn crossed the ground quickly to Miranda. "What's he going to do?"

"I expect something that will hurt a lot," Miranda said as a bitter taste coated the back of her throat. Her haughty resolve of only a few minutes before seemed to have evaporated, and she couldn't call it back.

A team of men and women bustled around the edges of the dome, digging holes and feeding in thick tubes, leaving the ends of each tube exposed.

The senator motioned for Miranda to follow as she strode up to one of them. "What are you doing?"

The man leaned on his shovel. "We're putting in more lines for oxygen. With more people in there, we will need more lines to increase our chances of survival. That hot box will fill with carbon dioxide in no time."

"Good thinking." The senator patted his shoulder and surveyed the area. The air smelled like a potent mix of anxiety and despair.

CHAPTER 40

RETRIBUTION

The grounds were empty, except for a few stragglers. Almost everyone had made it to the safety of the dome. The quiet left Miranda uneasy. *Why is he waiting?*

Out of the corner of her eye, she caught a flutter of Monrovia's hair on the wind. What was she doing over there?

"Rona," Miranda yelled in her direction, "come on, we need to get in the dome."

Miranda watched the sky. The clouds were darkening, a telltale sign that something big was on its way. "It's starting!" she shouted to anyone in earshot.

The workers dropped their shovels and ran to the tunnel.

Cloudlyn joined Miranda. "It's time."

"She's not moving." Miranda strained to see Monrovia behind a debris pile but only saw a bit of her hair.

A woman struggled with a heavy bundle. The ground rocked with the first impact of raining debris, not the major Falling yet. *She'll never make it.*

"I need help," Monrovia shouted.

"Get this woman to safety. I'll help Monrovia."

Cloudlyn gripped the woman's arm. "Drop your things and run!"

The last of the stragglers sprinted toward the tunnel.

Adrenaline rushed through Miranda. *I'm coming, sister.* She bolted away from the tunnel to Monrovia, her mind racing with terrible images of what might be wrong. A large piece of concrete slammed into the ground near her, knocking her to her knees. She got back up as dust and debris rained in her eyes.

"Monrovia!" The strip of white hair guiding her seemed to have vanished. She frantically scanned the dusty landscape. "Rona! Where are you?"

Another piece of jagged concrete slammed down, shaking the ground.

"Lost your sister again?" Alois' familiar voice echoed.

She spun around, looking for what form he had taken this time, but his voice seemed to be on the wind.

"Miranda!"

She turned back the way she'd come and saw Monrovia, waving frantically from the tunnel entrance, screaming for her to run.

It was a trick. Miranda's heart pounded louder than her footfalls as she bolted for the tunnel entrance. She was covering ground fast until a giant steel beam flew in front of her and she slammed into it, falling to the ground. She struggled to her feet, trying to shake her head back to focus, and dabbed at the tender bruise already forming on her forehead. *Which way?*

The steel beam had buried itself upright in the dirt while another swooped in, digging down like the first. They stood like goal posts. Miranda ducked as a volley of broken cinder blocks and discarded bricks swooped in from all directions.

The fragments stacked on each other, forming a wall of wreckage between the posts.

Panic set in as she sprinted to the left to get around it, but it grew wider and taller with each passing second.

"They don't need me to stop you." She shouted at the gathering clouds, hoping it was true.

There was no way around this growing pile. In desperation, she sprang onto the wall itself, but the higher she climbed, the higher the wreckage stacked, until something caught her foot.

"You always make me worse than I want to be," Alois said.

She yanked hard to free her boot, but it wouldn't budge. Cold fear gripped her chest as barbed wire snaked out of the crevices and looped around her other ankle, then her wrists. She inhaled sharply as the metal barbs sank into her flesh. Only her head was free.

"Thank you for gathering them all together. That makes it easier."

Miranda's heart raced as pieces of the wall she was now lashed to tumbled away. When it stabilized, she had a clear view of the dome and the darkening sky above it. Any minute now, something huge and heavy would burst through those clouds. Was there anything she could say to make him stop?

"Please! I'll go. I'll do whatever you want, just don't hurt them."

"Oh, we're past that now. You and Cloudlyn poisoned me to them. I've never revealed myself, here or on Earth. I'm not sure a simple reset could undo the knowledge of my existence. No, the people on Nibiru who were not present here will be spared, but this lot. Well, you've handled them."

"No, Alois!" Heat crept up her neck and flushed her face as she struggled against the barbs. "I am not doing this. *You* are doing this. It's you who needs to be banished!"

"Of course it is, *chère*, but who can do that?"

Miranda stretched her mind to reach Monrovia, to tell her it was time to push the people to end this, but her pleas were met with silence.

"We'll get to see how strong this dome really is," Alois tittered.

"Are you enjoying this?" Miranda spat the words out.

As the dark mass fell faster, people in the dome scattered, many racing for the tunnel.

"I almost forgot," he said, as he sent a mound of debris sailing through the air. It landed at the mouth of the tunnel, sealing the exit. "Fixed that problem."

She twisted against the barbed wire, each movement driving the spikes in deeper. *I can't get to them.* She hung limp, exhausted.

A spire sliced through the clouds, driving straight for the dome. "Beda said it would hold," Miranda whispered to herself. Her arms and legs shook as if they independently could no longer handle the stress. She chided her body for doubting. "It will hold."

"Still trusting in your *chère mère?* But she wasn't strong enough to see it through. You think she had an idea any of this would happen?"

The spire drilled for the crest of the dome, and Miranda fought to turn her head away, but the wire gripped it in place.

"Watch the show, *chère.*"

Metal, glass, and cinder blocks exploded. She shut her eyes, terrified of what she would see, but she couldn't hide from it. She squinted through the dust. She had to know. A long rift split along the dome, but it had held.

A smile crept across her face. *I should not have doubted.* "It's now or never, people," she whispered. She pictured the cold, rocky cliffs in her mind and envisioned Alois speeding toward them.

"Look at that crack!" He purred with excitement. "The next one is going to take care of this minor problem and I can start fresh."

It's an icy moon with jagged cliffs. The cliffs have deep cracks. He trapped your other half there. Send him back! She sent the thought out, knowing they couldn't hear her in the dome but hoping somehow her words would get to them.

The buzzing energy from the souls return surrounded her again now, dulling the ache of the wire's barbs. She imagined banshees whirling in frantic starts, ready for their prize and, in her thoughts, brought Alois back to his earlier one-dimensional form and imagined stuffing him into a crack.

She felt strong and sure, which made no sense because she was still lashed to a wall of rubble. *It's more than just me. They must be helping from the dome.* "We can do this together."

"Do you think I would let this go so easily?" Alois' voice cut through her thoughts.

A blunt concrete building broke through the clouds, plummeting for the dome at incredible speed. The surrounding energy spiked, and white light filled her vision. The building froze, suspended.

He hummed, "Impressive."

Blood rushed through her limbs. She pushed against the spikes, but the wire held firm. "They are whole now and they know about you. It's given them the strength to push your illusions back." She stretched her mind to ask for some of their resolve.

The thorny wires tightened against her flesh. "Do my illusions only work when someone believes in my power, Miranda? I should thank you for being such a loyal follower."

She gritted her teeth against the pain, but the spikes dug deeper, spilling blood and bringing forth a tortured scream. She took a ragged breath. "Your time here is done."

The building teetered over the dome, a paused concrete missile. Intention flowed from each hole the spikes had dug into her skin, and she imagined pushing the wire off her. Suddenly, her bonds loosened, forcing her to cling to the debris to keep from falling. She willed the banshees to collect him, but there was no screeching, no tattered gowns. Alois had gone silent.

Miranda blinked hard to be sure what she was seeing was real. Tendrils of light streamed through the rift in the dome, as if searching the air. She willed the light to find him, hiding in plain sight. *He's here.*

The tendrils stretched closer to her, searching for something to wrap around, something to hold and squeeze. Like octopus tentacles, the light landed, encircling a thing that had been invisible but now was flesh and blood. Miranda held her breath as Alois appeared, with his long beard, dusty-white tunic, and round, black glasses struggling against his bonds.

"What is this?" His panicked eyes searched for a way out as the glowing ropes wrapped tighter.

"Not fun, is it?" Miranda jeered as she quickly climbed down from the wall of wreckage.

The ropes looped across his face and knocked his tall, black hat off his head. It tumbled to the ground.

Her heart thudded. *Do we have him?*

Alois swelled in size, struggling as the ropes grew with him. Then he shrank to the size of a mouse and tried to sneak away. Miranda gaped as the ropes formed a basket, catching him before he hit the ground. A woven light top closed over his scant form. He snapped back to himself, a tired man looking for a way out, and the light lassoed him again. His eyes trained on the building still hovering over the dome, stalled but every bit a threat.

"I can still end this," he said.

As the massive building released, crashing to the damaged dome, Miranda willed it to freeze again. But instead of it slowing, she watched in amazement as a thick core of light stretched out of the crack and spread to cradle the plummeting building like a net. The lacework sagged from the weight of the brutal expanse, but the knitted light held.

"But I still have you," a pinched, panicked voice squeaked in her ear.

As quickly as he said the words, a loosely woven sack formed around her, trapping her. Alois dragged her over his shoulder, lifting her off the ground. He took off into the air. "No!"

She desperately worked at the netting with a piece of barbed wire still attached to her boot, but stopped when she realized she was already racing above the dome. She gasped for breath in the rushing air and her lungs burned as they had when she sank beneath the waves. The dome became a dot below. *Are they scared? Huddled together waiting for the end?*

As she climbed higher into the clear sky, her fear melted away and a flood of courage, relief, and love filled her from her toes through the top of her head as if they answered her question. Was this Kirasu filling her with hope?

"Alois, you split this world and its people, but I brought them back together. There is no going back because now they understand. No." She spoke the word with power and purpose. "Alois, you are done here, but I am not. Come and take him." The second the words were off her lips, two banshees flew howling and screeching out of the glare from the sun, lashing ropes around him, securing his arms as he screamed.

He met Miranda's glare and her net dissolved like foam in her hands. She plummeted, holding her breath and clinching her eyes, but feeling strangely calm.

If this is the end, at least they have him.

"They can't hold me." Alois voice grew faint.

This cage will hold.

A boney hand snatched her up by the ankle, slowing her fall. She let out her breath and whispered, "Thank you."

As they neared the ground, the banshee released Miranda's ankle, sending her crashing to the dirt. It flew straight up again. Miranda stayed where she landed, letting fat tears stream down her cheeks.

CHAPTER 41

REBUILD

Miranda crawled to her knees, letting the fear and adrenaline rush out with her tears. After several minutes, she collapsed back into the dirt, ready to lie there for days, but an intense banging interrupted her rest. She looked at the dome. The people lined the walls, smacking the sides with their fists, chairs, anything they could get their hands on. Miranda's eyes shot to the sky, but the looming brutal expanse of concrete was gone. They just wanted out.

She peeled herself up and stumbled closer. "Hey!" She grinned at her dirt-streaked reflection. "We did it!"

Monrovia drummed on the wall from the inside. She was obviously talking, yelling even, but not a word made it past the thick walls.

"How can I get you out?" Miranda kicked the ground, and her foot hit a shovel. The weariness in her limbs settled deeper. "This might take a while."

She sank the shovel into the fresh soil to widen the hole made for the oxygen tubes. Monrovia gave a thumbs-up and grinned. Miranda's biceps burned, but she dug until her fingers were numb and her wrists ached. It didn't take very long until her hand slipped, and she fell against the shovel, then crumpled to the ground.

"I can't do this."

Footsteps rustled through the wreckage. Miranda cracked one eye to see a man leaning over her. He seemed cautious. "Is it over?" he asked.

"Yeah." Miranda said, letting the weight of the simple confirmation settle on her. She sat up on her elbows. "But can you help me get these people out of there?"

The man nodded and ran away.

"Hey, why are you leaving?" But when no answer came, Miranda flopped into the dirt again.

Yet, a minute later, footsteps came from all sides. He had returned with an army and with all kinds of digging tools. Tears of exhaustion spilled down her cheeks. "You brought friends."

He put his hand on her shoulder. "Rest."

She let her head fall again while they dug holes around the dome with a furious energy.

***

She woke to something touching her head and flew up, brushing it off wildly, ready to smack whatever it was.

"Sorry!" Oren's grinning dirty face peered down at her. "It took a long time, but they finally got us out." Oren stroked her cheek. "You did it."

"We all did it. You guys caught him." Miranda felt like she was floating.

He nodded.

"Hey, do I get to give my hero sister a hug or what?" Monrovia pushed him aside and drew Miranda into a warm hug that seemed like home.

Miranda wiped away a few fresh tears.

299

A plaintive mew came from behind her sister. She pulled away saying, "Oh yeah, guess who stayed in the dome after everyone else evacuated through the tunnel?" Monrovia lifted Luna snuggling her cheek. "Smart kitty."

Miranda pet her head and thought the cat gave her a slight wink.

"And thanks for coming after me." Monrovia ruffled Miranda's hair. "But no more risking your life. I need a break from worrying about you. And why did you run the wrong way when everyone else ran for the tunnel?"

Miranda shuddered. "Alois tricked me. I heard you call for help and saw you trapped out there."

Monrovia sucked in a breath. "I was already in the dome. I should have told you."

"The trouble twins!" Tan dropped beside them, wrapping his arms around them. "My mother would like you both to report to her tent so she can check you over."

Hugo appeared from nowhere, and Monrovia tackled him with a hug. "Your mom can wait," Miranda called back, but every bone and muscle ached, and she rolled to her side. Oren pulled her close, and she snuggled against his chest, releasing into the heady security that came with using him as a chair. "Hugo?"

He took his eyes off Monrovia long enough to grunt, "Yeah?"

"Thanks for that crazy assist with the lasers, but seriously, were you trying to kill us?"

He rubbed the back of his neck. "I may have panicked," he said. "I can't believe I got Clyde to go along with it."

The image of the thin-faced man jumped into Miranda's mind, and she recoiled. "I guess I owe him an apology."

Oren snorted out a short laugh.

Tan gave Miranda's foot a playful squeeze. "When you're not so banged up, we should go skating again."

"If it's still there." She remembered the graceful swoops of the wooden structure that sheltered the rink. The crush of the celebrating crowd had been too much for her that day, but she'd like to try to stomach it now. If these people could tap into that happiness again, she might even learn a dance or two.

Those parties had been for Beda's funeral. Maybe they should all go back to Beda's waterfall and see what was left of it. It was still her special place, even if it was different. A pang of sadness gripped her as she thought of Carl and his smile that day on the balcony when he gave her the new boots. He was always happy to share. She hoped they would build a world he'd be proud of.

A line formed, stretching across the park.

"What are they doing?" Miranda asked.

Tan cocked his head and squinted, then his eyes widened. "They are moving debris."

As he said it, Miranda saw stones and bits of concrete pass from one hand to the next all the way down the growing line until the pieces of debris were out of the park.

Miranda looked up at Oren. "Let's go join them."

He smiled at her. "Always ready to help. Just one thing first."

He lifted her face closer to his and gave her a warm, deep kiss. She leaned into him, touching his cheek and letting her fingers trail along his strong jaw. Flutters danced in her stomach. It seemed unreal. They pulled away, both grinning at each other.

"Okay, now we can go." He helped her up, and they all found spots in a line that wound past the garden edge as more people joined.

Someone hummed a tune as they passed debris from hand to hand, and Miranda thought of Telos and Zoi. Had they stayed in Europa to become part of the banshee army now that their home was gone? Or were they really Kirasu now? Fully fused into that energy that guided them?

"Thank you," she whispered. She hoped they knew, even if they couldn't hear.

Tan passed her a rock, and she gave it to Oren. He handed it to Monrovia, and she sent it down the line.

Another came. Miranda's shoulders ached, but she didn't mind. Working together seemed right, and for the first time in a long time, she was not scared. She took the next stone and passed it down.

"We're going to be okay, aren't we?" she whispered, half to Kirasu, half to herself.

Rocks crunching into a faraway pile were her only answer.

ABOUT THE AUTHOR

Kristen Illarmo is a young adult, science fiction author driven to write stories with strong female characters in the backdrop of crumbling societies. She proudly calls New Orleans home, a fact that may only change if the perfect beach town reveals itself. When she's not toiling to improve efficiency in local government in her day job, she's writing about dark possible futures and thinking about the importance of the choices we make.

Don't miss *Without a World*, Book One of the Kirasu Rising series, and its prequel, *Behind the Red Door*. Visit Kristen's website, *www.kristenillarmo.com*, for more information.

Wait! Before you go…

Please consider sharing your thoughts with potential readers by leaving a review.

Reviews are an important part of the process for indie authors because they can help introduce this book to a wider audience. Please take a few minutes to leave a review at Amazon or BookBub.

Thanks so much!

www.ingramcontent.com/pod-product-compliance
Lightning Source LLC
Chambersburg PA
CBHW071401300726
48976CB00006B/1950